PENGUIN M
TILL THE LAST BREATH . . .

Durjoy Datta was born in New Delhi. He completed a degree in engineering and business management before embarking on a writing career. His first book, *Of Course I Love You . . .*, was published when he was twenty-one years old and was an instant bestseller. His successive novels—*Now That You're Rich . . .*, *She Broke Up, I Didn't!*, *Oh Yes, I'm Single!*, *If It's Not Forever . . .*, *Someone Like You*—have also found prominence on various bestseller lists, making him one of the highest-selling authors in India. Durjoy lives in New Delhi, loves dogs and is an active CrossFitter.

For more updates, you can follow him on Facebook (www.facebook.com/durjoydatta1) or Twitter (@durjoydatta).

Also by Durjoy Datta

Hold My Hand

*

She Broke Up, I Didn't!
I Just Kissed Someone Else!

*

Of Course I Love You
Till I Find Someone Better

(With Maanvi Ahuja)

*

Oh Yes, I'm Single!
And So Is My Girlfriend!

(With Neeti Rustagi)

*

Now That You're Rich
Let's Fall in Love!

(With Maanvi Ahuja)

*

Someone Like You

(With Nikita Singh)

*

You Were My Crush
Till You Said You Love Me!

(With Orvana Ghai)

*

If It's Not Forever
It's Not Love

(With Nikita Singh)

Till the Last Breath...

DURJOY DATTA

Penguin
metro reads

PENGUIN METRO READS
Published by the Penguin Group
Penguin Books India Pvt. Ltd, 11 Community Centre, Panchsheel Park,
New Delhi 110 017, India
Penguin Group (USA) Inc., 375 Hudson Street, New York, New York 10014, USA
Penguin Group (Canada), 90 Eglinton Avenue East, Suite 700, Toronto,
Ontario, M4P 2Y3, Canada (a division of Pearson Penguin Canada Inc.)
Penguin Books Ltd, 80 Strand, London WC2R 0RL, England
Penguin Ireland, 25 St Stephen's Green, Dublin 2, Ireland
(a division of Penguin Books Ltd)
Penguin Group (Australia), 707 Collins Street, Melbourne, Victoria 3008,
Australia (a division of Pearson Australia Group Pty Ltd)
Penguin Group (NZ), 67 Apollo Drive, Rosedale, Auckland 0632,
New Zealand (a division of Pearson New Zealand Ltd)
Penguin Books (South Africa) (Pty) Ltd, Block D, Rosebank Office Park,
181 Jan Smuts Avenue, Parktown North, Johannesburg 2193, South Africa

Penguin Books Ltd, Registered Offices: 80 Strand, London WC2R 0RL, England

First published by Grapevine India Publishers 2012
Published in Penguin Metro Reads by Penguin Books India 2013

Copyright © Durjoy Datta 2013

ISBN 9780143421573

Typeset in Adobe Caslon Pro by Eleven Arts, Delhi
Printed at Manipal Technologies Ltd, Manipal

To everyone who reads

1

Dushyant Roy

The curtains had been wide open for quite some time now, letting the sharp rays of the sun stream in through the open window, on to the face of a prostrate Dushyant, who lay in bed, covered in a worn-out hospital bedsheet, very uncomfortable in his sleep but still unmoving. His eyes flickered through the night and his fingers trembled. He was asleep and didn't wake up. It wasn't a good night's sleep.

Finally, after tossing restlessly from side to side, he woke up and tried opening his eyes. One of them refused to open, swollen from the huge gash just above his left eyebrow, which had been heavily taped and bandaged. He touched the bandage with his hands and checked for blood with his other half-open, groggy eye. He sighed as he found none . . . Only then did he venture to look around the hospital room. He was surrounded with medical equipment, a lot of it connected to him, a small television in one corner of the room and an empty bed on his left side. His thoughts wandered to what had brought him there. It wasn't the first time he was in one of these beds, but this time it seemed a little more serious than the other times. Landing up unconscious after a series of uncontrollable vomits and brain tremors was a way of life for him. It was his escape, his refuge. Being sober hadn't got him anywhere, and being drunk obliterated the possibility.

He had tubes attached to needles, which dipped into his veins and arteries, and pumped liquids from transparent pouches hanging from the stand on his right side. He was sure his parents had no idea of his whereabouts. He knew none of his friends would have given the hospital authorities his parents' numbers or address. He was in no mood to see or talk to them. Not now, not ever.

The hands of the watch on his cell phone touched. It was twelve—fourteen hours since he had been admitted. Last night, like many before, had been a night of debauchery, porn, poker, alcohol and smoke. Six of his friends in his cramped one-room apartment—a five-minute walk from college—and a few bottles of alcohol, some weed, nail-polish remover and just about everything which could get them fucked up.

The evening had started with casual banter about college professors, the new kids who had joined the college, girls and pornography. A few cell phone videos of girls bathing naked were transferred over Bluetooth amongst them. A little later the bottles had been popped open. Dushyant—who had graduated just a few months back—was mentor to these kids. He knew the exact proportions for deathly cocktails and the people who would have a steady supply of highly potent weed even during a nuclear holocaust. He knew how to get out of trouble. But more than that, he knew how to get *into* trouble. Like he had the night before, when he passed out only to wake up in a hospital bed. He remembered a seizure; he remembered feeling as if he was dying, but nothing more than that. He waited restlessly for the nurse to come in and tell him what the hell was going on. *I need to get the fuck out of here*, he thought.

On other occasions, he would just jerk off the needles that punctured his hand and walk right out of the ward, but there were too many of them this time and he wanted to know what was wrong, if anything. He was not scared, just concerned if it was serious enough for his mother to start crying and his father to start shouting at him for being irresponsible, disgraceful and a blot on the family name. *What family name? He is a bloody head-clerk at the MCD*, he said to himself. He never got the flawed definitions of *honour* and *family name*. He didn't give a fuck, and frankly, he knew they wouldn't come this time. His head hurt and he thought he could do without the nonsense his parents always put him through.

While he wallowed in self-pity and cursed the hospital, the door opened and a girl—short and fair—entered the room. She had big eyes—like the schoolgirls in Japanese cartoons—and looked like a confused kid in a candy shop with gold coins in both her palms, not knowing what to buy. But instead, her palms were clasped around the handlebars of her crutches. Her legs buckled at the knees and seemed to have no strength at all to bear the weight of her tiny five-foot-two frame.

'Excuse me?' he said and waved at the girl, who was in a robe slightly better than his. 'Can you call the fuc . . . ummm . . . nurse?'

'I think I can. But you know, I could have been a doctor. I am still studying,' she said, and looked at Dushyant and smiled. Dushyant didn't know how to react to that. He didn't remember the last time a girl had smiled at him.

'But since you're not, can you call her? Argh.'

'Being angry won't help your case,' she said, 'but if you pull off that needle with the blue cap out of your right hand, a little slowly, it might help.' She walked over gingerly to the bed next to him and drew the curtain between them. And then pulled it away.

'Excuse me?'

'Do it. There'll be no pulse. They will think you're dying and I hope, at least then, that someone will come running to check on you,' she explained and chuckled. 'And well, if no one does, you're in a really bad hospital. You should get a second opinion.'

'I am not going to do that,' he retorted.

'Then . . .' she said and slowly limped over to his bed. She picked up his medical chart which hung from the other end of his bed, her eyebrows knitted, and continued, 'You have to wait till three when a nurse comes in and draws some blood for some tests. Not a long wait, just two and half hours!'

'Whatever,' he said, closed his eyes and put his head back on the pillow.

'Fine, bye. Hope to see you again. I might pick this room. I am here for some tests, but they need to admit me for a little bit.'

'Yeah, right. You won't see me today. I will be out by evening,' he said rudely.

Pihu just smiled and walked slowly towards the exit. At the gate, she looked at the number and whispered to herself, 'Room 509.' Dushyant saw her nodding, and she disappeared into the corridor amongst other sick people. *I need to get the fuck out of here*, he said to himself.

~

'I don't know what the fuck they are up to!' Dushyant shouted on the phone.

It was four. The nurse had come and drawn some blood and given him zero answers. *Why am I here? When can I go? Did you tell my parents? Did you? What the fuck is going on?* She nodded to his questions unthinkingly, and told him the doctor would see him in a little while. He swore at her. In Hindi. He didn't think the Keralite nurse understood him. Cursing came as second nature to him . . . His sentences often started and ended with abuses, most of which had been improvised and perfected over the course of years that had passed by.

The first time he had hurled abuse was when he was in the eighth standard. Someone had addressed him as *bhenchod* and his comeback was that he didn't have a sister. Not too clever, but ever since that day, *bhenchod* became a way of life. It replaced emotions, feelings and entire situations, depending on how it was being said by him.

'Just be back soon, man,' said the voice from the other side of the phone and he disconnected the call. *Bhenchod!*

He had no visitors. He had no friends really. In the four years and the few extra months he had spent in the college, he had made drinking buddies, smoking buddies, getting-fucked-up-with buddies, but none who would come to see him in the hospital. Had it been six months before, some of them might have come. But now everyone who had graduated with him was either working or waiting for their offer letters. He had been placed, too, but the large IT-sweatshop company hadn't sent him a joining date yet. Stuck in a time warp, he didn't want to go anywhere. So days before college ended, he rented a flat just outside college and started to live like he was still studying—in his fifth year of engineering.

Dushyant was about to doze off when a doctor—presumably in his mid-thirties—entered the room.

'Hey,' he said. 'Are you fine?'

'Why wouldn't I be? I am just okay. When can I fucking go now?' he asked angrily.

'I am afraid you might have to stay here for a few days,' he said and looked at his chart. 'We are actually glad you woke up. It had been three days and we thought you were gone for good,' the doctor, Arman Kashyap, said with a smirk.

'Three days? Are you fucking kidding me? You have the wrong patient, Doctor. I came here yesterday. Is everyone here an incompetent fool? Get me out of these things!'

'Irritation. Forgetfulness. And confusion. Well, these are common symptoms for hepatic encephalopathy. As far as I see it, it's good news for you, boy. You have every symptom in the book. It's easier to treat that way,' he explained and smiled.

'Excuse me? I have what?'

'Hepatic encephalopathy,' he said. 'In other words, your liver has rotted and is playing games with your brain cells. You have had problems with urination for the past few days and you didn't tell anyone because you were embarrassed about it. And three days back, you had a seizure and passed out.'

'But I didn't. It was just—'

'I am telling you what happened, not asking you for your confirmation,' he said, with a heady mix of arrogance and confidence. 'Now, give me your parents' contact numbers so that we can tell them what a bad boy you have been.'

'You don't need to,' he mumbled, confused. And the confusion was not a symptom of the *hepatic whatever* he had, but what the doctor had just said.

'Hospital rules, Dushyant,' he explained. 'No matter how much I hate dead people, I hate unpaid bills more.'

Dushyant, dazed and caught off guard, wrote down an old, out-of-service landline number of his house and asked him, 'You're going to call them now?'

'Not really. Not unless you have to undergo some drastic medical procedure which requires them to be around. Or you are broke and can't pay the bills.'

'Fine,' he said. 'How long will it take?'

'If you don't die, you should be okay in three weeks,' he said. 'But if you go back and try to drown yourself in alcohol again, you might not get out of here alive. I have some other patients to look into, who are not killing themselves. I will check on you later today.'

'Will it hurt?'

'Did it hurt when you stuck needles inside yourself, Dushyant?' he asked. 'But don't worry, the best part of your disease is that just in case you die, you will die sleeping. Hepatic encephalopathy is a very lazy disease—somnolence and acting stupid being the main symptoms. You have already done with being stupid, so I guess there is just one left. Go, sleep.'

Before Dushyant could say anything to that, the doctor hung his chart on the bed and left the room. Frantically, Dushyant called his friend to confirm if what the doctor had said was true. It was. *This is seriously fucked up*, he thought.

He punched the words 'hepatic encephalopathy' into his cell phone's Google browser and it took him a few times to get the spelling right. A few search results popped up and he read through them hurriedly. Combing through the labyrinth of medical words and terminologies, he knew where his problem came from—his excessive drinking. *I don't even drink a lot!* He was right, but he was into all kinds of stuff and the more he read up on the disease the more he realized that he was at fault. A few sentences stood out and he lay there breathing heavily and cursing everything that he had ingested in the last five years, but still wanting some more of it at that moment. Ideally, he would have loved a couple of large shots of vodka mixed with a few shots, big shots, of tequila. If worst came to worst, a cigarette. Dushyant had never been an addict, and unlike addicts who thought they could kick the habit any time, he could actually do so. Or so he thought.

Soon, sleep took over and he closed his eyes, wondering if he would wake up again. What he had read circled his head for the entire time that he slept.

Those with severe encephalopathy (stages 3 and 4) are at risk of obstructing their airway due to decreased protective reflexes such as the gag reflex. This can lead to respiratory arrest. Intubation of the airway is often necessary to prevent life-threatening complications (e.g., aspiration or respiratory failure).

Are they going to cut my throat open? he thought in his sleep.

If encephalopathy develops in acute liver failure, it indicates that a liver transplant may be required.

Where would I get that! Even in his sleep, he wanted to get hammered. Vodka. Tequila. Whisky. Iodex. Anything.

2

Arman Kashyap

Arman Kashyap had stacked up medical degrees from premier medical colleges, but he was best known for his degree in attitude from God knows where. He walked the hallways of GKL Hospital with a confidence not seen in doctors three decades older and much wiser. His peers said he was arrogant because he belonged to a family of remarkable doctors and extraordinary businessmen. His father was the country's leading heart surgeon, his mom, a sensitive and highly popular psychiatrist amongst rich, bored and horny housewives, and his older sister, a paediatrician whose average day was littered with appointments with celebrities—medicine and excellence ran in his blood.

But the arrogance didn't stem from his impressive background. He just knew he was that *good*.

And he knew he wasn't just a jerk. Had he been one, he would have worked in the chain of hospitals his father had amassed in the last twenty years. He would have been sitting pretty in a corner office with a few brilliant doctors working under him, doing whatever he would have asked them to. But he didn't choose to be that, instead he chose to work out the grind and prove his worth every minute of every hour in a hospital where he held no influence. He had earned every bit of the reputation that he had got himself in the last three years. His sincere good looks—he stood at six feet, had short hair and wore expensive rimless spectacles—and savage drive to succeed had helped.

'So, you look like you made someone's life hell today,' Zarah said as Arman approached her.

'Hell? Guys like him make their own lives hell and come here with diseases which I have no intentions to diagnose or treat. It's a waste of resources,' he said and added with an evil smile, 'I was praying he wouldn't wake up. Wouldn't that have been so much better?'

'You wished he would die?' she asked, shocked. Just a few weeks had passed of her internship under Arman and she was still trying to come to terms with the genius doctor's behavioural eccentricities. Arman knew he wasn't the best boss or the most cooperative of colleagues to have. But he believed it was other people's liability to accept him for what he was. He was, after all, a rare genius.

'Don't you think he should die? A guy who cracks a competitive exam to a good engineering college only to drink and smoke himself to death. Should *he* live? Or should the people who die on the streets be given that chance?'

'Well, they can't afford it,' Zarah retorted, trying to outsmart him.

'I don't care about them. But the guy on that bed doesn't deserve to live,' he answered. 'Imagine what his parents must go through. Disgrace.'

'As if you get along with your parents.'

'How was it when you were growing up, Zarah? Did your parents tell you what *not* to do? Don't meet that guy, don't stay out that late, and *please* don't get less than 95 per cent in your examinations? And when did that stop? When you got through medical school in Delhi and they had no idea what you were studying and how much you should score? When they couldn't make sense whether 657/1230 meant good marks or bad?'

'Well, more or less,' she responded.

'Imagine that, only three times as bad. The hospital mails them details of every case I work on here and they keep telling me what to do. The patient coughs up blood, my dad calls; a seizure, my mom calls; and someone slips into a coma, my sister calls! It's a crazy house,' he explained. 'As if saving assholes like him was not enough, I have to answer to every damn question that my parents pose.'

'Is that why you don't work at your parents' hospital?'

'I don't work there because I think I deserve better than that.'

'I hope I start to understand what you mean some day, sir,' Zarah said and flicked her hair behind her ear.

'And that's not even the worst part. The worst part is—they are *never* right!'

'That's funny, sir.'

'You have to stop calling me "sir" first. It makes me feel, well, old,' he said. 'Anyway, we have a new patient. Pretty standard case. The good thing is that the girl is like you, only younger. She got admitted into medical school last year, found something wrong with her hands and diagnosed it herself. Impressive, isn't it?'

Looking at her face, he knew Zarah didn't know what to make of what he said, whether he was genuinely impressed or was being sarcastic. Anyway, he always felt something was wrong with Zarah. She was way too reserved for the way she looked. At five feet seven, she towered above even a few male doctors. She didn't have a shred of fat on her body, probably because she smoked a lot. But her lips, the lightest shade of pink, didn't leave any telltale signs of her smoking habit. Neither did her chocolate-coloured exotic skin, which was smooth and velvety. To be honest, the first time Arman saw her in her white doctor's coat and the three-inch heels, he thought she wasn't from India at all. Maybe Brazil. Or Chile. Or Uruguay. Some place not India. Usually, the prettier female doctors were outspoken; Zarah, on the other hand, was reserved. It was intriguing. Maybe she was a perfect case for his mother, the acclaimed psychiatrist. In her mother's words, she was *damaged*.

'Can you check her up and get her forms done?' he asked her and gave her the file. 'She is here for a few tests. We will admit her to the hospital in a day or two.'

'Right away, Arman.' Zarah took the file from his hand and started reading through it. 'It says in this file you were her external consultant? I didn't know you do that.'

'It's a special case,' Arman responded with a straight face, 'and it will be better if you keep it to yourself.'

Pihu Malhotra. Age 19. Arman saw Zarah's eyes rivet on the file. She didn't move a muscle.

'Is there a problem?' he asked.

'She has ALS? As in Lou Gehrig's disease?'

Arman could sense the shock in her voice—a definite marker of a young, inexperienced doctor. He had expected it. When he had first heard about the case, he had felt the same thing. Shock. Disbelief. Pity.

'Yes, why do you look shocked?'

'Isn't it something that afflicts people over the age of forty? She is just nineteen.'

'That's what makes it interesting. Have you heard about Stephen Hawking?'

'The super-genius scientist? The wheelchair-bound physicist who can't talk any more?' she asked, just to be sure.

'Yes, the same guy. He was diagnosed at the age of twenty-one. Doctors said he had three years. It has been forty years since then. His disease was progressing slowly. Hers, on the other hand,' he pointed to the file, 'is progressing at a faster rate. She was diagnosed one year back and she might not make it through the next three months.'

'What do we do? There is no cure, right?'

'No, there is not. I am on the research panel trying to find one. Let's see what happens. We will decide when the right time comes,' he said and got back to his work. He had no intentions of indulging in a 'poor girl' type conversation with Zarah. Clearly, Zarah was stunned and her face contorted to signify the pity she felt for the nineteen-year-old dying girl.

Zarah had studied to be in the *noble* profession and save lives and get people healthy, but she never really had the heart to overlook the pain of sick people in the first place. It reminded her of her own angst. She felt sorry for Pihu, and for the bastard who lay in the room with a damaged liver.

3

Pihu Malhotra

Pihu looked at the tall stacks of books lined up in front of her. Her lips curved into an embarrassed smile. She looked around and hoped nobody had seen it. Examinations were around the corner and everyone was stressed out and high on caffeine. Pihu was high on anticipation. She had finished the course. Twice.

Pihu's parents were ecstatic when she had cracked the All India Medical Examinations and decided to go to Maulana Azad Medical College, one of the best medical colleges in India. Pihu had smiled, shaken hands and hugged. She knew it was just the beginning. School never offered her the opportunity to bury herself in course books the way she had always wanted to. The course was never a challenge. The entrance examinations were a necessary evil. She knew she would sail through. When news broke out in her hometown that her AIR (All India Rank) was third, cunning pot-bellied owners of coaching institutes had flocked to her place, wanting her to advertise their highly qualified staff and fully air-conditioned classrooms with a picture of their most illustrious

14

student—Pihu Malhotra. A few days later, she was in the local newspapers. Her parents' dreams were fulfilled. Hers had just taken root.

These were the first set of exams in her college.

'You don't look tense?' Venugopal asked as he underlined his book with a fluorescent marker.

'I am okay,' she said, barely suppressing a chuckle.

She had the book *Human Anatomy* open in front of her. She had read it twice. She itched to read something else. Her eyes had been on the book on pathology lying on the side. A second-year student was sleeping on it. She wanted to peep in, worse still, whip it away from under the senior's head, but she didn't want to come across as a nerd.

'You have finished the course, haven't you?' Venugopal asked suspiciously.

'Yes,' she said and blushed. 'But I still have to revise,' she added.

'But when? You spent all the time with us. When did you get the time? I didn't see you study!'

'Promise you won't tell anyone?'

'I won't,' Venugopal asked and adjusted the spectacles on his hunched nose. Obviously, he wouldn't. Pihu knew that. Venugopal and Pihu were destined to be friends after the first roll call in their class of 335 students. Their roll numbers were consecutive, since Venugopal's full name was P. Venugopal where P stood for something unpronounceable for north Indians. They were partners in dissection and had cut open their first corpse together—it's the sort of thing that binds two doctors together for the rest of their lives. Kind of what it means for two engineering students to have the first peg of whisky together. Other than that, they were very similar. Middle-class families, dads in government service, mothers as housewives and CBSE toppers of their own regions. In a parallel universe where north and south Indians got along, it was a match made in heaven.

In the past three months, they had become the best of friends. They never kept anything from each other. They didn't have to, since they led simple lives. Simple people with simple desires. They had nothing to hide. They had never partied, never smoked, never drank. Neither of them had stayed out of their houses after eight. They never felt the need to.

'I had gone through a few books before I joined college,' Pihu said.

'You had? Which ones?'

'Anatomy. Physiology. General Pharmacology. A few others.'

'A few others? That's like the whole course,' Venugopal gasped.

'I always wanted to read them ever since I started preparing for medical entrances. That's all I have ever wanted to do.'

'You're crazy. Why would you?'

'I have always wanted to be a doctor. Ever since the time I was a little kid. At first, I thought I liked the candy my paediatrician gave me! But slowly, it became an obsession. I used to fake illnesses as a kid so I could go to the clinic and hear the doctor talk about various medicines and cures. It's everything I have ever wanted to do. Haven't you?' Pihu purred and batted her eyelashes shyly.

'I have always wanted a career. And being a doctor was one,' Venugopal responded. 'But you're awesome. You will be a great doctor.'

'Thanks.' Pihu blushed. 'So will you.'

'I hope so. But why didn't you tell me before? You could have taught me. I am struggling here.'

'I can still teach you,' she said.

Venugopal pushed the book towards her, rested his chin on his knuckles and commanded, 'Teach.'

'I didn't want you to think I was a freak,' Pihu said softly.

'I don't need to tell you that.' Venugopal laughed.

Pihu always thought of Venugopal as a sweet, well-mannered guy. He was from Chennai, Tamil Nadu, and barely spoke any Hindi. Pihu had spent the first few weeks forcing him to talk in Hindi and laughing her head off. Somewhere between the lectures on human lungs and lymph nodes, Pihu knew she had found a friend for life. She loved the way he cursed the Delhi food, complained about the egregious hostel canteen's sambar and how he pronounced 'mall' as 'maal'. Their bond strengthened over countless meals of butter chicken and shitty sambar, and arguments about which tasted better.

~

Pihu stared at the books again wondering what had gone wrong. Fear clouded her mind. A million possibilities battled each other and she cried. She had read about 'hypochondriasis of medical students', a condition in which medical students diagnose themselves with diseases they don't have. It stems from the paranoia one suffers from after obsessing over different symptoms throughout the day. But she knew for a fact that she wasn't imagining things.

She had left the examination hall thirty minutes before the scheduled time. She knew all the answers. She had wanted to write them. The pen was in her hand, and the answers in her head. But her hands had cramped. It wasn't the fear of the examination; she didn't know what it felt like to be afraid of an examination. There was something wrong with her hands.

It wasn't the first time she had felt it, but she had chosen to ignore it earlier.

She had tried moving her hand in vain. After struggling with intermittent pain and the lack of sensation for half an hour, she had started to write. She had written three beautiful answers when the pain and the lack of sensation came back. She had tears in her eyes. She didn't know what was wrong with her hand. Every page from every medical book she had read came rushing back to her mind. Her head hurt. Tears streamed down her face. Half an hour before the exam ended, she left the hall, tears in her eyes and strange cramps in both her hands.

'Why haven't you been picking up your calls?' Venugopal asked, worried and flustered.

Venugopal had been calling her for quite some time now. Pihu had disconnected all calls till she asked him to join her in the library.

'There is something wrong with me,' she explained. 'I had not given it too much thought earlier, but I know something is definitely wrong with me.'

'Yes, I know. You study too much,' Venugopal suggested and smiled.

'It's not that. It's the examination.'

'What? You did well, right? Everything you taught me was perfect! It was like you knew the questions beforehand. You are teaching me everything from now on!' he chortled.

'I didn't write anything after the third question,' Pihu said, tears flooding her eyes.

'Hey . . . Hey . . . Are you crying? What happened? Were you nervous? But you knew everything, didn't you?'

'I knew everything.'

'Did you blank out?' Venugopal asked, concern writ across his face.

'NO! I knew the answers.'

Shhh. The librarian asked them to be silent.

'Then what happened?'

'I couldn't write. My hand . . . I had no control over it,' she said and broke down in small sobs. Venugopal looked puzzled. He took her hand in his palms and applied pressure at a few points. He asked her if she had any sensation in her hand. Pihu could feel the warmth in Venugopal's touch, but she knew something was wrong. *Why can't I feel it!*

'Can you feel my touch?' Venugopal asked.

'I am scared,' she said. She picked up a pencil from her neatly arranged geometry box. She tried to write her name on the piece of paper in front of her. She couldn't control it. Venugopal watched in horror as she scribbled. It wasn't the usual curvy, artistic font she used to write in. It was hardly legible. It looked like she was using the wrong hand. 'I can't control my hand.'

'Let's see a doctor?'

'I wanted to be a surgeon,' she said and put her head down on the books. She cried.

'C'mon, Pihu. You don't know what it is. It could be something as simple as Vitamin C deficiency. There are cases reported where Vitamin C deficiency causes paralysis. Even if it's not that, there could be a million other innocuous reasons! I think you're overreacting,' Venugopal assured her.

'What if it's not an *innocuous* reason? What if it's something more?' she asked, her voice breaking off in sobs.

She looked at her hand. Pale and useless. *Stop being so negative! Maybe it's not that bad. This can't happen to me. Maybe Venugopal is right.* All the possible causes for the symptom started to shadow her mind. She was freaking out, her tears were uncontrollable. What was it? Stroke? Nerve injury? Poliomyelitis? Botulism? Spina bifida? Multiple sclerosis? Guillain–Barré syndrome? All of a sudden, it looked as if she could have every disease she had read about till now. The deadlier the disease, the more convinced she was about its possibility. Sleep evaded her that night as she looked up every possible cause of her problem. By next morning, she had a list of eighty-nine possible causes. She scheduled herself for a plethora of blood tests the next day.

Venugopal had a horrendous next exam. Pihu and Venugopal had spent the night looking over all the possible causes of Pihu's loss of control of her hand. They narrowed it down to twenty types of blood tests and visited a pathology lab at night, rather late for them. She didn't want to trouble him, but he had insisted. Pihu waited for him outside his examination hall the next day with her blood test results in hand.

Her blood work was clean, eliminating eighty-eight possible causes.

～

'I never thought I would be the first person I would have to diagnose,' Pihu said on the phone.

There were no tests left to be done. Blood tests ruled out pathogens and other common diseases, breathing tests to check the lungs, MRIs to rule out any neck injury, electromyography to check the nerves in her hand, a head MRI to eliminate other conditions and nerve conduction studies to sum up the rest.

'You can never be too sure,' Venugopal said from the other side of the phone.

'I wish I didn't have to,' she whimpered and heard the rustling of pages. 'Are you still in the library?'

'No, I am not.'

'You *are*. Go out, Venu! The exams just got over. Go out and party with the guys.'

'Not without you. I want you to be here,' he said.

'I don't think I am coming back,' Pihu responded.

'You can't talk like that. You haven't even seen a doctor, yet. You have to be positive.'

'He must have read the same books that we have. I am sure of what I have, Venu. I can't be in denial,' she lied.

'You mean to say that experience counts for nothing? See a doctor. It could still be something else,' he argued.

Pihu didn't want to pursue it any more. She knew he was going through denial. A certain part of her was going through the same. Except for this call, she had not stopped crying since the time she discovered what she was afflicted with. She had cursed the unfair balance of nature. What she had was not something she deserved. She had cried and pored over the reports again and again, hoping there would be a mistake. She wished she was wrong in her self-diagnosis. She could be. She was only a first-year medical student and she wasn't supposed to diagnose it correctly in any case.

'Are you going to tell them?' he asked.

'I think I will let some doctor do it,' she said. Her eyes watered up. She heard the flipping of papers from the other side. 'I will talk to you later. The signal is cracking up.' She disconnected the call. *I hope I am wrong about this.* She sighed. The tears returned and they never stopped during the three hours it took for her to reach her home from the college hostel. All her dreams washed away in an instant.

~

Once home, she stood in front of her parents, complaining about the strange sensations in her right arm. Her mother started to ask her about the examinations. Dad asked her if she was eating right. It took her an hour to make them take the cramps and the loss of sensation in her hand seriously. Her mom suggested stress. Dad suggested infection. 'Delhi's water is riddled with parasites and germs. You're almost a doctor, you should know,' he said. She insisted on seeing a doctor. Her dad smiled at the irony. Pihu knew what he was thinking about. He had imagined her as a doctor. Something that Pihu knew would never happen. *I hope I am wrong*, she sighed.

On the way to the hospital, she tried to be her chirpy self, even though all she wanted to do was cry. Maybe she was wrong. The doctor in the hospital asked her a few questions and prescribed her some blood tests.

'It could be anything. Let's wait for the blood test results,' he assured the worried parents. 'Come back tomorrow and we will find out what's wrong with her.' He pushed the bowl of candy in front of her. Out of habit, she stuffed a fistful of Éclairs in her pocket.

Pihu knew the doctor wouldn't find anything abnormal in the tests and would order some more tests. Back home, she fished out every research paper and every document ever written about the disease. Looking through various reports she found a research team in a hospital in Delhi which specialized in stem cell research and developing experimental new drugs for the disease. She found the email ID of one of the doctors on the team—Arman Kashyap, supposedly a genius, and shot across an email giving him the details of her disease. She was desperate. She didn't want to die and she didn't deserve to.

That night, when she was done reading about her disease and had cried enough to make herself tired, Venugopal called again. He had been texting her constantly. Pihu knew for sure he had been doing some reading on the disease too.

'What did he say? Did he order all the blood tests? Did he guess anything? Any alternative causes? Differential diagnosis?' he asked, the panic in his voice apparent.

'The reports come tomorrow. I know they will be clean. He hasn't guessed anything yet.'

'Maybe they will find something that we didn't. We did the tests just once. And these government pathological labs make mistakes all the time. Where did you go? Apex Hospital?' Venugopal blabbered, hoping against hope. This time he wasn't even convincing. He had checked and rechecked the reports; Pihu was sure of that. They weren't incorrect.

'Let's wait for tomorrow.'

'Are you okay, Pihu?'

'Yes.'

'Are you scared?'

'Very,' Pihu said and started sobbing softly. She had promised herself that she would be strong and not cry. She couldn't do it. She had read about the suffering of people who had the same disease as hers, and she felt terrible. Having read horrendous accounts of how patients lose control of their body as it slowly rots away, she started to question the fairness of it all. *Why me? Of all people!* She cursed the mirror in front of her for it was lying. She wasn't healthy. Her insides were rotting away, slowly, bit by bit.

'It's going to be okay,' he assured her.

'Nothing is going to be okay. You know that! I am dying, Venugopal . . .'

She cried a little more on the phone and eventually drifted off to sleep. She didn't know if Venugopal had waited for long before he disconnected the call. It didn't matter. She was alone in this. She had to get used to it.

~

Things only became worse the next morning. Her denial had given way to acceptance, and the acceptance of her condition depressed her. With a heavy heart, she checked all the websites

she had bookmarked the day before, searched for cures on the
Internet even when she knew there weren't any, and checked
if Dr Arman Kashyap from GKL Hospital had replied to her
long, ranting mail.

A little later, they were in the car, negotiating the early-
morning traffic to the hospital. Pihu sat on the back seat,
wondering if the doctor had any inkling of what was wrong
with her. She hoped he would. And she hoped it wasn't what
she thought it was. The anticipation of the pain her parents
would go through was getting unbearable.

'Good morning,' the doctor from the day before said. He
was smiling. 'The blood reports came clean.'

A smile shot across her parents' faces. Pihu remained
expressionless as she looked at all the branded merchandise—
pens, diaries, clocks and notepads—from the big pharmaceutical
companies. Her mom folded her arms as if to say, *I know it's
because of the stress.* Her father absent-mindedly played with a
plastic model of the human brain.

'Are you still having some problem with your hands?'

She nodded.

'Any other problems? Difficulty in breathing? Anything?'

She nodded. Now he's getting it. Maybe. *I would have made
such a good doctor.* She tried not to buckle and weep. Her parents
were still distracted. She felt sorry for them. Again, she stuffed
her pocket with a fistful of Éclairs.

The doctor looked at her parents and started to ask them
about their families. 'So Pihu's grandparents? They are still alive?'

They let the doctors know whatever he needed and the
doctor noted everything down on a small pad. She knew he
was yet to make any sense of it. But he had a hunch about
what Pihu had.

'We need to do some more tests,' he said, 'to check the nerve reactions. Nothing major.' The doctor smiled. Pihu smiled back at him. *Does he know? Why is he smiling?*

'I am sure it's because of stress. She is a medical student, you know. Lots of pressure, big books, late nights, you know? She is a brilliant student, topped the region in her board examinations. She wants to be a surgeon.' Her mom's chest swelled with obvious pride. The doctor nodded approvingly.

'Do you know what's wrong with her?' her father asked, keeping down the fake brain.

Please don't ask, Dad. I am dying. Slowly. Please don't ask.

'Let's wait for the results,' the doctor answered and whisked her away to the testing room.

It took the doctor three hours, a battery of tests and consultations with other doctors to come to the conclusion Pihu had reached days before. She had noticed the expressions of shock on their faces while her doctor discussed the case with other doctors in her presence. As they talked and looked in her direction, with pity on their faces, she was sure they didn't know that she already knew. Some of them even called their counterparts in other hospitals for a second opinion.

'Did you figure it out yet?' she asked the doctor, who shifted restlessly in his place.

'We are just getting a final confirmation from an expertdoctor in Mumbai,' he said. She felt sorry for the doctor, too. Why should he be a part of the gloom that was about to engulf her family?

'I know what I have, doctor,' she said, her head hung low. *'Excuse me?'*

'I am a medical student. First year, Maulana Azad. I did the tests myself.'

'What tests?' The shock on the doctor's face snowballed into concern and pity.

'I have ALS. I know there is no genetic history. I know
there is no cure. I know that I am slowly dying. I could be
gone this year or the next. But I will die eventually. I have
read all there is to read about the disease. I know what's
going to happen. I will not be able to eat on my own, go to
the bathroom or even breathe. You will cut a pipe into my
throat to help me breathe or I might choke on my own saliva,'
she explained. She hadn't discussed her painful future with
Venugopal for she didn't have the strength to. It looked like
it could never happen to her. As she finally described her own
death to the doctor, she came to terms with it. The news finally
sank in. In that moment, all her dreams, her aspirations, her
visions of herself as a doctor melted away and the morose faces
of her parents stared back at her. Her eyes glazed over and
she resolved to not weep. *There is some mistake! This shouldn't
happen to me. I have done nothing to deserve this. I am perfectly
healthy!* Her heart cried out loud.

'There are treatments—'

'Riluzole, diazepam, amitriptyline. They will give me a few
months more. A few days more of breathing on my own. I
have read all about it.'

She tried not to cry. The doctor didn't want to give her any
false hope. She had to be ready for what was coming next.

ALS is a cruel disease. It starts with the patient becoming
clumsy. You drop things, get tired easily, and the sensations
in your limbs keep getting dimmer till paralysis sets in. After
that, you're at your helpers' mercy. You can't eat because your
tongue and your jaw muscles will be too weak to chew the
food. You can't talk fast or for too long because your mouth
will become tired after the first minute or so. You will be on
crutches . . . before the wheelchair comes in. Soon, even that
will be a problem because you won't have the forearm strength
to roll the chair. You will be paralysed and bedridden. There

will be tubes running in and out of your body to help you eat, breathe and defecate. Machines will keep you alive. It's a sorry way to die.

'I am sorry,' he said. 'I wish I could do something. I can give you some books you can read about people who have fought the disease. They didn't win, but they died happy. You can't lose to the disease.'

'I would just wish for you to tell my parents. I don't have the courage,' she said and the tears came again. She tried to stifle her sobs the best she could. Never had she thought her parents would outlive her. What greater misfortune can there be for a parent?

'You're the most courageous patient I have seen in the longest time,' he said and added with a pause, 'I have a daughter. She is seven.'

'Does she want to be a doctor too?'

'Yes. You remind me of her,' the doctor said, looked down at the reports in his hands and closed his eyes. Pihu wondered if he was praying for them to be wrong. She wondered how many death sentences the forty-year-old man had given before hers. The watery eyes of the doctor told her that he was still not used to it.

'Let's tell my parents?' Pihu said, and clutched the doctor's hand and slipped in some Éclairs. 'Give this to your daughter from my side.'

'Sure,' he nodded and took a deep breath.

Pihu took one too. The wails of her mother and silent groans of her father already resonated in her head and she felt dizzy. They entered the doctor's chambers. Her parents' eyes met hers and she knew they could see the horror. Their faces fell as if they knew what the middle-aged doctor was about to tell them. She went and sat next to her mom and held her hand. The doctor started to explain. The world blocked out.

Her mind was blank. The denial of her parents, their shouts, their screams, their accusations against the incompetent doctor and the irresponsible hospital, their claims of their daughter being perfectly healthy—nothing registered in her brain. She had just one image seared on her retina.

She was going to die, motionless on a hospital bed with a tube cut into her throat.

4

Kajal Khurana

Kajal paced nervously in her hostel room. The news of Dushyant lying unconscious for three days had just reached her. It wasn't the first time she had received such a call. When they were dating, she was used to going to the hospital, picking him up and cleaning up his shit. But the last such call was two years back. Today, she had suppressed the impulse to drop everything and visit him. *He wouldn't want to see me*, she argued. *Do I want to see him?* Two years had passed since the last time they had talked.

Kajal dialled the number.

'Hello, GKL Hospital? Can I talk to the doctor of a patient admitted there? The name is Dushyant Roy.'

'Hold on,' the voice from the other side said. The waiting sound piped up.

'Hello? This is Zarah Mirza.'

Two summers before this one, Kajal was a second-year student and Dushyant was a year senior to her. It wasn't until a few friends pointed it out that Kajal realized she was constantly being stared at by a senior. It was none other than the swearing, belligerent, infamous, drunkard of a senior with a penchant for getting into trouble—Dushyant Roy. Kajal hadn't noticed his stealthy moves earlier, but slowly she started to spot him everywhere. She hadn't made much of him earlier and thought of him as one of the many roadside ruffians from the mechanical department. Little did the rich daddy's girl know that he was going to change her life forever. Forever began on the day Kajal was sitting idly in the library, looking blankly outside the window . . .

~

Kajal looked at the open grounds of Delhi Technological University and felt disconnected. Two years had passed since she had started studying electronics engineering and felt more disillusioned with every day that passed. She wasn't meant for Schrödinger equations and Fourier transforms, like many others studying with her. While many had resigned themselves to their fate as engineers for life, Kajal still believed she would be something more. At least she hoped. People with money can always do that—hope, change careers, do crazy expensive things, and call themselves travellers after buying travel packages to posh European countries and staying in beautiful resorts. Though Kajal had never been that type; she was just directionless.

Her latest direction was to turn to writing. She had always been a voracious reader. From Sweet Valley High, the Hardy Boys, Enid Blyton when she was young, to David Baldacci, Dan Brown, Nicholas Sparks when she got older, to the heavier works of authors like Mohsin Hamid and V.S. Naipaul, she had read it all. She picked out a corner in the library and started to read from the page she had folded the day before. It was the latest book by Nicholas Sparks. Like every other girl, she had spent countless nights crying to his books, even though she steadfastly maintained that she wasn't into romance novels and that she had never been a fan of Indian authors and their amateurish love stories set in engineering colleges.

'Hi,' she heard a voice from behind her.

She turned around to see the guy who had been following her around college for the last few days, standing just over her shoulder. Her first feeling was of revulsion. His hair was tousled carelessly, his clothes looked like he hadn't changed in days and his four-day beard just looked annoying. He wasn't that tall; maybe 5'10" or 5'11" or even taller, she couldn't tell because he was well-built for his frame. She imagined an Indian Vin Diesel. Not her type; she liked leaner men. Like Edward Norton. Like Imran Khan. Maybe a little darker.

'Yes?'

'Do you mind if I sit there?' he asked, and pointed to the seat next to Kajal.

Kajal hesitated and he took the seat before she could respond to the question. *Rude*, she thought. She liked that.

'I have read that book,' he said. 'It's just like the last one. The girl dies and everyone cries. All his books are the same book. I don't know why girls still like him. They're so predictable.'

'I didn't need to know that,' Kajal retorted. She started reading, mindlessly. She forgot which paragraph she was on. It didn't matter. A little later, she said, 'Even if it's the same book, the people are different and so are the emotions. It's an entirely new experience every time. You wouldn't understand. I don't expect you to.'

'As a matter of fact, I do. That is why I read all of them. Well, initially I just read one because I saw you reading it and thought we would have something to talk about. I ended up reading all of them,' he claimed.

'You're such a girl!' she giggled.

He nodded approvingly. She wouldn't have guessed that the guy who sat next to her shared the same taste for books as hers. She would learn later that he didn't. Dushyant had always been more interested in books that took him beyond the realm of the obvious. He read books people hadn't heard about. A memoir of a serial killer. An out-of-print trilogy about a deranged doctor. And more.

Her eyes roved around nervously as an uneasy silence hung between them. He looked sturdy, the veins in his forearms were consistently thick and they disappeared inside his T-shirt, which fit him snuggly. He was undeniably muscular. He smelled very strongly of cologne, as if he had tried to look presentable at the last moment. *He could have shaved, at least!*

'Dushyant,' he said and stuck his hand out.

'Kajal,' she said and left his hand hanging mid-air. He retracted it, blushing. He didn't meet her eye. She could tell he was nervous. His legs shook. Kajal started reading again. The same paragraph, over and over. Dushyant sat there looking at her, and at his palms, rubbing them together, looking here and there, shifting his feet and fidgeting with his phone.

'I have been following you,' he said, finally.

'I have been told that,' Kajal responded.

'For two years . . .'

Two years? Creep! Or . . . really sweet? Dushyant had turned beetroot red. He couldn't meet her eyes. Instead, he gazed at his own weathered palms. He looked vulnerable, embarrassed and needy. Maybe even a little high. Kajal let a little smile slip. Dushyant caught that and blushed a little more.

'So, tell me, what do you read?' Kajal asked. *Two years?*

Dushyant smiled, and his eyes lit up like the fourth of July. Quite frankly, his choice in books scared her.

~

They dated for eight months. They had come a long way from the time they had first met in the library and had talked about books, his waning obsession with weight training, her growing dissatisfaction with her career choice, his problems with his parents, her loving sisters, and last but not the least, his enduring fixation with her.

Dushyant was never the perfect boyfriend. Her friends hated him with all their heart, but not as much as her sisters. Kajal was tall—almost 5′5″—and never had a hair out of place. One could imagine a news presenter for an idea of what she looked like. Her clothes, understated, were always perfectly matched. She wasn't fond of bright colours and never aimed to stand out. She aimed to soothe. Her fair skin, the defined nose and the confident walk meant business. She wasn't a pushover.

Dushyant was abrasive. He was quarrelsome. He was possessive. It took Kajal one month to realize that Dushyant was beyond obsessive, almost to the point of being schizophrenic. He drank too much, he smoked too much, and he loved her too much. He had waited two years to tell her he loved her. He swore he would spend a lifetime doing it. Sometimes, it was sweet. It looked to her like he cared; on other occasions, she was scared. Not scared that they would break up and never see each other again, but scared of what he would do to her. Within a month, she had changed into someone she didn't recognize any more.

At first, Kajal used to like the little tabs Dushyant kept on her. He used to get jealous at the mention of her ex-boyfriends, fume at her for spending more time with her friends, chide her for staying out till late, and ask her to not to drink in his absence. Kajal found it thoughtful. Who wouldn't? Dushyant made her feel wanted. Loved. No matter what the time of day, no matter what he was doing, one call from her and he would go running to her. He never let go of her hand, hugged her whenever she needed it, and made love to her like no one else had. Kajal felt like she was enveloped in a protective bubble wrap, something that would absorb anything with the potential to harm her. But soon, the bubble wrap would become suffocating.

Kajal loved Dushyant with whatever she had. Their relationship wasn't one of the two-hormone-charged-college-students type, but of two mature people who saw themselves together for the rest of their lives. When they lay on the open grounds of their college late in the evening, his rough, gym-scarred fingers wrapped around hers, she felt complete. As evenings turned into nights, nights into days, and days back into evenings, their love for each other grew.

Kajal learnt to overlook Dushyant's little flaws. Dushyant always said Kajal had none. Kajal always smiled, even when she felt pushed to the edge by her control-freak boyfriend.

'Do you think this will last?' Kajal said as Dushyant wrapped his hand around hers in a movie hall.

'How can it not?' Dushyant said, and brushed her ears with his lips. He had done that many times since the first occasion, but Kajal still felt the chills run down her spine like the first time. Dushyant wasn't Kajal's first boyfriend. But he was the one she would remember forever; she was sure of that. His touch, the things he said in her ear whenever they were in the back alley of the dark library, the lingering feeling of his hands on her bare stomach, his loving fingers on her creamy inner thighs, the wet, gentle touch of his tongue on her ears . . . she would never get over them.

'You're the best thing that has ever happened to me,' Dushyant said as soon as an action sequence ended in the movie and there was silence. The conviction in his voice was very unsettling; it often made her wonder what would happen if, God forbid, they ever broke up.

'And still you can't quit drinking and smoking for me?'

'I have cut it down a lot.'

'You need a cigarette every hour, Dushyant,' she said. 'You will kill yourself.'

'I am trying. It will take time. You just can't let it go overnight,' Dushyant retorted irritably. Kajal never liked to talk about his drinking problem. She loved him, so she had to. But she had had enough. The steroids he took as bodybuilding supplements, the marijuana, the never-ending cigarettes . . . his addictions kept piling up. She didn't know where to begin.

'If you loved me enough, you would have stopped by now.'

'I have stopped taking steroids,' he defended himself.

'That's because it's been months since you have been to the gym. I don't like to see you destroy yourself. I hope you understand that. I have nothing to gain out of restricting you from your addictions. It's just that I don't want anything to happen to you.'

'Nothing is going to happen to me. Okay, fine,' he said. 'You stop talking to Varun. I will stop smoking. That's a fair deal?'

'*What*? How's that even connected?'

'You're addicted to Varun. I am addicted to my cigarettes. You leave him, I'll quit smoking. I am not comfortable with you being friends with your ex-boyfriend and you're not comfortable with my smoking habit. It sounds fair to me.'

'You talk to Smita too, Dushyant. I have never pointed my finger at that.'

'Fine, I will stop talking to her. I never call her anyway. But you do call Varun. There are times you put my call on hold to pick up his. Sometimes you talk till the dead of night or early morning. What do I make of all this? If you need more friends, why not someone else? Why do you have to be friends with your ex-boyfriend, of all people?' Dushyant accused.

It wasn't the first time Dushyant was being paranoid about Kajal still being friends with Varun—her best friend for the longest time and a boyfriend for two years.

'You're being childish. I have told you a million times that there is nothing between us. He is just a friend and will always be,' Kajal asserted. She thought about all the times Dushyant had got drunk and harped on about how he hated Varun with every cell in his body.

'I don't think so. Why don't you just accept that you still have feelings for him?' He shrugged, trying to act as if he didn't care. Kajal knew he did. It didn't take long for Dushyant to change from being nonchalant about something to start breaking things.

'I don't. He is a friend. I've known him for fifteen years. How can I just stop talking to him?'

'Why can't you? He dumped you. He was dating someone else while he was still dating you. I don't understand how you can forgive him. Don't you have a speck of self-respect? I just don't like the fact that you have forgiven him so easily. How could he do that to you? He doesn't even respect you,' Dushyant grumbled.

The movie ended and they exited the movie hall. Kajal felt odd as Dushyant walked in front of her and didn't even hold the door open. Clearly, he wasn't pleased.

'Our relationship was not working. I don't blame him,' she reasoned.

'You don't blame him? You spent days crying for him.'

'I spent days crying because he left. I felt alone and lonely. Not because I missed him as a boyfriend but because I missed him as a friend. I had no one to go to.'

'And now that you have me, you still miss him? How does that work? You have a boyfriend. You shouldn't need him,' Dushyant argued as they entered a coffee shop. All this time he walked three steps ahead of her, not meeting her eye and behaving like they weren't together.

The waiter promptly rushed towards them and Dushyant swatted him away rudely. The shocked waiter lingered on.

'Water,' Kajal indicated to the waiter. 'And a cappuccino for him.'

Dushyant picked up the menu and acted as if the conversation was over.

'He means nothing to me. Believe me. He is just a friend. And it doesn't matter if I talk to him. I love you and nothing changes that.'

'Well. I am fine. Whatever. You talk to him, you sleep with him. I don't care.'

'That's just unfair.'

'Whatever,' Dushyant said. 'Can we not talk about this?'

Dushyant didn't bring up the topic again that evening. The rest of the evening, he was rude to her. They went back to his friend's flat and slept there. Dushyant was rough with her that night. For a change, they weren't making love, they were having sex. There were no intermittent, passionate love-yous exchanged during the course. There were just grunts and groans. It was almost like he wanted to hurt her physically. He didn't hug her to sleep. Kajal hoped he would be okay the next day, but it only became worse.

The next evening, Dushyant was drunk out of his wits again. Old Monk. Smirnoff. Chivas Regal. Nail-polish remover. Iodex. He called Kajal and told her, 'You love *him*, I love *this*! I will never quit drinking or smoking!' He called her names, abused her family and Varun, and disconnected the call. Later that night, Dushyant's friends called her to give her the address of the hospital he was admitted to. He had passed out and was frothing at the mouth. Kajal filled out the paperwork in the hospital the next day and got him back to the hostel. It was the first time she'd had to bring him back from the hospital that month. Within that month, it happened thrice. Each subsequent time, it was worse. By now, Kajal was used to his druken tantrums. The abuses, the name-calling, the threats—she had become used to everything. It was the price for true love, she told herself. There wasn't a fourth time.

A few days later, he crossed a line he shouldn't have. Her patience was tested, and she didn't think she had the strength to carry on. She vowed she would never go back to him.

~

Kajal lay with her head on the pillow, her thoughts going back to every time Dushyant had said they would last and that he would never hurt her. She believed in him. It was all lies.

The memories of the day they had broken up were imprinted on her brain, and she knew she would never forget what had happened.

That day, Kajal's phone had been lying unattended and he had seen pictures and text messages that were more than a year old. He had not reacted at first. But as the night progressed, he started to get drunk. And angry. He hadn't talked much. Shot after shot was downed. His eyes were bloodshot. Later that night, after an argument, he had struck Kajal on her face while he cried and howled like an animal. Everyone, friends of both Dushyant and Kajal, had watched helplessly as she fell and hit the chair, reeling from the impact of his heavy hand on her face. He had locked himself in a room. All his friends had banged on the door relentlessly, scared that he might overdose inside. Kajal had pleaded with him to open the door. He had let her inside. There were no words exchanged. For the first time, Dushyant had forced himself on her. He had paid no regard to her cries and pounded her with disdain. He had treated her worse than a whore and violated her repeatedly. Once done, he had rolled over, drunk from the bottle of vodka, and passed out. A crying Kajal had left the flat and gone back home. She had texted Dushyant telling him they were over and he was dead to her. For the next six days, he had kept calling her. With every missed call, Kajal's temper had risen. Her decision to stay away from him had strengthened. Tired and angry, she had told him that she had never loved him and that she was thinking of getting back with Varun. The calls had stopped immediately.

Again, she had no one to talk to. After fiddling with her phone for hours, she dialled Varun's number. *You have me; you don't need him,* Dushyant used to tell her. *Lies.* 'Hi, Varun,' Kajal said, fighting her tears.

'Hey? Long time. Where have you been? You don't pick up my calls, you don't call me back? I dropped you about a million texts. What's the problem?'

'Dushyant never liked you, you know that, right?'

'Yes. I never liked him either. He asked you to stop talking to me, didn't he? That narrow-minded bastard. I don't know what you're doing with him. Really, he is worse than the Taliban,' Varun joked.

'Yes, he asked me to stay away from you, but it's okay. No boyfriend likes the ex-boyfriends of their girls.'

'But your guy is very childish. He is immature and hot-tempered. He is not right for you,' Varun preached like he always did.

Kajal choked on her words.

'Are you there?' Varun asked. 'Are you okay?'

'Yes, we broke up a few days back.'

'Oh, you did? Why?'

'He hit me.'

'What? That bastard! How could he? What else did he do? Why didn't you tell me earlier? Wait, I am coming over,' Varun said and disconnected the call before Kajal could respond. He texted her to ask whether she was at her college hostel or home. A little voice inside her wanted to ask Varun to stay away, but it was silenced by the tears that trickled down her face. Kajal needed her best friend. She tied her hair back loosely and ran her fingers on her cheek where Dushyant's hand had struck fair and square. Her pale-white skin still bore the marks of his rough hand. Dushyant was a strong guy, and he had not tried to restrain himself when he'd slapped her.

She saw Varun park his car in the parking lot of the Defence Colony market. The car number ended with 0002, like every one of Varun's family's cars. Varun belonged to a family with means. His father owned one of the biggest printing presses in Delhi. Within the first year, Varun's sharp business acumen landed them their first multinational clients and helped them grow at a faster rate than his father had imagined. Their 200-acre plant swelled to 600 acres, the number of workers tripled, and they had more clients flying in from Europe and North America than any other printing set-up in the country. Varun had transformed a *lala*-type family business into a seething, angry corporate giant.

Contrary to what Kajal thought of him at first, he was not just another rich pretty boy in an Audi A4 labelled *Dad's Gift* on the rear windshield. He was ambitious and cut-throat. He worked eighteen hours a day, travelled extensively for business and took his work very seriously. Kajal liked that in him, but it was also the root of discord between them. The meetings, the late-night flights, the investor presentations, the bank-loan agreements—between all this, he never had time for Kajal. For the major part of their relationship, Kajal was too awestruck to notice his absolute lack of commitment to the relationship. Kajal had always wondered what he saw in her. They broke up when he slept with someone on a business tour to Shillong. She didn't think the break-up was because he slept with someone else. They had drifted apart long before that. What surprised her was her indifference to his betrayal.

Without waking anyone, Kajal sneaked out of her place. 'How are you doing?' Varun asked. He looked as if he had aged ten years in one. *Long hours in the office*, she guessed. He had even lost some hair.

'I am good. Much better now,' she said. 'How's work?'

'Let's sit and talk?' he said and led the way to the nearest Subway outlet.

'Eating healthy these days?' she mocked.

'Doctor advised me to. He has asked me to start exercising too, but who has the time?'

'You don't, for sure,' Kajal taunted. 'You should take care of your health. You look like you have a couple of kids already.'

Varun shrugged. 'So, tell me, what happened?' he asked.

Kajal narrated her side of the story. She broke down a couple of times and realized that everyone had turned towards them. He listened patiently, ignoring all the uninvited looks from the nearby tables. Varun finished the salad and they walked towards his car. She didn't want to cry in public. A girl like her, pretty and docile, why did she have to cry at all?

'Will you be okay?' Varun asked as they sat in the car.

'I think so,' she said and dug her face into her palms. And wept.

'I still can't believe he hit you.'

'He was drunk,' she murmured. She didn't tell him the whole story.

'Whatever the case may be, you're in an abusive relationship, Kajal. Before this, he used to shout at you and threaten you. Now he has hit you. If you let him get away with this, he will keep doing it. First to you, then to the others he dates after you. You have to realize that he is mentally unfit to be in a relationship. He has no sense of boundaries. Hell! He doesn't even respect your privacy. You've got to see that. The sooner you do, the better it will be for you. It's a good thing you broke up. You just can't be in such a restrictive relationship.'

'I don't want to talk about it any more,' she said and tried to hold back the tears. Varun hugged her, and told her that everything would be all right. She wanted to believe him like she had believed him earlier, like she had believed Dushyant.

~

For the next few days, Varun often dropped in after college timings to check in on Kajal. She was doing better, but she still missed Dushyant. She felt bad for herself that she did. Dushyant, on the other hand, tried his best to apologize and make things better. Kajal told him she didn't want to hear a word from him. Dushyant stopped trying after he spotted Kajal get into Varun's car one day. He called her that night, abused her and called her a slut. He told her that she must have cheated on him, that she was sleeping with Varun all this time.

Kajal spent the next day crying. Varun was there to hold her hand. And to kiss her. She kissed Varun back. She was no longer in a restrictive, abusive relationship with a guy with an appalling lack of respect for her. She had broken free and walked right back into her past.

5

Zarah Mirza

Zarah had fifteen cases to file that day, each of them more boring than the last. Broken arms, sprained ankles, torn ligaments, et cetera. Her boss, the enigmatic and brilliant Dr Arman Kashyap, was not fond of filing reports and that's why he had the most number of interns working for him at one time. Usually interns worked in pairs, but Arman was never a big fan of rules. No one knew what he enjoyed more, flouting them or challenging the hospital authorities afterwards.

'If you work in pairs, you get complacent about what you do. If you work alone, you become cautious from the word *go*,' Arman had said on the first day. Zarah had not been able to forget those words. She used to check every medicine thrice, sometimes even more, before administering it to any patient. Even if it was just cough syrup.

'You look busy?' A fellow intern walked into the room the interns had been assigned. Though Zarah usually worked in the opulent office of her boss, his overbearing presence used to made her jittery. The presence of any man made her feel jittery. She clearly remembered her first day in the hospital, with men crawling everywhere. Patients. Doctors. Ward boys. Their eyes like slithering snakes on her body—undressing her, violating her and rubbing their naked, sweaty, hairy bodies against her in their heads. In those moments, all her latent hatred for men bubbled over and she had a severe mental breakdown. Zarah had never been in a co-ed school or college and it was on her insistence. Staying away from men was the only way she could banish the horrors of her past.

'I have a lot of filing to do,' she said, trying to act busy. Ever since she had started her internship, an alarming number of interns, resident doctors and senior doctors had showered her with attention. It fuelled her need for sleeping pills and antidepressants.

'Your boss is an asshole,' the fellow intern said.

'He's not that bad. People are jealous because he is good . . . and young,' she defended him. His searching eyes made her feel uncomfortable, like she had been doused with a bucket full of rotting maggots.

'He is reckless and has no regard for rules. He doesn't file reports or keep a history of the medicines he prescribes. The other doctors keep mum but I am sure many patients have died under his watch because of his crazy ideas,' he argued. Zarah noticed the restlessness in the intern's eyes and his body language. Or was it lust? Maybe he was trying the primal, old-fashioned way to get her into bed. Take out the threat, the opposition, and any other contender who's trying to bed who you want to bed first. Zarah wanted to run away. *No, I've got to fight this!* Like every rape victim, Zarah, too, had read all the books, documents, reports and guides that helped victims move on with their lives. Funny, no book prescribed sleeping pills, Xanax or Valium, because that's what worked for her.

'He gets the job done. He wraps up the most number of cases. If other doctors are men, he is God. Plus, he now has

me for filing his reports. He doesn't need to do that any more,'
Zarah defended him further, trying not to look at the intern.
She was agitated. She could sense him licking his lips greedily.
The maggots had entered her clothes. They were everywhere.
Small, slithering and slimy.

'The rules are made by doctors much more experienced
than him.'

'Experience doesn't count for everything,' Zarah grumbled.
She could feel his hands on her thighs. The maggots reached
her face. They entered her nose, her ears. She was losing it.

'Fine, go defend him,' he said, irritably. 'Okay, anyway, junk
it. Want to go for lunch?'

'NO! I DON'T! WILL YOU LET ME WORK, PLEASE!'
she yelled.

'F . . . Fine . . .' the intern spluttered and left the room. Zarah's
thickly veined eyes followed him outside the room. She wanted
him dead. The maggots were gone. She still felt filthy.

~

Zarah had lunch with a girl intern that afternoon, like the
many afternoons before that. She liked her. She was sweet,
caring and very hard-working. She liked that. But the best
part about her was she didn't talk about boys or marriage
or family.

'Hey, listen . . .' she said.

'Yes?' The girl looked up from her files.

'What do you know about Lou Gehrig's disease? ALS?'
she asked nervously, even though she knew.

'Fatal. Multi-organ failure. A nerve-related problem. You
can't really expect a patient to live beyond five years. Why are
you asking? Do you have a patient?'

'Yes, a girl.'

'A girl? It's not seen in anyone less than fifty years.'

'She is nineteen. First year, Maulana medical school.'

'Are you serious?' she asked, shocked. Zarah handed over the file to the girl, who pored through it from behind her blue-rimmed spectacles.

'Yes. She is getting admitted here. It says here she experienced a lack of sensation during an examination. I just googled her name. She was All India Rank 3 this year.'

'That's sad,' she whimpered and handed the file back to her. It was no secret that the patient was dying.

'I know. I hate these diseases. No underlying cause and absolutely no fault of the patient. I wonder how she must be feeling,' Zarah said and sighed.

'Don't get too attached to the patient. Remember what Dr Mehra taught us. Be emotional about the disease, not the patient.'

'Yeah, right,' she replied and shook her head.

'I am serious.'

Zarah kept mum and they continued to eat their food in silence. She flipped through Pihu's file to go over the basic details of the disease's progression in her case. She spotted something very uncommon, if not downright strange. None of the effects of ALS on the body are reversible, but Pihu had regained some use of her hands, and her speech had become clearer over the last few months. *How can that be? Can that be the reason why Arman is trying to treat a person whose death sentence has already been written? Is she the answer to the disease?*

She knew that Arman was on the research panel of doctors looking for a cure for ALS. She made a mental note to ask him. After all, he did admit to being an external consultant to the patient. There was something definitely amiss with this situation.

Just as she finished eating, her phone rang.

'It's someone asking for the doctor of Dushyant Roy. Dr Arman is not available. Should I put the call through?' the voice from the other side said.

'Sure,' she said and heard the call-transfer beep. 'Hello? This is Zarah Mirza.'

'Hi…Umm…Hello, Doctor, I am Kajal. I wanted to know about a patient admitted in your hospital. Dushyant Roy?'

'Oh, yes. He has a liver problem. Are you a relative?' she asked.

'Is it serious?'

'He will live,' Zarah said. 'Serious, but curable. May I know who you are?'

The line disconnected.

6

Pihu Malhotra

Pihu looked around the room she had grown up in. The room on whose walls she had always imagined she would hang her diplomas and degrees. She looked at the photo frames with pictures of her as a toddler, the bedsheets and the tonnes of books she had so lovingly arranged. She wondered if she would get to read even a third of them. She was distraught. For all the times she had craved to be in a medical school, she got only three months. It had been nine months since then. The loss of sensation meant she had to drop out of medical school as soon as four other hospitals—one in Delhi, two in Bangalore and one in Mumbai—gave the same verdict, each one with more finality than the last. Her disease had progressed faster than anyone had anticipated. Within two months of detection, she had trouble walking without crutches. Soon, eating had become a problem and she couldn't chew for very long. Fifteen minutes of activity made her breathless and tired. Her muscles were slowly losing their strength and integrity. The paralysis slowly set in. Life for her became a constant battle for survival—to see the next morning. To see her parents around her, to hold their hands and recount memories till it felt like she had lived them twice. It became a constant struggle to forget what was coming for her. She had committed herself to her impending death sentence. She had just a few excruciating months to live.

All this while, she made sure she sent across a mail every day to the young doctor, who was a part of the research team looking for a cure for ALS, in New Delhi. Sometimes, it was about the pain of being an ALS patient. On other occasions, it was something interesting she had read in a medicine book. His mailbox had become like a personal online blog-cum-punching-bag-cum-stress-ball for her. She knew for sure that he must have marked her mails as spam after the third one. But she kept sending them . . .

Pihu Malhotra <p_malhotra198@gmail.com>
To Dr Arman Kashyap <ArmanKashyap@GKL.co.in>

Hi Dr Arman,

My mom still hasn't stopped crying. She tries not to cry in front of me, but she doesn't make it. Dad is a lot better. I got myself checked again. Six months, they say. Give or take a few months. I can't walk for very long.

Regards
Pihu Malhotra

Pihu Malhotra <p_malhotra198@gmail.com>
To Dr Arman Kashyap <ArmanKashyap@GKL.co.in>

Hi Dr Arman,

Sorry to disturb you again. But I am crying. For the past two days, I haven't been able to sleep. I think of all the bad things that are going to happen to me. Why? Why me? I didn't do anything wrong to anyone. Neither did my parents. I just . . . I am sorry.

Regards
Pihu Malhotra

Pihu Malhotra <p_malhotra198@gmail.com>
To Dr Arman Kashyap <ArmanKashyap@GKL.co.in>

Hi Dr Arman,

I finished the book on cancer diagnosis. It's very nice. Wish I was in the lab and could see the carcinomas myself. I envy my classmates. They must be having so much fun. I wonder how Venugopal is doing and whether he still misses me. And I hope he has made good friends there. I wish I was there. I am sorry to disturb you again. I am sorry.

Regards
Pihu Malhotra

Pihu Malhotra <p_malhotra198@gmail.com>
To Dr Arman Kashyap <ArmanKashyap@GKL.co.in>

Hi Dr Arman,

I can't walk any more. I see a shining new wheelchair in the corner of the room. I don't want to use it. I want to stay in bed. I am scared. I also choked on my food once. People say I am dying. They tell me time is running out. Why doesn't it feel so? Why does it feel that time has slowed down? Every moment lingers like it will never pass. It feels like death is moving away from me and I am running to get there soon. The sooner it comes, the

better. I just want to be put out of my misery. Is a dead
daughter better than a dying daughter?

I am sorry.

Regards
Pihu Malhotra

~

The mails never stopped. It was like a vent for her frustration
and her growing anger.

Four months after the first email, she received a mail from
Dr Arman Kashyap, GKL Hospital. She jumped at the sight
of it! And had wondered later why she had done so. Arman
Kashyap was a handsome man, tall, fair and with rimless
spectacles that made him look very intelligent. But the short-
cropped hair made him look like a badass and he stuck out
like a sore thumb in the group photograph of all the doctors
at GKL Hospital.

There was no formal introduction, no asking how she was
or even who she was, instead there were a set of questions he
wanted her to answer. She had answered them to the best of
her ability, like she would do as a student. Along with her
answers, she attached a report on what she thought about the
various researches that had been done on ALS. She wondered
if she was being a smart-ass, but then thought she had too
little time to care.

To her surprise, Arman had replied almost immediately. The
language of the mail suggested he was impressed, but it was
cleverly concealed. It was late in the night and Pihu typed out
a long mail. It took her four hours to type it, one slow clumsy
letter at a time. She had to take breaks because it was hard for
her to sit up straight for that long. She didn't forget to mention

that in the mail. Minutes after she had hit the send button, exhausted, she crawled to her bed and drifted off.

The next morning, the first thing she did was to log into Gmail and refresh it till her fingers hurt. *Inbox (1).* The mail contained just one line. It was a link to a website and beneath it was a combination of letters, numbers and special characters. She clicked on the link, which took her to a zealously protected website, and punched in the combination in the field that asked for a password. The website opened up like a whore's legs on a payday and lay open a world of information on her disease. In the next few hours, she had devoured whatever she could find on the website. What really grabbed her attention were the clinical trials GKL Hospital was carrying out on ALS patients. They were only moderately successful. Just as she was reading through it, she received another mail that explained how she was ineligible for it.

Dr Arman Kashyap <ArmanKashyap@GKL.co.in>
To Pihu Malhotra <p_malhotra198@gmail.com>

I am sure you have gone through the clinical-trial reports. Unfortunately, you're not eligible for it. Section 5. Para 6. I apologize.

Regards
Dr Arman Kashyap

Pihu looked for Section 5. Her face drooped. Since it was a disease which only inflicted older people, clinical-trial permissions had not been granted for anyone below the age of thirty. She had slumped in her chair and switched off the computer. She was tired.

For the next two months, she hadn't sent a single mail to the doctor in GKL Hospital and she didn't receive any. Her condition had been worsening steadily, her spirit and body slowly dying. She and her parents had braced themselves for the inevitable. She was going to die. Her parents were going to cry and lament for the rest of their lives. There was nothing that could have changed that. She was in a wheelchair. Only liquids were allowed, chewing food was out of the question. There were times she had tried to eat solid food and had choked on it as the muscles in her food pipe gave way. One day when her suffering had reached a peak, she sent a mail to Arman, updating him about her pitiable condition. She wanted it to be a long mail, but her body gave up within half an hour.

Pihu Malhotra <p_malhotra198@gmail.com>
To Dr Arman Kashyap <ArmanKashyap@GKL.co.in>

Hi Dr Arman,

This could be my last mail. To you or to anyone. The disease has progressed to its last stage. It took me twenty minutes to type this. I am constantly exhausted. It's like a big boulder is crushing my lungs, snuffing the life out of me. I need assistance for everything now. I can't even clean myself after going to the washroom. I am sure you know what happens. My parents are being brave. They don't cry in front of me. I spend my hours sleeping or smiling at my relatives. They know I am dying too. It's a strange feeling. I am scared at times. Sometimes I think about how I am going to die. Will my lungs collapse? Or my heart? And then I am relieved at times. It's going to be over. I ask my father to read me my books from medical school.

Maybe I will be a doctor in some other life, if there is anything like that. I just want to thank you for replying to my mails and showing me your research website. It meant a lot. Thank you. I need to go now. Best of luck.

Regards
Pihu Malhotra

~

From what she had learnt about the disease, she knew she didn't have more than three months to live; some doctors gave her even less. The fear in her parents' eyes multiplied every day, their grief slowly becoming unbearable for them. During those days, her relatives and cousins had started to drop in to see her for the last time. Pihu, confined to her bed, would smile at them. And cry when she would be alone. For the most part of the day, she would sleep. Her body, whatever was left of it, was constantly tired and exhausted.

She began to get bedsores. Her mom would spend hours shifting and rolling her on the bed to prevent the infections from the bedsores from spreading. They only became worse. She would stay up and cough for hours on end. Saliva drooled from her mouth but she couldn't bring a hand up to wipe it. Day after day, she would spend all her time lying on the bed, staring at the ceiling as her father read to her from medical books and journals. She could only talk in mumbles; her tongue had become weak too. She was trapped in her dying body, waiting for death to come.

Her father clicked pictures of her every day, trying to capture his daughter for the last few times. Visiting doctors always left the home with their heads hung low. They knew the next time they could find her dead.

A few days after she sent her last mail, a package arrived at the front door with Pihu's name on it. Her father opened the box gingerly. The contents were wrapped very carefully in bubble wrap. There was a spiral-bound file of papers and a box with syringes, bottles of coloured liquids and capsules.

'What's this?' her father asked as he sifted through the contents.

She shook her head and looked at the letter that lay with everything on the bed. Her dad read the letter, which stated in clear, simple words that these were the medications they were trying out on the clinical-trial patients at GKL Hospital. The handwriting was lucid, not like a doctor's.

Dear Pihu,

Follow the instructions as written in the file. Keep it to yourself and your family. Don't get doctors involved. The drugs have a reasonable success rate at our hospital. They stall symptoms in some cases. They reverse the effects in others. Think before you decide. Don't hold me liable.

Regards.

Her father looked at her for an explanation and she told him about the mails and the website. She asked her dad to read the file that had all the details about the progress of the patients the medicines had been tried on. They spent the whole night reading through every case, every patient and every dosage that she had to take. Whether she should take the medication or not was a no-brainer. She was dying. She had just three months to live, give or take a few weeks. A 20 per cent chance of living was an infinitely better option than to continue living like the undead for the next few months, and then, in any case, die. She made her father learn how to use the syringes. After a few times of puncturing his own veins, he got the hang of it. From the next day, she was on the medication. For the first few times, his fingers trembled every time he had to pierce Pihu's flesh. And then it became easier.

Slowly, things changed. Two months later, she mailed the doctor again.

Pihu Malhotra <p_malhotra198@gmail.com>
To Dr Arman Kashyap <ArmanKashyap@GKL.co.in>

Hi Dr Arman,

I am better. It is working. For the first time, I took solid food. Thank you.

Regards
Pihu Malhotra

With the mail, she attached a report she and her father had maintained for tracking her progress. The experimental drugs were working on her. She wasn't coughing relentlessly any more and had regained some of her strength. She could sit up and read on her own. The sensation in her hands was coming back, though they were still far from being perfect. Her parents were happy they were getting their daughter back.

But things weren't as rosy as they seemed to be. A month later, Dr Arman asked her father to get her admitted to the hospital. The symptoms had shown relapse in the case of many patients in the clinical trials.

7

GKL Hospital

Three boxes and most of them were books. Pihu had finished packing her life into boxes labelled *'FRAGILE'*. Her parents were waiting outside, their eyes hollow and devoid of hope. They held hands. Occasionally, a teardrop streaked down their cheeks. For the last two months they had been the happiest they could have ever been. They had watched helplessly as their daughter almost died lying on her bed, and then saw her gain her strength back. Now, they were scared she would go back to her previous condition. The drugs, after the initial promise, had stopped showing combative properties against the disease. As a result, all the symptoms were back in the case of a large chunk of clinical-trial patients in New Delhi. Dr Arman had asked them to admit Pihu into the hospital too.

'Let's go?' Pihu said and held out her hand. Her mom held it with both her hands and caressed it. She could see the pain in her mother's eyes and false hope in her dad's. They got into the car they had hired to take them to Delhi. Her father had taken a transfer to Delhi. His boss, for the first time, was sympathetic.

The taxi reached Delhi at eight in the morning. They went straight to the hospital instead of the apartment they had rented. Dr Arman had scheduled some tests for her. By mid-afternoon, they were done. She also selected a room which she would move into later that night. Her parents wanted her days in the hospital to be comfortable, but she still chose a double-bed room.

'Beta, why don't you take a single room? It will be much more comfortable,' her mom suggested.

'Mom, I don't need a single room. Plus, it's very expensive, Maa.'

'As if . . .'

Her mom broke down and Pihu wrapped her arms around her. She kept weeping and mumbling in sobs till the time they reached home. The taxi driver unloaded the boxes and carried them to the apartment. He was instructed to keep the boxes near the door itself. Her dad went back with the driver to get some food and check in with the hospital about the arrangements.

Pihu felt bad for her dad. Not a single teardrop had escaped his eyes. He knew it would make his wife feel worse. But Pihu had noticed every time her father tried to look away from her. He did his best not to make any eye contact with her, to stem the barrage of overwhelming feelings he had held back behind those stoic eyes. At times, she would think that it would've been better if she had just died the first time around. She hated the false hope the experimental drugs had momentarily generated.

'Dad's not talking to me,' Pihu said as her mother laid down lunch. 'I am not going to be here for long, I think he should.' Her mom's mouth went dry and the colour drained from her face. Seeing that, Pihu apologized, 'I am sorry. I won't say that.'

Sometimes, she felt suffocated. She wanted to crib and cry and shout at how unfair it was. But she couldn't, because it wasn't just she who was suffering. Her suffering would end with her last breath while her parents' would just start.

'I have cooked everything you like,' her mom said.

'I can see that.' She giggled and loaded her plate till it almost tipped over. She didn't know if she would be able to eat solid food again. They smiled at each other.

'Your dad was saying that the doctor might try some new treatment on you? Do you think the new treatment will help? Has anyone been cured? How many patients have shown signs of relapse?' her mom asked as she ate.

'A few. The next stage has not been tried on anyone else. They might start with a few patients next week.'

'Hmmm.' Her mom's eyebrows knitted. Even though her daughter was to be a doctor a few years from now, she never believed a word other doctors said. She always viewed them with piercing suspicion.

'We can hope for the best,' Pihu assured her.

Her mom stayed quiet for a while. 'I don't know why God did this to us. We have never cheated anybody. You have been such a good girl. I pray every day. Then why us? Why my little daughter?' she said and patted Pihu's head as she ate. Pihu tried hard not to cry. Seeing her mom's tears made her maddeningly sad. But she had asked these questions a million times and had never got around to finding an answer. It was time to stop asking.

'Maa, I don't want you to cry. If you cry, I will too,' she said.

'But I had so many dreams for you. Your wedding, your kids, my grandchildren. What had we ever done to deserve this?' her mom wailed and rushed to the other room.

Pihu knew she would not come out of her room before she cursed God countless times for their pain. But she would still pray, and light *diya*s and incense sticks. She felt sorry for her mother. Though she wanted to hug her and assure her, she wanted her mom to prepare for the worst. She concentrated on the food instead. A little later, the bell rang and her father brought in twenty more boxes of their stuff, which were unloaded in her room. Her father paid the driver and he left.

'Mom's crying again,' she said as her dad joined her at the table.

'What else can she do?' he asked.

Pihu served him. He had not been eating a lot those days. She dumped a lot of rice and pulses on his plate. His attempts to stop her fell on deaf ears.

'Eat. You need it,' she commanded. 'You're under a lot of stress.'

'And you?'

'I am okay.'

'Are you sure, beta?'

'I will be fine. Plus, I have the best parents in the world to help me deal with this.' She put her hands around her father's neck and kissed him lightly on the cheek. Her father didn't say anything. After they finished the food, they washed the dishes together—something that they had always done together.

'Did you like the room you saw?'

'Yes, I did. There is another patient in there. He is young, so it's better. At least not like the other rooms where there were only old people,' she laughed.

'Is it a boy?'

'Not really a boy. Five–six years older than me. Are you scared I might have an affair with him?' she chuckled.

'I wish you could. And then I could take away your cell phone and scold you,' he said wistfully.

'Aw. You're the best dad ever,' she purred and clutched his hand.

He put his arm around his daughter and his eyes filled with tears. Pihu knew how difficult it must be for him. No matter how hard he tried, she could always see it. At least things were a little better now. She had got a second chance to live. Though she didn't know how long it would last, she still wanted to thank the doctor who had made it all possible.

~

The taxi pulled over at GKL Hospital. The three boxes were in the trunk of the car. Sealed. Pihu got off the car without any help. She was feeling a little better. The hospital was made of red-brick stone and was preposterously huge. One of the hospitals she could have worked in, had she graduated. She was yet to meet her doctor, Arman Kashyap, and was *dying* to meet him. She stifled a giggle at her choice of words. He was the man with all the answers. And he was good-looking too!

They walked to the reception and filled up the elaborate patient-admission and insurance forms. They were asked to wait so that the room could be prepared for her. Pihu was asked to accompany one of the nurses into a changing room.

Unlike others, Pihu loved the stale, nauseating formaldehyde smell that hung around in a hospital. It smelled like a dream to her. A *broken* dream now. The nurse handed over a robe and pulled the curtain so that she could change. Tying the knots of her robe was a little difficult as her fingers failed her. The nurse asked if she needed any help and Pihu called her in. She felt naked and embarrassed as the nurse tied the knots behind her back. But she had been through much worse. Before she took the experimental drugs, she was used to a nurse bathing her and seeing her naked every day.

'I am going to die,' she said to the nurse and smiled.

'Don't say that,' the nurse replied.

'No, I just said that because you might be the only one who will see me naked before I die. That is, apart from the other nurses who have seen me naked before. Why don't we have hot guys as nurses? I mean, I wouldn't mind that. Even you wouldn't, would you?'

The nurse laughed and Pihu laughed with her. 'Shall we go?' the nurse asked.

'Only if the knots are tight enough.'

'They are,' she said. 'Which ward do I need to take you to?' She picked up her chart and read out the room number. '509 . . . Oh, seems like you have another patient with you in that room.'

'I know. I've met the guy,' she said and grabbed her crutches.

She stopped by a few mirrors to look at herself. And prayed that her robe wouldn't fall off. Even with the flimsy robe on, she felt as good as naked, as if everyone could see through it. The nurse offered her a wheelchair, but she refused. She staggered on to her crutches and walked to the elevator, which took her to the third floor. She didn't know how long it would be before she lost the strength to walk again. She walked towards room no. 509.

Hepatic encephalopathy. She read out the words written on the chart of the guy who was to be her room-mate in her last, dying days. *It's curable*, she thought. *In most cases.*

'There.' The nurse gestured. 'I will set you up and call your parents?'

'Sure.'

She saw the guy again.

Dushyant Roy.

He was sleeping. She thought he looked gorgeous with his unruly hair, four-day stubble and carefree arrogance. *He drinks. He smokes. Probably does drugs too. Hmm. Probably owns a bike and drives it really fast.* Within minutes she had imagined him as a bad boy straight out of old English movies. Or more like Ajay Devgn, with his legs in a 180-degree split on two Yamahas, from the cult Hindi action movie *Phool aur Kaante*!

In the eighteen years before her disease was diagnosed, she had never looked at boys like a girl usually does. They were always classmates, not potential boyfriends. Over the last few months, she had grown fat on a healthy diet of her mother's old Mills & Boons, the *Fifty Shades* and the Sylvia Day trilogies, and felt an insuppressible urge to be amongst the opposite gender. To feel what it was like to be attracted to a guy, to feel the little goosebumps when a guy touches you, to be in the naked company of a man. To . . .

'There,' the nurse said as she tucked Pihu in. Pihu thanked the nurse, who asked her to push the button if she needed anything and left.

'It's not that bad,' Pihu mumbled to herself. She fiddled with the controls of the bed. Up. Down. Stop. Up. Down. Stop. Up. Down. Up. Down. Stop. She giggled.

'Can you stop?' the voice from the other side of the curtain said. It was hoarse and demanded attention.

'Oh.'

Dushyant. She drew the curtain to the side and met his piercing gaze.

'I am trying to sleep here,' he grumbled.

'You're not trying to sleep. It's a symptom of the disease you have. You will feel sleepy for the next month or two,' she explained, her playful enthusiasm anachronous with the news she delivered.

'Whatever. Will you just stop making that noise? It's annoying.'

'Hi, I am Pihu!' She thrust her hand out.

'Umm . . . I don't need to know your name. I am leaving in a day or two,' he said, 'and your voice is more annoying than the noise you were making earlier. Let's not make it any more difficult than it already is.'

'Fine. By the way, you're not leaving in a day or two. Your

liver is shot. Your treatment is going to be long. So it's better if we became friends.' She forced a smile on her face.

'I don't want to be friends with a kid. And mind your own business,' he growled. He paused. Pihu waited for him to realize that they had met earlier. His eyes widened. 'Aren't you the—'

'Pihu.'

She stretched her hand out again for him to shake. Reluctantly, he shook it. Just then, her parents walked in with a few bags in their hands. Pihu felt Dushyant jerk his hand back and saw him bury his face in his pillow.

Such beautiful eyes, Pihu thought to herself. *Snap out of it! You pervert!* Lately, the urge to be with a guy had peaked. She didn't want to die un-kissed. Being a good girl for nineteen years hadn't yielded anything, maybe being bad would.

'Are you comfortable?' her mom asked. 'Is the air conditioning okay? Are you cold?'

'I am fine, Maa.'

She clutched her mom's weathered hands. Her mother sat next to her, patted her forehead and mumbled some terms of endearment she used to call her when she was a kid. Her father opened the bags, arranged the bottles, the books and a couple of framed photographs from the thirty-six-photos-a-reel days.

'I wish I had a brother. I always missed a sibling,' she said as her eyes fell on the picture in the photo frame. It was from the time they had gone on a ten-day vacation to Dwarka-Puri to celebrate her tenth board examination results. She would never forget those ten days of scrumptious food, parental pampering, sandy beaches and long walks.

'Our world was complete when you were born,' her mom said. 'Plus, it's such a problem raising young boys. Girls are like little angels.' She ran her hand through Pihu's hair. Pihu didn't know if she had ever felt better.

'Do you need to sleep?' her father asked.

'I think I will read for a bit,' Pihu answered. She could sense Dushyant writhing uncomfortably in his bed. Was he in pain?

'Which one?' her dad asked.

She pointed out to the book *Pathology of the Liver* by R.N.M. Macsween. Her dad handed over the book, which was thickly bound and cruelly heavy, and she opened the book from where she had stuck small yellow and red Post-its.

'I will be outside if you need anything,' her dad said.

She nodded. Her mother took the couch and scrunched up to fit in. The room suddenly felt silent. The medical instrument beeped. Beep. Beep. The drips dripped. Drip. Drip. She rustled through the yellowed pages. There were diagrams and pictures. Her eyes widened. It was fascinating as well as disgusting. Dushyant was snoring now.

Pihu read through the night. Near morning, she fell asleep.

8

Dushyant Roy

It was a painful morning for Dushyant. The sedatives wore off and the pain escalated. He had rung the bell twice but he hadn't been attended to. He clutched his stomach, rolled in his bed from side to side and whined. Had Pihu and her parents not been nearby, he would have screamed his lungs out. His guts were on fire.

'Can you call someone?' he heard Pihu say to her father. Her father promptly left and came back with a nurse.

A transparent liquid was injected into his bloodstream and he felt immediate relief, followed by a spinning, whirling sensation in his head. As if he had just got off a merry-go-round. The nurse left just when he was about to ask her for more. His hand was stretched out, wanting more of the liquid that had just got him high as a kite. Slowly, his eyes closed and the boundaries between truth and fantasy began to blur. He heard the woman—Pihu's mother— say to Pihu, 'He used to drink and smoke. The nurse told me. He needs a liver transplant, but he has no donors. I don't know why you chose this room. He will give you some infection.'

'Maa, his disease is not contagious and it is too late for him to give me a drinking habit.'

Her mom gave her an icy stare. 'Whatever it is. I wonder where his parents are. Since the time we have come, no one has come to meet him.'

'Why are you so worried?'

'I just feel bad for his parents. Such a young boy with such bad habits. Disgraceful!'

'It's okay, Maa.'

'What okay? My daughter is such a nice girl and she has to . . . and he will live. It's so unfair,' he heard the exasperated mother say. Would his death make it any better for the woman?

'Maa, can you keep your volume down?' Pihu begged. 'He can hear us.'

'I don't care,' her mother said angrily.

He tried not to move and concentrate on what they said about him. Getting fucked up has its own advantages. It's as if people assume you are deaf when you're not. But they had shut up. Soon, he was in wonderland. Darkness. Clouds. Flying. Kajal.

~

The ground beneath him shook, then his bed and then he. He woke up with a start and saw a familiar face staring at him. It was the offensive doctor with a rod jammed up his behind.

'Good morning. Though it's almost noon,' the doctor said. 'I am Arman. I believe we have met before. You're the one who almost drank himself to death. I'm the unfortunate one who has to save you so that you can do it again.'

Dushyant felt embarrassed and angry. He could feel the girl's and her parents' eyes on him, judging him, cursing him. The cocky attitude of the doctor made it worse, and the dreadful pain in his stomach made him want to slap the doctor across the face.

'Can we get on with this?'

'Yes, we can. I heard you were whining with pain this morning? Did he cry?' Arman asked. The nurse nodded in affirmation.

'I wasn't fucking crying!' Dushyant protested.

'Shut up and keep your voice down. This is a hospital, not your house. If you're not crying, the pain is not much. And for future reference, please don't cry. You're a grown man, for heaven's sake. No more sedatives for you. We will start you on a fresh batch of antibiotics. The first ones didn't work like they should have,' he said.

'Are you even sure what's wrong with me?' he asked, trying to get back at the doctor.

'As a matter of fact, I am,' he retorted. 'You are stupid and throwing your life away. Now the fewer questions you have, the better for you.'

Dushyant felt offended, but before he could say something, another doctor, a girl, entered, dressed in a doctor's coat that fit her snugly around her tiny waist and well-endowed chest. Her heels looked a little out of place in a room where someone was dying, but they looked good on her well-built yet slender legs. Her naturally tanned skin shone and Dushyant's pain died out for the few seconds that he spent looking at her, imagining her in various scenarios, with and without the heels and the overcoat.

'This is Dr Zarah. She will take the tests and try to keep you alive if you decide to cooperate with her. Do you understand?' he asked him condescendingly.

He was stumped and didn't know what to say. The girl standing behind Arman looked more amicable, even though her expression remained unchanged. Arman piled the girl with medical mumbo-jumbo before he moved over to the other side. He saw him pull the curtain and block the disgusted faces of Pihu's parents out of view. Was he that repulsive?

'Is he always like this?' Dushyant asked Zarah as she tied a strap around his arm.

'More or less. It's been just a few weeks for me too. But he is a brilliant doctor and he will end up saving your life,' she answered. He noticed the sharp nose and the light-brown eyes. The lipstick was immaculately done; the outline matched her bronzed skin perfectly.

'My life? You guys already know what I have, don't you?' he asked, a little scared. He wanted a smoke, a beer and maybe a snort of a line of cocaine.

'You had another seizure last night. The problem can be neurological too. We are still looking at it.'

'What? Neurological? You mean something is wrong with my *brain*?'

'We're not sure. It might be a tumour or a clot somewhere. We need to do a full-body scan and an MRI.'

'When?'

'Right now,' she said and pressed the bell. Two ward boys came rushing to shift him from his bed to the other stretcher.

'I can move.' He got up and climbed on to the stretcher. The ward boys started to wheel him away from the room. Zarah walked by his side, her heels clicking against the sandstone beneath, her hips swaying alluringly with each step. Dushyant wondered how old Zarah was. He really needed an ecstasy pill. Or at least a joint.

'How come they never came when I was pressing the bell all morning?' he complained.

'They have been working here for years now. They know when they are needed and when they are not,' she explained. 'There.' She pointed to the MRI room.

'Really?'

'No. Not really. Arman had asked the ward boys to keep you off any kind of sedatives.'

'Why? Why would he do that?'

'He doesn't like you.'

'A doctor hating a patient? That's new. Well, fuck him.'

He was sure he saw Zarah smile. For the first time, he saw an expression on her face other than her constant icy stare. A little later, he was frisked for metallic objects and asked if he had any plates or screws in his body. Despite the multiple fractures his body had sustained from falls off stairs, bike accidents and such, his bones still held up on their own. *Bones of steel and a heart of stone*, he thought and smiled.

'Now, this will take a while. Don't move while you're inside and shout out if you feel strange. Am I clear?' she asked.

Dushyant nodded. He felt a little ashamed in Zarah's company. In the outside world, he would have talked about her with his friends and wondered if she was single. Maybe he would have fantasized about her a little. But now, he was naked in a robe, helpless and at her mercy. A pretty girl's mercy. His body ached for a smoke. He felt defeated. Like he had when Kajal told him she never wanted to see him again. That day was a cursed day; a day he never wanted to remember. A little later, he was swallowed by the gigantic circular dome of the growling MRI machine. He felt unsettled. His head ached and he wanted to scream. *You're a grown man.* The words came back and he stayed shut. He didn't want to shout like a scared pussy in front of her. Why did he care?

'Did you always want to be a doctor?' he said, just to distract himself.

There was no answer. A little later, a voice answered back. 'More or less.' The voice echoed. He felt better.

'This thing is bloody noisy.'

'I know it is,' Zarah said. 'Let me concentrate on the unflattering images of your brain.'

'How does it look?'

'It looks perfect to me. Though we will have to take Arman's opinion on this. I am no expert.'

Dushyant stayed shut for a while. The white shell made him claustrophobic.

'Are you okay in there?' Zarah asked.

'I guess.'

'Just a few more minutes,' she said.

He closed his eyes and tried to relax. He thought about Kajal and the other guys in college. The guys he had got sloshed with that day. None of them had called, let alone visited. The sound slowly came to a stop.

'Done,' she said and instructed the ward boys to pull him out from the machine.

His eyes never left Zarah's lithe body as her shapely behind sashayed in front while he was being wheeled back to his room. Zarah was engrossed in the few printouts she had in her hand. The stretcher was pushed into a lift. Zarah followed; her eyes still hadn't left the sheets in her hand.

'Oh, by the way, your girlfriend called,' Zarah said. 'She sounded concerned.'

'I don't have a girlfriend.'

'Well. I just guessed. Kajal, if I remember correctly. Sister? Friend?'

'We used to date. She called? Here? At the hospital?'

'Yes, why?'

'We haven't talked in years. She is dating her ex-boyfriend now. What did she say?' he asked, desperately trying to hide how crushed he felt. Zarah's eyes seemed to see right through him, her sharp gaze looking for their own answers. He felt naked, his secrets spilling out.

'She wanted to know if you would live.'

'What did you say?' he asked. A montage of black-and-white Polaroid images of his life from two years back flashed in front of his eyes. He felt guilty. Ashamed.

'I told her there's nothing to worry about.'

'Anything else?'

'No,' she said, her frosty voice giving nothing away.

Zarah left for Arman's office after they reached the fifth floor. Before leaving, she said she would check on him in the evening and update him on his condition. He nodded. His mind was clogged with the sudden reappearance of Kajal, and the images of his brain in Zarah's hand. What was that he saw on Zarah's face? Concern? Was he dying? Or was she always this cold?

The lack of answers from the doctors, the indistinguishable expression from Zarah and the battery of tests confused him. For the first time, he was scared. He wanted to see Kajal and tell her he was sorry. Then he brushed the negative thoughts away, cursing himself for thinking too much. He tried to think about the good things in life—weed, alcohol, poker and the young female doctor with caramel skin and taut muscles.

As he climbed into his bed, he wondered what might have driven Zarah to try to kill herself. In the elevator they had taken to the fifth floor, he had noticed the tiny slit marks on both her wrists.

~

Arman had left by the time Dushyant was in the room again. He was thankful and felt relieved. Next time, he would punch the guy in his face, but only after Arman figured out what was wrong with him. First they said liver and now the brain. He was freaking out a little. Hospital, MRIs, tests, diagnosis—you see these in movies; they never happen to you.

'So, did they do an MRI?' the irritating girl on the next bed asked him as soon as he was in his bed.

Give me a break, he thought. 'Do you just *have to* talk?' he asked as the niggling pain came back. It started in the stomach, then travelled to the limbs, the tips of the fingers and slowly, his entire body started to throb with pain. 'Do you have to play the nice girl? It's just irritating! Don't you have a boyfriend to call? Or anyone?'

'Excuse me?'

Pihu's face shrivelled. The upturned lips didn't melt Dushyant, for he hadn't asked for her company. She, her parents and her effervescent happy, optimistic face made him nauseated.

'I don't want you to ask me how I am doing or what they did to me. I have no interest in talking to you or anyone around you. Just keep to your business and don't bother me!'

'But—'

'You're irritating me. So are your parents. Go, choose another room. Your mother will like it. She thinks I am scum and a bastard. Do her and yourself a favour and just fucking stop talking to me,' he grumbled. Pihu cowered. He smirked. The girl scrambled for words, made a face, and pulled the curtain between them. Dushyant felt good venting it out. Little did he know that the cute ball of energy on the next bed was more persistent than he would have ever imagined.

The outburst reminded him of the times he had shouted at Kajal. Kajal used to shout back and eventually break down into uncontrollable sobs. He thought he could hear little sobs from the other side of the curtain. Or were they in his head? What had Kajal wanted when she called?

He didn't feel pity for Pihu or sorry for what he had just done. Instead, he loved the silence. Of the medical equipment. Of the drips of medicine. Beep. Drip. Beep. Drip. His own uncertain heartbeat. Lub. Dub.

~

It was late at night. Dushyant was writhing on his bed with pain. It felt as if his stomach was being ripped apart and hung to dry. He was sweating and the bed was wet with his perspiration. He had to adjust the temperature of the room twice. There was no relief. He had rung the bell twice for painkillers but no one had come. He wanted to drive a broken bottle through Arman's throat. He wanted to jam an injection in his arm. Pop a pill. Snort a line of cocaine. Get fucked up again. He had tried getting down from the bed but had fallen. His body went numb with pain.

He started to cough violently, and pressed the button twice. Reluctantly, he pulled the curtain away and groaned, 'Pihu.'

'Huh . . . Yes?' Pihu woke up from her sleep.

'I coughed.'

'So?' She rubbed her eyes, trying to shake the sleep off.

'It's blood,' he said and pointed to a pool of blood at the foot of his bed.

9

Arman Kashyap

Arman crushed the stress ball in his hands as he paced around the room. He was annoyed. A few more patients had shown relapses, and Pihu would show the same signs too. The next step in their research—the stem cell approach—was progressing like bloody snails on a rainy day. No one in their hospital thought it would work. Treatments of the sort had been tried on patients in the US and a few patients had had their lives extended by a year or two. A few had died on the operating table. To make his day worse, the asshole in room no. 509 had just vomited more blood than he could have had in his alcohol-ridden veins. He, too, seemed to be dying.

But even then, Pihu was top priority. He had noticed Zarah standing at the door with a file of reports, while he struggled with the analysis of the research results. It was one way or the other. The stem cell approach was a huge risk, a risk that he was willing to take.

'Yes? Are you waiting for something?' he asked.

'Dushyant is not doing that well. He has a fever now. The pain in the stomach is getting worse. His liver is getting worse.

He has had two seizures in the last two hours. His systems are shutting down.'

'But the antibiotics made him cough blood.'

'So what do we do now?' she asked.

'Exactly. I want an answer and I want it from you. And give him the sedatives. Make him shut up and take down a list of every drug that he has done in his lifetime. Let's see if we get something there,' he said without flinching, his mind somewhere else.

Zarah nodded and left the room.

Arman frantically pored through the research reports in front of him one more time. They were wasting time. People were losing to the disease without even a shred of hope. But he knew that it would take him and his team years, if not decades, to ascertain and prove that the stem cell approach could work. The girl he thought he had saved, the girl who thought she had been saved, would be long dead by then. He saw her file lying across the table and flipped through it. *Pihu Malhotra. 19. Medical Student.* The words floated in his head, refusing to settle down in an undiscoverable corner. Why was he so hell-bent on trying the treatment before it was time? Was it desperation? Was it the guilt from having someone believe that he had cured them? He didn't know. With her file in his hand, he left his office and headed for the third floor. In the lift, he read through her file twice, nervously flipping through the pages, wondering if she had lost herself in the disease. He wondered if she, like the many patients he had seen dying, had let the disease define her.

'I was diagnosed three years back.'

'I first noticed it when I was driving.'

'Is there a cure?'

These were often the first responses Arman heard from his patients who had lost to the disease way before it eventually consumed them. From the little he knew of her, she was different.

He entered the room and saw Dushyant lying on his bed, his eyes rolled over, sleeping under the effect of the powerful sedatives. *Such a burden*, he thought. On the other side of the curtain, he saw Pihu reading a book. Her mom was reading a book too.

'Hi. I am back,' he said and smiled. Arman knew exactly when to put his charm on. He was quite the guy to date back in medical school. Since he had grown up around medical books and people from medicine, expecting him to excel in medical school was like expecting a fish to swim. With plenty of time on his hands and with big wads of cash from his father's hospitals, he was the perfect guy to be with. But the girls who dated him back in those days admitted that his charm didn't lie in his wealth or his big brain. It was in his disarming smile and his perfect behaviour. Even as a college student, he dressed impeccably. Characterized by his crisp white shirts, traditional dark-blue jeans and white sneakers, one could easily spot him in a crowd. To this day, he had stuck to his dress code like a priest—white shirt and a pair of blue jeans. He wouldn't be caught dead wearing anything else.

'Hi, Dr Arman,' Pihu said. 'I see you are not wearing your doctor's coat.'

'I am off duty. This is my free time,' he answered and sat beside Pihu.

'I am glad you think of me in your free time.' Pihu giggled, and Arman was sure she winked. Not like grown-ups wink, but like little kids do—closing both their eyes and smiling, hoping they have closed just one.

'Are you flirting with me, Ms Pihu?'

'I am just making the most of my time here,' she said. Her cheeks were now a deep shade of pink, her eyes glinted with life and she bared every one of her thirty-two pearly teeth. Arman could no longer look at her like the diseased body he had seen the last time. Like a physical manifestation of the words in her file. He had looked at her eyes to look for imperfections, her skin for lesions and her body for flaws. But this time, he looked at her and saw a person brimming with childlike fervour. The cute face with the high cheekbones promising a beautiful woman in the future, the perfect eyes, the short hair that covered one half of her face, and the smile that never left her.

'I am glad to hear that from you. Often patients lose hope a little before we would want them to,' he said. He fell silent. Had he not felt Pihu's hopeful eyes on him, he would have been a lot more comfortable doing this.

'Is there something you want to say?' she asked.

'Yes. In fact there is,' he answered and paused. 'Do you understand the progress of your disease?'

'Yes, I do, Doctor. I was almost dead when you saved me,' she beamed. *Why did she have to say that?*

'I didn't save you. A few more cases of relapses have been recorded today. It's only a matter of time before you start showing the same symptoms too. I thought I should let you know. There is only so much that I can do.'

'What you have done for me is more than enough, Doctor. In those days when I was dying, I used to stay up all night thinking that I would choke and I wouldn't even be able to call for help. I was confined to a bed for months. I couldn't eat, I couldn't talk, I couldn't even do the smallest thing without someone helping me . . . My body was dead. You gave me a few extra days to live. I don't think you will ever know what that meant for me. I won't ever be able to thank you enough for what you did for me. You had no obligation to save me. In fact, you could have lost your licence if you were caught. You still can get barred. I don't think there is anything more you could have done.'

'It's sweet of you to think like that,' he said, barely recovering from what he had just heard. Beneath the chirpy, smiling demeanour, there was a grown-up girl, armed to fight the disease with all she had. All of a sudden, he didn't want to talk about her disease any more. He didn't want to be responsible for snuffing out the glimmer from her eyes. 'So, how was your college? Did you like being there? Why don't you tell me about it?'

Her grin got wider. After that, she was unstoppable. She told him everything there was to know about her fascination with medicine right from the eighth grade when she first decided that she would become a doctor. Arman heard her out patiently. Not much registered in his mind. Lost in the narrator's boisterous laughter and enthusiasm, he couldn't keep track of the conversation. Just to stamp his presence in the conversation, he started to ask her a few trick questions about medicine. After she got twenty of them right, she said irritably, 'Everyone knows these!'

Even I didn't know the answer to a few of them, Arman thought and looked at her in awe. She was brilliant. She reminded him of a young *him*, who was hated because he was annoyingly brilliant.

'How was yours?' she asked.

'Huh?'

'Your college? You went to AIIMS, right? I've read all about you,' she said.

'Yes. And then I went to a medical school in New York. I worked there for a few years and then came back.'

'Oh. How old are you?' she asked with an impish smile.

'How old do I look?' Arman played along.

'Your educational details say thirty-three, but you don't look a day older than twenty-five!' she blurted out.

Arman chortled and tried to hide his happiness on hearing that. It wasn't the first time though. Arman had often had problems in the past making people take him seriously because of his boyish looks. Luckily, he was finally growing up.

'So?' she asked again. 'How old are you?'

'A little older than twenty-five, but young enough to date you,' he said and smiled. He saw her blush and melt into giggles.

'Let's go out some time, then. You can carry the drips and the injections for me. I am sure it's more interesting than carrying handbags. Plus, I won't really take time to get ready. I have come to like this robe.'

Arman nodded and tried to ignore the hint of dejection in her voice.

'There is something I wanted to talk to about,' he said. 'I called up your college.'

'You did? Why?'

'I wanted to know about you. They told me that you were a brilliant student. Surgery, that's what you wanted to get into, right?'

'Yes. Since always. You have no idea how many carrots I ate because they told me that you need a 6/6 vision to be a surgeon. My mom always said carrots were good for the eyes!' she chuckled. Arman laughed with her. She was strangely amusing for a girl.

'You would have made a funny surgeon.'

'Not with these hands,' she said and pointed out.

'We can get you all right,' he mumbled.

'Can you? Because I would hate to operate on someone like this.'

'We are not sure though.'

'I know what you're talking about,' Pihu purred. 'The stem cell research, right? But that hasn't been approved yet, has it? Has it ever been tried on anybody?'

'It will take twenty years to confirm that the treatment works,' Arman replied. He was impressed at the girl's retentive power. The research website had published a few articles on the stem cell research and how it should *only* be tried on patients in their last stages because of the high risk involved. Arman never bought the argument and thought it was stupid.

'So?'

'We can do it on you,' Arman weighed his words. He didn't want Pihu to freak out since those articles clearly stated that deaths resulting from those procedures were far too many to try it on comparatively healthy patients.

'Aren't you like the best young doctor in the country? A sensation in the field of medicine?'

Her words made Arman a little uncomfortable, a little proud of himself and a little happy. The science conferences where people used to glorify his successes never mattered to him. Not even a bit. But her words did and he felt strange about that.

'Some people say that.'

'And won't you be risking your medical licence, and probably find yourself in jail if anyone finds out about this?'

'More or less,' he answered.

'So either you are crazy or very confident that this will work,' she said. Arman noticed her forehead crease. He wished he could tell her that it was neither. Simply put, it was the only way to save her from dying.

'A bit of both.'

'I think it's your call then,' she said and smiled. Her doubtless confidence put him slightly off balance. If the treatment didn't work, he knew he would just accelerate her deterioration and make her die sooner, if not instantly.

'I will think about it,' Arman said, shaken. He got up from the bed.

'Fine,' she said. 'If it doesn't work?'

'Let's not talk about it.'

'Like the lyrics of that song, *What doesn't kill you*? "What doesn't kill you makes you stronger"?' she asked. He nodded.

Arman shook her hand and said, 'Our date is still due.'

'I am looking forward to it. Though I might have a problem with choosing what I'll wear. I am thinking of being a little bold and wearing the blue robe instead. Or . . . I don't know. I am having trouble deciding.'

They laughed till their stomachs hurt and till Dushyant writhed in his sleep.

'I will be back soon,' Arman said and headed for the door.

'Dr Arman?' she called out.

'Yes?'

'Did you really call my college?'

'No, I didn't. But no one who's dying would read all the books lined on your side table. Four out of those fifteen books are on surgery,' he said.

'You're smart,' she said and winked. 'And you're cute!'

'People tell me,' he replied. 'And I am not thirty-five. I am younger. Much younger.' He left the room.

His steps were unsteady as he trudged back to his office. His head felt strange and for the first time in years, he didn't feel like going with his gut. In other cases, he would have just started the treatment, putting everything on the line. Never ever did he think twice before putting a patient's life at risk for what he believed in. He knew he would save them. Eventually.

But this time, he wasn't sure.

The smile. The childlike wink with both eyes. The promised date. They haunted him, pricking him like little pins in his heart and in his head, a strange mix of pain and pleasure quite like acupuncture, through the day, as he mechanically worked around patients and reports.

She is just a kid, he told himself.

10

Zarah Mirza

Zarah woke up that day with a severe back pain and a blinding headache. If medical school was tough, working in a hospital was a nightmare. While hers was a 24/7 job, all her friends were now engineers and management graduates with jobs that ended at six in the evening, allowing them enough time to get sloshed, act silly and wake up in each other's flats. Having said that, hers was a satisfying job. Sometimes. Mostly, she was just administering medicines. Being a doctor was tough; saving lives was a different ball game. Often in medical school, she had wanted to quit and aim to become a cosmetic surgeon. Or a dentist. Something that wouldn't put anyone's life in her hands. There were no holidays or margins of error in her profession. Other people's sick days were her working days. She felt guilty for thinking the way she did. She had not become a doctor for making people beautiful but to relieve them of pain and suffering. But she was too damaged herself for that responsibility.

She swallowed a couple of aspirins from the rapidly depleting bottle on her bedside. Alcohol had been a steady companion for the last few years. Over time, the sleeping pills had stopped working and doctors stopped prescribing them to her, calling it a worsening addiction. No matter what, she never visited a psychiatrist for her *problem*. Her hatred for men had only aggravated as the years passed by and she could see the perverse, animalistic instinct in their eyes every day. It was odd that she was at ease with Dushyant, the patient with the liver disease. His eyes were cold and it didn't feel as if he was trying to despoil her in his head. He was one of the few men by whom she didn't feel threatened. Maybe it was because he was weak and dying.

She checked her cell phone. There were no missed calls or messages. She felt relieved. After lazing around in her bed for an hour, she stepped into the shower and felt the hot water spray against her skin. It felt good. She felt relaxed and thought about the good things in life. Years of self-administered therapy had taught her how to cope with pressure and pain. The water clung to her skin as she stepped out of the water. Drops of water slid down her toned legs and wet her kitchen floor. Wrapped around in her towel, she made breakfast for herself—scrambled eggs and toast with butter. Living alone had its own benefits. Even though she missed her mom a lot, she didn't want to spend a lot of time at home. Her dad had just retired from the army and she felt it was better if she stayed away from him. Staying away from him meant staying away from the horrifying memories of the night she was chafed of her innocence by old, wrinkled hands on her frail body.

She drove with the windows pulled down in her red Hyundai Santro. It was passed down from her mom to her when she earned her doctorate. The stereo blasted out old Shahrukh Khan songs. As a kid, people had a hard time explaining to her that it was not the actor who was singing.

'Hi,' she said, smiled at the receptionist and swiped her card at the reception. Her long dark-brown hair was a mess.

She had shampooed it in the morning and let it dry during the drive to the hospital. Now, it was all over the place, but she managed to rein her tresses into a bun.

She prepared the coffee to brew in the coffee maker, arranged the files of the patients she had to attend to that morning, and had just caught her breath when her phone rang.

'Hello? Is this Dr Zarah Mirza? There is an emergency. Patient from room 509 is missing,' the voice from the other side said.

Simultaneously, there were announcements on the PA system regarding the missing patient. Dushyant Roy. Zarah rushed to Dushyant's room and found the bed empty. *Obviously!* Pihu was missing too. *Maybe she is undergoing some tests*, she reasoned. Zarah rushed out and ran arbitrarily in the hallways of the hospitals. She checked the stairwells, waiting rooms and the lifts. He was nowhere to be found. The morgue, the pharmacy, the clinic. Nowhere. Exhausted, she went to the reception again to ask if anyone had found him. The receptionist shook her head. Half an hour had passed by and there was no sign of him anywhere. Her concern about him baffled her.

With her head hung low, she left the lobby and went out for some fresh air. Mindlessly she walked towards the parking lot, wondering where Dushyant might be. The feeling that she would never see him again filled her with a strange, uneasy sensation. Normally, she would have been happy to have one less man in her life, a minuscule reduction of the hatred she held for men, but she was not.

She had been out for just about a few minutes when she spotted *him* on a concrete bench. While still in his hospital robe, he was blowing smoke rings and smiling at them as they drifted away from him. Zarah ran towards him. A few steps from him, she slowed down. Her guard was up again, her eyes flitted around for the easiest escape just in case Dushyant decided to lunge at her.

'What are you doing here?' she asked, out of breath, her hands on her knees.

'I thought I would excuse myself for a smoke,' he said. 'It's good for the pain.'

'Wait. Is that marijuana? How did you get it?' Her heart rate slowed down, her fear melted away. His uninterested yet warm eyes confused her, even drew her closer.

'A friend got it for me,' he answered and took a long drag again. His eyes were glazed over. He was clearly high.

'Don't you want to get better?'

'I want to, but you guys seem to be getting nowhere. My organ systems are behaving strangely. My body feels like shit and I am constantly in pain. Just two days back I was fine and now I am not,' he complained and smoked.

'You will be fine. Your insides are a cocktail of a million things that you have ingested over the years and it will take us time to find out what's wrong with you,' Zarah explained. 'Can we go back in, please? We have to run a few tests.'

'Tests again?'

'Yes, we have to check for tumours,' she said. She felt sorry for him. The first man she didn't imagine or want dead.

'Is there anything I *don't* have?' he asked.

'We suspect the steroids you took could have caused the tumours in your kidneys and liver. Studies have shown it is a delayed side effect. We believe excessive drinking made it worse and that's what's taking you down.'

'I never told you that I took steroids,' he said and smirked at the perfect smoke ring he had just blown. The rolled-up joint burnt to its end and he threw it on the ground.

'Arman knew.'

'He knew? How?'

'He looked at you and he could tell you had been a sports guy or a gym guy during some part of your life. He inferred that since you were a rash, irresponsible and impatient guy, you would take steroids to grow bigger or get stronger faster.'

'Such a bastard,' he muttered. Zarah saw a brief smile on his face.

'Is he wrong?'

He shook his head and lit another one. Zarah snatched it from him and threw it away. 'Enough,' she said.

'But he could have been wrong,' he grumbled and got up. They started to walk towards the hospital entrance.

'He confirmed it. He talked to Kajal.'

She saw the blood drain from Dushyant's face. Whatever was left of it. He looked at her shocked, violated.

'Why? That fucker!'

'We took your medical history and you never told us anything about steroids. Had you told us, he wouldn't have talked to her,' she responded.

Dushyant's discomfort was apparent. Zarah wanted to ask him about Kajal but she didn't want to poke around. They got into the lift and walked in silence to his room. His hands brushed against her a few times, but she didn't panic. No sweating. No freaking out. No horrifying images in her head.

'Next time you need a smoke, call me. Don't do the disappearing act again,' she said.

'I will try not to,' he answered and climbed up on the bed. 'But the smoking is good for me. It numbed the pain and I feel better now.'

'Can I ask you something?'

'Sure. You're my doctor. That's your job. I wonder if Dr Arman knows what his job is!'

'Why don't you tell your parents about this?'

'They don't need to know.'

'I think they do. In any emergency of a transplant, they will have to be the first ones we'll need to check for a match,' she explained.

Zarah was never a good liar. Over the years, she had bonded with whoever had a troubled relationship with their parents. Ever since she got to know that Dushyant had been hiding his illness from his parents, she felt a special connection. Two broken people make for a wholesome friendship. Even though she had never been friends with any guy.

'You couldn't possibly understand what I have been through.'

'I will. You can try me,' she said.

'I am tired. Can I sleep now? It's starting to pain again, unless you want me to run off for a smoke again.'

'I will put you on some painkillers,' she said and pushed a medicine into his IV.

'We can talk about this later? At night?' he said.

'Sure.'

'And am I dying?'

'Too soon to tell,' Zarah said, not wanting to assure him falsely.

He closed his eyes. Zarah waited for him to drift off and then left his room. *Talk about it later?* Why would she ever talk to a man? Hateful, vile men who wanted their hands on her body and . . .

~

Zarah was fourteen. It was the year 1999.

She always felt out of place at the parties thrown by her father's superiors at the huge farmhouses they owned, bought with money they had made from defunct arms deals. Her mom was drunk and playing poker with the other aunties. Dad was, as usual, drinking and discussing paltry pay cheques and cursing the government for being soft on Pakistan. All the army kids were too old for her, and they were all trying out vodka and rum and anything else they could get. The older kids were snogging behind the bushes.

She felt bored. Her tummy felt strange after the gallons of aerated drinks she had gulped down out of boredom. A little later she couldn't hold it in any more. At the far end of the farmhouse, there were washrooms for guests and she walked towards them. There were drunken generals, colonels and other rank holders all over the farmhouse grounds. She felt awkward and strange. Just a few yards away from the washroom, she felt a rough, overpowering hand on her mouth and another hand across her waist. She saw two men with demonic expressions on their faces.

She only remembered partly what happened next. Over the years, she had tried to slowly erase that memory from her head and had succeeded to an extent. Her rape on that fateful night now seemed like a figment of her imagination. Something that had happened in a parallel universe. Though to this day, she still woke up in the middle of the night with a cold sweat, the faces of those old men—as old as her father—staring down at her, between her legs, scratching her bare body, grunting and moaning as they inflicted pain on her. They took turns for about half an hour. She still remembered the pain, she still remembered the curse words, and she still remembered the egging from one old man to the other, urging each other to violate her harder. She still remembered lying in her own sweat, urine and blood, crying and waiting for help. Her screams were hollow and soundless. No one came. She remembered how she had put herself together, looked at herself in the mirror and felt dead inside. She wondered if she had done something to deserve it. More than that, she clearly remembered how they had threatened to kill her family if she ever told anyone about what had happened. She had lived in fear ever since. For more than a year, she stayed quiet. But one day, she tried.

The first time she tried telling her father about it, she was slapped across her face. And she just told him that a friend of his had tried to manhandle her. He refused to believe her and told her she was imagining things. Her own father denying her the right to get back at the people who destroyed her.

'He is a respectable man and a senior of mine,' he said. 'Dare you talk like this again!' He walked off.

For months, Zarah was in severe depression. Her mother thought it was puberty which was causing it and brushed it off. She would shower five times a day, eat soap to cleanse herself from the inside and was referred to many doctors for OCD (Obsessive–Compulsive Disorder). Slowly, she cured herself. She shut her mind off to all her memories and created new ones.

Sometimes, she felt vindictive. She tracked the two army men years after the incident. One of them died a year after the incident, three bullets to the chest in an attack on the army base camp in Srinagar. Since he was a veteran Kargil hero, his funeral was covered on television. She laughed demonically, faintly similar to how those men had that night at the farmhouse. Her father watched silently.

The other man slipped into a coma after slipping on his bathroom floor five years after the incident and suffered a concussion. He got better with time but would be confined to a bed for life. Seeing him lie helpless on the hospital bed made her feel better. Telling her rapist's nineteen-year-old daughter what he had done to her made her feel ecstatic. When the man's daughter asked Zarah how she knew the whereabouts of her father, Zarah replied, '*I have never forgotten him. He is a monster.*' The horror in the daughter's eyes quenched her vengeance. She laughed when she saw the man's daughter confront him with her newly acquired news.

She was over it now. Her rape did take away her innocence, but it also took her family away from her. Her father and she never looked each other in the eye after that day.

~

As she sat in Arman's office that evening, completing all the paperwork for the day, she wondered what Dushyant's story was. She had visited him again that afternoon and had scheduled him for a full-body scan. During the entire procedure, they had not talked. There were other doctors overseeing the procedure and Zarah didn't want to be seen socializing with a patient.

Late at night, she headed towards room no. 509.

11

Pihu Malhotra

The day had been exhausting. MRIs, nerve biopsies and a million other tests were carried out to track the progress of her disease. Arman oversaw every blood draw, every biopsy and every current wave that was made to pass through her body. It was comforting for her. The battery of tests, the pain and the constant tension were scary. In the middle of her third test, she asked her parents to leave. She knew she was the weakest with them around.

'Are you still thinking about the stem cell thing?' Pihu asked Arman again.

'Yes, I am,' Arman responded. If they went ahead with it, it would be a long treatment that would require her to pop fifty pills a day till the time of her surgery.

'These tests are off or on the record?'

'You don't have to worry about it. The medical expenses will be paid by the hospital. I got you into the pre-trials but I have told them we won't be testing the stem cell treatment on you till we get the permission to do so . . . which we won't.'

'Fine,' she said with a sad smile.

'Let's hope things go as per plan,' he said and tried hard to concentrate on the screen. They were checking if the disease had won the battle against the antibodies.

She sensed that he was either uncomfortable or he didn't like to talk when he was working. The creases on his forehead were incredibly sexy. The taut veins in his outstretched hands were signs of a man who had played some sport in his younger days. She started to imagine him on a football field, on a rainy day, his T-shirt stuck to his toned torso, his hair wet and his legs dirty. In her fantasy, she was with him on the field. Alone. Soon, they were rolling in the mud. *I am losing it! Stop it!* She snapped out of her wet 1990s Jeetendra-movie fantasy. It was only one of the dozens of various situations where she found herself being intimate with Dr Arman.

'Do you have a girlfriend?' she asked with a twinkle in her doe-like eyes.

'No, I don't.'

'Why don't you? You're smart and successful. You should have one,' she said and smiled at him. The nurse drew blood and she winced. Arman winced, too.

'I don't have the time.'

'Oh yes, I forget! The great Dr Arman Kashyap. How can you have time when you're too busy being a genius?'

She chortled and Arman looked at her in fake anger. He said, 'Are you making fun of me? I don't think anyone has told you but you should know better than to fight with your doctor or your waiter. They can kill you or pee in your food.'

Pihu felt good to see him joke and loosen up. Usually, he was too busy cranking his brain muscles to full capacity and bringing people back from the dead.

'That's gross!'

'The pee thing? Yes, I know. That's why you shouldn't mess with us.'

'Or what will you do? Kill me even faster?' she said.

Silence. Arman's face contorted. She was happy to see that her absence would matter to him. Then, she immediately chided herself for thinking too much. Arman was at least a decade older, even though her mind reasoned that it only made him more desirable. Successful, sane men, with experienced hands and tongues make for better fantasies than young, immature boys. Going by the scores of Mills & Boon books she had read, older men always knew where to touch, where to place their tongues, where to hold and caress . . . *Snap out of it!*

'I thought you would be used to people dying around you. You must see it every day, don't you?' she asked, breaking out of her imaginary world of muddy football fields, crackling fireplaces and deserted metro stations.

'I thought so too,' he said and walked away from her. He started to check the numbers and figures on the monitors.

'Can you guide me through the numbers and things you're checking for?' she asked out of curiosity. It had been more than a year since she had attended medical school, but her thirst for knowledge was still insatiable.

For the next one hour, they discussed her tests in excruciating detail. She felt good when Arman admitted that she was smarter and more knowledgeable than even a few medical-school graduates. At one point, he even called her a freak, a mutant with an extraordinary memory for medicine. Her schoolgirl cheeks turned scarlet as if he had complimented her smile.

'I think we are done for the day,' he said. 'Now, we just have to compile the results and see what happens.'

'Great!' she said and smiled.

'By the way, I talked to a few doctor friends in the US who are trying out the same treatment. They are very hopeful about its success. Who knows?'

Arman didn't look at her while he said that. He clasped

his palms and rubbed them together, like a young kid lying to his parents.

'Thank you.'

'You don't have to thank me.'

'I do. After a long time, I felt I was in a class again. It was perfect,' she purred and wondered if she was still blushing.

Arman leant towards her and held her hand. Her breath stuck in her throat. The warmth of his hand, the look in his brilliant black eyes and the creases on his forehead almost knocked her heart out. For a moment, she was back in the muddy football field, in front of a crackling fire in a big house, in a deserted metro station with just the two of them.

'Everything will be okay,' he assured her. She wasn't listening to the words. The words floated in her ears and she turned her to him with a blank head and a rapidly beating heart.

'I am sure it will,' she said.

Arman hugged her and she lost herself in his arms. 'You will be okay,' he muttered. He jerked his hands away as he saw Zarah walk into the room. 'I will see you later,' he said and left the room abruptly.

~

Pihu was smiling as she stared at the ceiling. She could still feel his hands around her. Slowly, she closed her eyes and wished she could stay there for ever. Her daydreams knew no bounds that day. Her mom was sleeping scrunched on the tiny bed and Pihu didn't want to wake her up. Her dad was at home. Venugopal cut her calls and she guessed he must be busy peering down cancer-ridden lungs or rotten pituitary glands. In the past few months, Venugopal and Pihu had spent hours talking to each other about her symptoms, his crushes, her fears and it always felt like they would be back together, on the last seat of the class, scribbling notes together, nudging each other whenever the class would hover around penises or anything of that sort.

She texted him.

The doctor hugged me today. I think I'm in love. Not like teenage-I-love-you-so-I-need-you love, but eternal, true, dying love.

Venugopal:

You've got to be shitting me. I thought I was your eternal love. We would be a perfect example for racist bastards.

She laughed and remembered the times they had placed their hands together and compared her pale-white complexion to his smoky black tinge.

She replied:

Aw! You will always be the one. But he's so cute! I mean, not really. He's just hot. Like really hot. Like unbelievably hot. I wouldn't think twice checking him for hernia.

Venugopal:

Nothing beats a tall, handsome and a really dark guy. Anyway, I get it. And stop being gross. Are you high on something?

Pihu:

No! Call me as soon as you get free. And tell me everything what you're doing/cutting/reading/screwing up! Miss you.

Venugopal:

Miss you more!

With no one to talk to about how spectacular her day was, she turned to Dushyant, who looked engrossed in a book. A part of her was surprised to see the brat with a book. *He can read?* It was hard to imagine him doing anything else but loitering around with an empty bottle of alcohol in his hands and a half-burnt cigarette on his lips. She wasn't far from the truth though.

'I heard you had gone missing today?' she asked, trying to make small talk. She really wanted to tell him about the gooseflesh and how she thought she would faint when the doctor touched her.

'None of your business,' he said and turned on his side.

'Why are you so bothered by me? Anyway, I am the only one who talks to you. Oh! Apart from the hot female doctor, that is. I tell you, having a background in medicine myself, doctors usually aren't as gorgeous as her. Or Dr Arman,' she said hoping he would latch on to the conversation.

He shrugged. 'I don't like you in my room. Your parents wanted another room for you, why not take a single room? Why still be here and eat whatever is left of my brain?'

'Are you still pissed at what my mom said?' She recalled the time when her mom had labelled him a degenerate, profligate son. 'I am really sorry about that. Sometimes, she is just—'

'No, I am not. I just don't see a reason why we have to talk.'

'I am sorry for what she said. Can we—?'

'You don't have to be. Can I get back to my book?'

'I don't know what your problem is with me,' she said, exasperated. Pihu never saw any reason to be rude to someone. Concepts like rudeness, jealousy, hatred, et cetera baffled her. People, for her, were either black or white, with no shades of grey.

'I don't like you. Do you get me? I don't like the fact that you're constantly smiling when my whole body feels like it's burning up, turning to ashes. I am scared to death and when I look on the other side, I see the smiling face of a carefree girl, with her parents hugging and kissing her. It's irritating. Why couldn't you just take another room and let me suffer in peace?'

'You're not dying. I talked to Dr Zarah. She just said you have some tumours. You will be okay,' she assured Dushyant whose body shook in little tremors. *Was he crying?*

'I coughed blood. I even peed blood today. They are clueless about what I have. Please let the real doctors do their jobs and don't meddle,' he bellowed at her.

'You will be okay. I am sorry if my smile bothers you so much,' she said, almost guilty. Like she always did, she rationalized his behaviour as an outcome of his frustration and fear.

'Just get your treatment and get the hell out of here,' he growled.

'Fine,' she said and drew the curtains between them.

From the other side, she could hear Dushyant ring someone from his phone and call his room-mate—*an irritating girl named Pihu . . . a bitch*. Her eyes welled up. His tone was hurtful. She wanted to pull the curtain away and shout at him. *You're not the one who's dying, I am!* All of sudden, she choked up. She was no longer delighted by her thoughts of an imaginary romance. She was going to die soon. He was going to live. Her pain was going to be a lot more. She had been through it earlier and she was doubtful she had the strength to do it again. She hated her body and wished it had destroyed itself the first time. A dreadful time was staring right in her face and he reminded her of it.

~

She couldn't sleep. Her conversation with Dushyant had left her shattered. It reminded her of now now-numbered days. She picked up the book—a multimillion-copy bestseller and a guidebook for patients afflicted with ALS; it had been recommended to her by the first doctor who had diagnosed her—*Tuesdays with Morrie*. It was about a seventy-year-old man named Morrie who had the same disease as her—ALS. It was about the life lessons the old man shared with a student of his across a time frame of thirteen Tuesdays. He eventually dies, slowly and in pain, but content and victorious.

She tried not to think about the time before the experimental drugs had worked, but that's exactly how she started to think about it. When she had to be fed with someone else's hand, when her tongue used to be paralysed and she would choke on it. She had been trying not to think about it, but Dushyant brought those memories flooding back into her head. She imagined someone cutting her throat open and inserting a tube so that she could breathe normally. She was crying now.

Just then, she heard the door open. The curtain hid most of the person who had just come in, but she could make out from the silhouette that it was a girl. The lack of a doctor's coat told her it wasn't Zarah. She strained her neck to see who it was but couldn't.

'What are you doing here?' she heard Dushyant say.

'I wanted to see how you were doing. I was worried.' The girl's voice quivered. It was a very feminine voice. Almost like whipped strawberry cream on chocolate. Sweet as hell.

'You didn't need to come. I don't need you. And I am fine,' Dushyant grumbled. Pihu noticed the same rudeness again.

'Don't say that,' she said. 'They called me up. Your doctors . . . They said you could have tumours. I was scared. What's happening, Dushyant?' she prodded, her sweet nightingale voice almost putting Pihu to sleep. Her voice was the truth.

'Why do you care?'

'Because I do.'

'You don't need to,' he said. 'Does Varun know you're here?'

'No, he doesn't.'

'Are you going to tell him?'

'It doesn't matter whether I do or not. I don't think he needs to know,' she said.

'Are you guys still together?' he asked.

'Yes.'

'Good,' he said and paused. 'So now that you have seen that I am okay, I think you should leave.'

'It doesn't have to be like this,' the girl said. Her voice still shook as if she was scared of Dushyant. Pihu strained her ear to listen closely, Dushyant's nails-on-a-blackboard voice in stark contrast to the girl's opera singer's voice.

'It has to be like this.'

'Why are you acting so difficult, Dushyant?'

'I am acting difficult? You leave me and then don't talk to me for two years and now that I am here, you come to me? Why? To make yourself feel better? I am not going to give you that pleasure. I had a hard time forgiving and forgetting you; please don't make me go through that again. Go back to your rich, smart boyfriend you have always been in love with. I don't care about you any more.'

'We didn't have to end up like this.'

'You chose it to be like this. You walked out of my life and fucked your ex-boyfriend! It wasn't me, it was your fault,' he growled.

'I didn't . . . but I am sorry; after what happened, I couldn't have stayed and you know that. After what happened between us . . .'

'Had you loved me enough, you would have stayed. You definitely wouldn't have gone running into his arms. I was begging for you to come back. I almost destroyed myself to get you back. What didn't I do to catch your attention? For a little pity? Why didn't you come when I was drinking myself to death? Why? Didn't you think for once how I would feel?'

'I did—'

'Fuck off. Please. I don't want you here. I would rather die than talk to you,' she heard Dushyant shout.

'But—'

'Just *get out*.'

'Dushyant—'

'One last time, GET OUT.'

She heard the rustling of the bedsheet and saw the feet leave the room. She felt sorry for the girl with the hypnotic voice who had just been disparaged by Dushyant. Too bad, she couldn't see her beyond the soft, beautiful ankles. For the first time, her judgement about Dushyant changed. Maybe it wasn't the disease or the tumour, maybe Dushyant had always been a sick person.

12

Dushyant Roy

The needles tugged at his skin as he rolled over and tried to get some sleep. He knew he wouldn't get any that night. The pain had slowly become permanent. Painkillers were less effective now and the pain was now a part of him. He tossed and turned, thinking about Kajal and the argument from moments earlier. He wondered why she had bothered after all these years. Was it because she still loved him? Did she still think of him when in bed with Varun? Maybe it was because she felt guilty about what she had done.

It was ten. The curtain was still drawn between them. The girl on the other bed had been a constant source of irritation. His skin crawled every time he looked at her. Even on the verge of death, he wasn't at peace. The last thing he wanted was to have the image of a chattering young girl gnawing at his eyes in his last moments. Instead, he needed a smoke.

There were still twenty rolled joints safely tucked into one of the books a friend of his had dropped at the hospital. He took three of them out and stuffed them into his robe. Slowly, he unscrewed the drips on his hand and pulled them off. He walked out gingerly, trying not to attract attention to his tottering self. He had taken just five steps away from the room when someone called out his name. He turned around to see Zarah leaning against the wall, her eyebrows knitted and her lips curved into a sinister smirk.

'Going for a smoke again?' Her voice a measured mix of sternness and playful exuberance. He nodded. 'What did I tell you about not vanishing again?' she asked.

'Come along? I have enough for both of us,' he responded. Usually unmoved when challenged, his eyes were like a cowering dog who had pooped in the hallway.

Zarah smiled and motioned him to follow her. Together, they went to a rarely used balcony on the sixth floor. Usually, patients want to get out of the hospital as soon as they enter and don't look for hang-out spots to smoke. But Dushyant was different. The lack of direction or purpose soothed him, made him feel unshackled. The need to get high and fucked up ruled him.

Zarah took one of the rolled joints from his hands and lit it up. As the pungent fumes snaked up from the smouldering joint and hid her face momentarily, Dushyant stood there, ogling. The irritating girl's words hung uncomfortably in the air. *The hot female doctor*. With a lit joint in her hand, a careless strand of hair wandering aimlessly around her face, she leant dangerously close to the edge of the railing. An air of unabashed freedom surrounded her.

'You shouldn't be smoking, should you?' he queried. Zarah didn't answer; instead, she looked at the neon-lit city, her eyes already glassy from the weed. She closed her eyes, let open the bun and allowed the breeze to play with her hair. She took another long drag and let the smoke curl out from her slightly parted lips. *She is a regular smoker*, he thought. Long drags of a joint as potent as the one in her hand often made even old-timers wheeze and choke. Not her.

'Neither should you,' she said and turned towards him. The joint was working its way into her body. He could see it in her elegant and almost sexual turns and the deliberate flips of her hand while managing the unruly tufts of hair around her face. 'You fought with her?' she asked.

'Her? Her, who?'

'Oh, well. The girl who shares your room and the girl who came to see you today,' she answered. Another long drag. She wasn't an amateur, even by Dushyant's standards.

'I had my reasons,' he said. 'The girl in the next bed irritates me. She behaves like a life coach. She fiddles with things, gets excited as if she has just checked into a spanking new hotel suite and not a hospital ward. I can't stand her.'

'And what happened with Kajal? The other girl?'

'How do you know I fought with her?'

Another drag. Her responses were getting slower. So were his. It wasn't the weed clouding his senses that drew him to her. It wasn't her overpowering scent, her piercing brown eyes, the olive skin or the supple body that he wanted to feel in his rough hands and leave savage bite marks on. What drew him to her was her nonchalance, the hidden anger, the restlessness in her eyes, the tiny slit marks on her wrists and the belief that she belonged to the same tribe as his. One of dejection, longing and crushing loneliness. 'I was standing outside when I heard your voice. I couldn't help but eavesdrop. I told you I would see you in the night, didn't I?'

'Could you hear us talking?'

'You were shouting.'

'Shit.'

'Ex-girlfriend?' she asked, even though she knew the answer to her question, her eyes firmly on him.

Dushyant didn't answer for a bit. At a distance, he could see the bunch of lights he recognized as his college hostel.

He wondered if Kajal was back in her hostel room . . . or with Varun. Was she still thinking of him? Was she crying? Did she tell Varun where she'd been?

'Yes,' he said. 'We broke up two years back. I did something stupid and she left me. I tried to win her back, but she was gone. I hadn't seen her since then,' he mumbled and wondered if he should tell her what had happened that night.

'She wants to come back?'

'I don't know what she wants,' he said and climbed on to the ledge. Unlike Zarah, who was at ease with her legs dangling on the other side of the ledge, he was petrified. The hundred-foot drop made his heart pump fiercely.

'Careful,' Zarah said and laughed boisterously. Unhindered and unpretentious. He looked admiringly at the sharpness of her nose, the cheekbones and the perfectly fitting trousers. *Too stunning to be a doctor*, he thought. With the mild hallucinogen in his bloodstream, he could see images of a bikini-clad Zarah turning heads on an exotic beach in Brazil.

'Why haven't you told your parents yet?' she asked. 'And how long do you think you can keep up with the medical expenses?'

'I have more money than it looks like,' he said.

'Rich parents, eh?'

'My father is a clerk and my mother is a housewife. They haven't sent me a single buck since my second year,' he answered.

'Then how?' she asked. He searched for signs of shock on her face but found none. She was too high to care.

'I am a face that people forget. But I am also a brain that forgets little.'

'So you do little brain-trick shows for people?' she chuckled.

'Not really, but close. You remember those multiple-choice questions we had to answer to get through entrance examinations?' She nodded and he continued, 'I was brilliant at that. In eleventh grade, my coaching-institute teacher had noticed that and made me take an exam for a rich kid in the senior batch. I cracked three exams for the kid. All we needed was to click a picture of his which looked like me, and it was done. It was five thousand for each exam. My teacher had a new car the very next week.'

'So?' Zarah looked disturbed. *Finally!*

'Business slowly grew. I started taking every type of exam. BBA, MAT, CAT, engineering and even medical entrances. I have taken the board exams, tenth and twelfth, every year since then. I know all the textbooks by heart. I make more money in those four months of examinations than people make in years. I am a safer bet than a leaked paper or two years of expensive coaching classes. If I am not caught, I have a zero rate of failure. And I come cheap.'

Last season, Dushyant had taken thirteen board examinations, nine engineering entrances, four BBA entrances and a few MBA entrances. He took the GRE five times and a whole host of other exams which now he couldn't even remember. None of the surrogate examinations went cheaper than twenty thousand rupees. He made 8 lakh that year. What with his failure rate of zero, people clamoured at his doorstep, even paying the entire sum upfront.

'How long have you been doing this for?' Zarah asked and lit up the last joint.

'It's been five years now,' he said. 'And I have been saving up. I don't go out on expensive dates or have any indulgences. I have a lot of it with me.'

'All you spend is on alcohol and drugs,' she murmured.

'A lot of that comes free for me. I took an exam for an army officer's kid one time. My alcohol comes cheaper than you can imagine. For other things, I have my sources. I am a loyal customer and I never get into trouble with the police or anything.'

Zarah threw the burnt joint away. She turned silent.

'What happened?'

'Umm . . . Nothing.'

'Something is wrong. I thought we were discussing stuff,' he said.

'I am an army kid, too,' she conceded.

'You don't come across as an abrasive brat.'

Zarah shot an icy stare at him. Dushyant had always thought of army kids as extrovert bullies. The constant variation in environment and the change in schools made them competent to handle any social exchange with ease. They grew up a lot faster, matured faster and came across as extra-smart brats.

'Is that what you think about army kids?' she asked.

'I am not putting them down or anything. In fact, as a kid I wished I was as cool as them. So, are you like that?'

'Not really. I don't think so,' she answered and added with a pause, 'I don't want to talk about it.'

'What? Did they beat you or something? Because that's okay. Mine did. You wouldn't believe how much my father beat me when I couldn't clear the IIT entrance examination. Before the exam, I was more scared about what he would do to me if I didn't clear the exam rather than the exam itself. It's ironic—since that year, I have cleared it thrice for other people,' he said. 'See this,' he pointed out to a few circular scars on his left forearm.

'Are these cigarette butts? He burnt you?'

'More times than I can remember. Every time I didn't score well in a coaching-class examination, he would thrash me mercilessly,' he said. 'And this one is a belt-buckle wound.'

'Didn't your mother say anything?'

'I think sometimes she wanted to. But she was used to it. I think she thought I deserved it,' he explained. 'Plus, I used to get beaten up once a month. Or less. The frequency wasn't any higher. Sometimes, it was just a few slaps. Everyone gets those. But he constantly kept me in fear. It was a nightmare,' he said. For a moment, he wondered what made him blabber so much that night. Was it the joint? What was it about this girl that gave him verbal diarrhoea all of a sudden? He hadn't shared the agonizing details of his troubled teenage years with anyone other than Kajal. Everyone who knew him was aware that Dushyant hated his monstrous parents with all his heart, but no one knew where it came from.

'What happened after that?'

'Nothing. I put up with their bullshit till the first semester. They stopped sending me money after I finished third in class. So, I started earning on my own. Then, I didn't need them,' he claimed.

'How did they react?'

'They struggled to understand what was happening for the first few months. I didn't call them. I didn't ask for money. They came to my college a few times to check what had gone wrong. Eventually they found out that I had started smoking and drinking. Dad whipped out his belt again, but I fought back. I was much stronger . . .' His voice trailed off. He felt Zarah lean into him. Suddenly, he became conscious of her physical proximity.

'And?'

'They have softened up a little. I didn't talk to them for six months. Sometimes, they had to come to the hospital after my episodes of drunken madness. They still try to tell me that I am a failure and how they wished they had brought up a dog, not a son. But I have a choice now of not listening to them. I exercise that. They are dead to me.'

'Is that why you do this to yourself? Torture yourself to torture them? Like you did when Kajal left you.'

'Are you a psychiatrist now?' he asked, and then moved on.

'I don't know. Maybe. I just want them to feel sorry for what they did. Make them feel that they lost me because of their behaviour. And yes, I do want them to feel miserable.'

'You're destroying yourself to do that?'

'I am not destroying myself . . . Well, maybe, I am. But I like my life. I like doing what I do. It might have started out like that, but it's no longer that. I used to be bothered at first. Now, I don't care that I don't have a family to go back to.'

Zarah was quiet. Dushyant knew his story forced people to consider their previous judgments about him. He never had any illusions about his failures in life or his detestable nature, but he knew he wasn't the worst either. No matter what he did, he knew he would always be better than his father. With his eyes stuck firmly on her, he waited for Zarah to respond. People usually did, expressing sympathy for him, and then moving on with their lives. At the end of the day, he was a raging alcoholic and an addict who was meant to be hated, not understood.

'We should go back,' Zarah said.

'So soon? After all this, don't you think I should know about you a little too?' he asked as he jumped down the ledge. Every bit of his body hurt. His heart eased a bit now that he wasn't gazing at a hundred-foot drop.

'Maybe later.'

'A little bit?' he asked.

The inquisitive tone in Zarah's voice had changed to a cold, professional pitch. 'Let's get you into bed,' Zarah said and led the way back to his room. He followed soundlessly. She put him in bed, reattached the tubes and screwed them back on.

'If you keep sneaking out like this, you will take more time to get better,' she whispered.

'More nights like these and I won't mind staying here a bit longer,' Dushyant said and felt someone else had said it. He had just flirted with her. *Why did I do that?* Zarah smiled and told him she would see him tomorrow. They shook hands and she left the room. There was something about her, this doctor.

He knew she was hiding something from him, something about her parents. Whatever the reason for her sadness, it only made her alluring and desirable. Like an antique table that has character, the flaws—the tiny slit marks on her wrists—made her more beautiful. The layers to Zarah made her more intriguing. Even more beautiful than she was. For the first time since he had woken up in the hospital, he felt better.

He was still dazed from the weed and the calm Zarah had helped instil in him when he heard someone sobbing softly from the other side of the curtain. He leant in the direction of the sound and saw Pihu's father sitting near her feet. Pihu was sleeping and so was her mom. The man just caressed the toes of his little girl and kissed them lovingly, with tears in his aching eyes. His eyes were pure, black sadness.

Dushyant's breath stuck in his throat and he felt hollow inside. He wondered what Pihu had. He put his head back on the pillow and wondered if his dad would ever sit next to him and cry for having lost him.

13

Kajal Khurana

Kajal was the third daughter of a rich business family based in Punjabi Bagh, New Delhi. Aseem Khurana, her father, dealt in converting unsuspecting animals into bags, shoes, clothes and the like. Getting into fashion and leather designing seemed like obvious career choices for the two elder daughters in the family. Kajal, younger by ten and twelve years to her sisters, was the spoilt one. By the time she entered college, both her sisters were happily married and, more importantly, incredibly successful businesswomen. The leather factory now had showrooms and boutiques all over the northern region. Money was never an issue. The smallest car she had ever driven was a puny Volkswagen Beetle that cost her father a small fortune. In spite of the abundant money and the cradling comfort, Kajal grew up to be a very sensitive, simple girl with a magical voice and a penchant for reading. She never shopped, never hankered for an iPhone or that awesome-little-black-dress-for-the-party-next-weekend, and was never comfortable in chauffeur-driven cars. Her only loves were music and books, which she indulged in with wholesome passion.

No one expected her to choose science after her tenth board examinations, but she did. The bigger surprise came when she cracked the entrance examination and made it to a premier engineering college. Her parents—not really impressed with their daughter getting into a *boys'* field—wanted her to go to London and study literature. But she was dead set on studying engineering. Her sisters, headstrong and no-nonsense, asked her to chase her dreams and make something of herself. They were sure Kajal would bring in the next wave of technology.

Three years later, Kajal was disillusioned and wanted to quit college. Fluid dynamics, Fourier transforms and the like were not things she was interested in; she was just good at them.

Kajal was the apple of her parents' eyes; her wants were always put first. When she had first mentioned her discontentment—after her break-up with Dushyant—her dad had arranged for prospectuses of colleges in London where she could study literature. Or journalism. Or whatever young girls with kohl-lined eyes, dressed in kurtas, studied abroad. A little part of her had wanted to go. Not because it was the calling of her life, which she had conveniently ignored, but because she had wanted to run away. Only if she had left for London instead of continuing here, she would have never gone through the turmoil she faced now. The news of Dushyant's illness had shattered her. The severity of his disease had been keeping her awake for days now. Varun hadn't been helpful at all. With his eyes glued to the presentation on his laptop, he had asked her to *get over it. Dushyant would have listened to me and not asked me to get over it if the roles were reversed*, she thought. Against her good sense, she had gone to see him at the hospital, only to get ridiculed and be thrown out.

As she made her way back to the auto she had come to the hospital in, she felt her grief first swell her heart, and then her eyes. For more than two years, she had tried to cut off that part of her life which Dushyant had been a huge chunk of. But the moment she set her eyes on him, her heart called out to her, jolting it out of its slumber.

The contours of his face had hardened, the eyes were sunken, the beard was unshaved, but the sincerity in his eyes screamed for attention. The goodness of his heart, which nobody else but she could see, called out to her. It was as if two years had meant nothing, just a blip on the time–space continuum. Within an instant, she was back to the day he had first talked to her in the library. Since the break-up, she hadn't gone back there. There were a lot of places they had been to together and a lot of things they had done together that had lost their charm once they parted ways. The library didn't feel the same, the golgappas had lost their tang, and the late-evening walk in the park felt like a chore.

The autorickshaw drive to Varun's place was shorter than she would have liked. *Don't go*, a voice inside her screamed as she paid the auto driver and then climbed up the stairs to the lobby of the fifty-storeyed apartment building in Connaught Place where Varun lived alone. His apartment was on the thirty-eighth floor from where one could enjoy a brightly lit view of Delhi at night. She had lost count of the nights she had spent staring aimlessly into space while Varun prepared for his next big meeting.

'What took you so long?' Varun asked as he opened the door. He was still in his office clothes. A finely striped shirt, now hanging over his crisp, ironed trousers. Varun was ageing faster than normal and looked more like thirty-two. He was ageing gracefully, though; the greys in his hair were patterned and looked good on him.

'I stopped by at the hospital. I wanted to see how Dushyant was doing,' she said. She searched for any change in the expression on his face. Disappointed, she looked away.

'Want a drink?' he asked.

'I don't drink.'

'Oh,' he said. 'Yes.'

Kajal was annoyed. He had known her for ever. How could he overlook such details? It wasn't the only thing, though. Time and again, she had chosen to forgive him, blaming it on the age difference, on the difference in the kind of lives they led and the kind of people they inherently were. They were both born into money, but while Varun had grown up to appreciate the luxuries of life, Kajal still loved her novels, her music and the dirty spice of street food more.

'Won't you ask how he was? How things went?' she said, trying to incite him, to elicit a reaction of any sort from him. His calm demeanour, his uncaring self and absolute lack of possessiveness irritated her. Sometimes, she wished he would shout at her, scold her and threaten to leave her. Do something that would make her feel important, loved. Anything that would make her feel more than a useless piece of furniture you turn to when tired. A few months back, she had even posted pictures of her with a guy Varun didn't like, on Facebook. Still no response. Just a shrug and he moved on.

'How's he?'

'He is alive. He has tumours and a failing liver.'

'Will he live?'

'I think he will, but he is in real bad shape,' she said and added to exaggerate, 'Though the doctors aren't very hopeful. They are still to figure out many symptoms.'

'I hope he gets well soon. He was always a little screwed up,' he said and sat at a distance. One leg calmly crossed over the other, and he reached for the remote. 'Want to watch a movie today?'

'Isn't that what we do every day?' she asked, now angry. 'And I just told you someone is dying and this is your reaction? *Let's watch a movie?* Do you even care about what I want?'

Her eyes sized up the guy she had been with for two years. He wasn't the same guy she had known when she was younger—the older, wiser guy who could make everything all right with just a few kind words. Their perspectives were different now, and that had more to do with her discontentment than the seven-year age difference between them.

'I am not having this fight again today!' he growled, his voice rising.

'WHY NOT? It's not that we meet every day. Half the time, you're out of town, and when you do have time for me, all you do is get drunk and fuck me. Or well, watch a movie.'

'Excuse me—'

'I am tired of this, Varun!'

'Is this because of that guy you saw in the hospital?'

'His name is Dushyant. Do you remember? Dushyant. I dated him before I dated you.'

'I DO REMEMBER,' he snapped. They were standing right next to each other. Varun towered over Kajal who was staring right at him. 'The bastard who hit you and you came crying to me!' he shouted, his hands flailing all over the place.

'Just because he hit me doesn't make you better, Varun. Day after day, I wait for you to come back to Delhi so that we can spend a little time together. And what do you do? You just call me over. I am done being your slut—'

'I never said that.'

'But you do treat me like that, Varun,' she argued. 'I wasted so many years on you. Understanding you, being with you when your meetings didn't go well, trying to get what you're going through . . . and what do I get? The guy I am with still offers me a drink when he knows that I don't drink!'

'I am sorry—'

'No, *I* am sorry!' she said, tears flirting with her eyelashes. She got up and started walking towards the door.

'You can't go—'

'I need some time,' she said and closed the door of his plush apartment behind her. Deep inside, she knew she was never coming back. By the time she got into an auto to go back to her college, the tears had dried up. But the realization of what life had come to struck with full force. She decided she would go back to the hospital again some day. As the kilometres clocked in between her and the posh building Varun lived in, she wondered how far away they were from each other. She had never been the one for him. His work was his only passion. She was always the mistress.

The voices of her sisters rang in her head as she snuggled into bed that night. They hated Dushyant as much as they loved Varun. The news of Dushyant slapping her was hard for them to digest. *It's just the start of an abusive relationship*, they had said. And she had believed them. *That's how it all starts*, they had insisted.

During the years she had spent with Varun, she had missed the passion, the madness, her torrid relationship with the guy she knew the best—Dushyant—and most of all, she missed the way she was when she was with him.

14

Arman Kashyap

The reports were a mess. A million different problems and a zillion possible reasons behind them. Treat one symptom and it might play havoc with the other problem. Arman's brain had reduced to slush, concentrating on Dushyant's case and isolating the primary debilitating cause. There were too many things tripping over each other in his head. He had been thinking about Pihu and her progressive condition. But it wasn't just the disease he was thinking about, and that's what bothered him the most. He was thinking about *her.*

He was itching to see her again, to watch her regale him with her silly stories, see her giggle like a little kid and get excited by the littlest of things. She was unbelievably alive for someone who was dying. He was thinking about the promised date but alternately, he was also thinking about adopting the tiny ball of cuteness.

The clinical trials were not the reason for his sleepless nights, it was *her*—the infectious smile, the exuberance, the will to live, the courage and the undying love for medicine. Being a specialist in ALS cases, Arman knew what lay ahead of Pihu if the treatment didn't work. Pihu knew it too. Just like the last time, she would die a slow, excruciating death . . . The very thought made him shift uncomfortably in his seat. Worse still, she would die on the operating table.

He had seen his patients lose the use of their limbs, breathe laboriously, lie on a bed for days, wallow in self-pity, curse their lives, and die. He shuddered.

Dushyant's reports were leading him nowhere. A smattering of guilt crept in. Every minute he spent thinking about Pihu and her affliction meant a minute of extra suffering for the patient on the other bed. Not that he ever cared for patients like Dushyant who had a death wish. From steroids to drugs to other banned narcotics, his body was a noxious cocktail of toxic chemical compounds. Arman left the room to talk to Dushyant and check if he had missed something in the preliminary tests. He walked the empty hallways of the hospital alone. It was three in the night and he could hear the incessant snoring in the hallways, the creepy crickety sounds of the crickets and despite these noises, the deathly silence of the hospital. A handful of people still hung around. The night-duty ward boys, some odd doctors going through the motions like zombies, the nurses, and a few grieving relatives sprawled on the benches.

In the past month, he had been to his house just thrice, and that, too, when he'd run out of his white shirts. He had now resorted to ordering his shirts online from an e-retailer—*White Shirt, Large, Quantity: 5, Cash on Delivery*. It was convenient. Not having to choose what to wear meant a few hundred hours more to live. What would Dushyant and Pihu not give to have those extra few hours?

'Still here?' a voice said from behind. It was the Head of Department, Oncology.

'Had something to do,' Arman answered.

'You always have something to do,' the man said and walked off, smiling. He would probably go home, gorge on home-cooked rice and dal, and curl up with his wife and sleep. For Arman though, it was a constant state of insomnia. His body had adapted to endure long hours without complaint. A few hours a day of sleep on his couch sufficed. Of late, his mom had started flooding his inbox with the CVs and pictures of *Slim, Convent-educated, MBA/Engineer/Doctor girls from Good Family Backgrounds* whom he could get married to, but he never opened any. His family thought pinning him down in wedlock was the only way to slow him down.

He pushed open the door to the ward. The lights were switched off and he slowly adjusted himself to the ambient light of the room. He checked the numbers and the crooked lines on the small monitors. Dushyant was lying on his side, peacefully for a change. Arman picked up the chart and looked over the sheet. *What bullshit*, a voice screamed inside him.

'Hi!' a warm, fuzzy voice greeted him. He turned to see Pihu's half-open, sleep-battered eyes on him. Her smile made him feel enveloped in a warm blanket with a hot coffee on a rainy Sunday, the kind of smile that shines on an office-goer's wife's face after he returns from a long, harrowing day at work.

'Hi!' Arman responded.

'Did you come to see me?' Pihu asked. Her expectant, doe-like eyes made him lie.

'Yes,' he said.

'You're even cuter when you lie. I told Venugopal that. He said I was crazy.'

'Who's Venugopal? Should I be jealous?' Arman played along. He hung the chart back on Dushyant's bed.

'You could be. He's very good-looking, after all.'

'Better than me? I doubt that. Did I tell you how many girls I dated back in college? I was pretty popular, you know?

I don't think this Venugopal guy could beat me. So, is he better than me?' Arman grinned playfully.

'No, I lied.'

'You shouldn't lie to a doctor, you know?'

'You shouldn't lie to a patient, you know?'

'I didn't,' Arman argued.

'You did. You're not here for me, are you?' She scrunched her nose in fake anger.

'What if I am?' Arman asked and sat on Dushyant's bed, facing her. It wasn't really a lie. Going all the way to Dushyant's room was his subconscious making a decision to be close to Pihu again.

'I told you it's hard to stay away from me,' she said.

'You never said that.'

'I am saying it now and you better believe it,' she quipped. 'Will he be okay?' The worry in her eyes bothered him, made him feel responsible.

'You seem to be concerned. You picked this room after you met him, didn't you? Zarah told me.'

'You seem to be concerned about why I picked this room,' she giggled. 'Oh, now I get it! That's why you never liked him—because you thought I have a thing for him. And you know, I *could* have a thing for him! He is quite a badass and badasses are cool. You know he snuck out of the hospital to have a joint? How ridiculously cool is that?'

Even in the darkness and the inherent depression of the hospital room harbouring two half-dead people, Pihu's eyes shone bright. Her spirit was indomitable even when it stared at an inevitable death. But then, what choice did she have but to fight?

'I never like any of my patients, especially his kind. The kind who ought to be dead before they reach the hospital.'

'Now you're just being mean! I don't like him *that* much!

You really don't have to be that possessive about me. Oh my God, I need some space. Like—*really*,' she said and jerked her hands around like a spoilt, high-maintenance girlfriend with Gucci shades and razor-sharp five-inch heels. He laughed at her imitation.

'I was serious though,' he said finally.

'You can't be serious. Isn't that why we took up medicine? To save lives and to heal people? No one deserves to die,' she reasoned.

'I am not being mean. And I am not saying he deserves to die. I don't like people throwing their lives away.'

'You're throwing your life away too.'

'I'm not.'

'You work too much. I know you have a responsibility towards the patients who come here. But you also have a responsibility to take care of yourself, which you clearly aren't doing.'

'Fine, grandma! And this from a girl who keeps smiling all day just because she doesn't want to see her family cry? Are you taking care of *yourself*?'

'Yes, I am.'

'You're taking care of *them*, Pihu. You and I, we are not that different.'

'We are!' she defended.

'Don't lie to me. I just told you that. Don't tell me there aren't times you want to cry out loud and curse everyone and everything, and throw stuff around, and break people's heads. Don't tell me that sometimes you don't want to grab your crying father by his collar and ask him why it is happening to you and not the guy on the other bed, and that you don't want to ask your mom to stop sobbing and let you sob instead and throw a tantrum as well,' he said and fell silent. Pihu didn't say anything and Arman realized his folly. 'I am sorry,' he said. 'It just kills me to see you lying there, smiling at everyone, when I know it's crushing you inside.'

'I am smiling at you because I am glad you understand,' she murmured. Arman took her hand in his and caressed the skin which had been punctured time and again with needles. 'And yes, I do smile for them. But I smile for myself too. My memories of them will be gone as I leave; their memories will stay with them forever. Don't we all smile for the pictures we click even on the worst picnics? That's all I want to do. I want to smile for their last pictures of me.'

Arman didn't know what to say to that. 'By the way, I notice your parents have finally decided to go home?'

'Yeah, I threatened them. They had to,' she answered. Arman chuckled and she wasn't pleased to see this. 'Why are you laughing?'

'You threatened them?'

'Why? Can't I? I can be very assertive if I want to be.'

'I am sure you can. But just to confirm, you threatened real people? Like what did you do? Puffed your mouth and refused to breathe? Who would feel threatened by you?' he barely suppressed a chuckle.

'Whatever,' she grumbled. 'So tell me, why are you here?'

'Didn't you just say it? I found it hard to stay away from you.'

'Oh, c'mon. I know I am cute and whatever but why would you want to see a dying girl?' she said and added after an excruciating pause, 'I am just kidding! You are here to see him, right?'

'Yes,' Arman said. 'You want to know what's wrong with him?'

'That's what I like the most about you. You just know how to turn me on!' She batted her eyelashes.

'I'm sorry to disappoint you but we are yet to figure out what's wrong. I could use your opinion.'

'Sorry? That's like multiple orgasms! I can play a real doctor then,' she said excitedly.

'Here, then,' he said and wrapped his stethoscope around her neck. She grinned.

He narrated the reports to her, explaining to her every detail of Dushyant's case. For the next half hour, she shot dozens of questions at him and he was more than glad to field them. Arman let her put forth her ideas, and though a lot of them were stupid and inane, he didn't shoot them down outright. After all, the disparity in experience and education was gigantic, and for her age and experience she was annoyingly exceptional.

'I hope I am not wasting your time?' she queried after her twentieth idea on how to treat the guy was shot down, after careful consideration and deliberation, by Arman.

'No, you're not. It's good to get some external opinion. Anyway, the doctors around here are not that great!' he said to encourage her. 'And if you were to apply for a job here you would so get it. Though I do have to admit we have a strict sleep-with-the-boss policy here.'

She smiled shyly and said, 'I would take up the job just to be applicable for the policy!'

They laughed till their stomachs felt like they would explode all over the ceiling. Their conversation went from how to treat Dushyant to their respective time in medical school. She regaled an amazed Arman with a multitude of stories from her brief stay in medical school, while a struggling Arman admitted he had no memories of professors, labs and operation theatres or the feeling of cutting open his first corpse. As she described her first incision on her virgin corpse, Arman started to feel as if he was there, with her, holding her hand and guiding the knife as it moved deftly along the ribcage. As if he was a part of that memory. He took pictures of her, of them and of the imaginary corpse.

Once finished, Pihu wanted to know more about the patients he had miraculously treated in his much-talked-about career. 'There are no miracles, just logic and knowledge,' Arman said pompously.

'Fuck off,' Pihu replied.

He knew he was gifted. He could see beyond the obvious and take radical decisions that no one else would dare take. People wondered at his competence and called him a freak and a genius, but he never gave it a thought and accepted his talents humbly as a gift.

'So aren't you worried about him?' she asked.

'You really like him, don't you?'

'No, I don't. As a matter of fact, he never talks to me nicely. He abuses me and asks me to mind my own business every time I try to talk to him. I don't know what his problem is. Maybe he doesn't like me.'

'You're too sweet for your own good,' he said and added, 'Let's teach him a lesson then? No painkillers for him tomorrow.'

'No, you don't have to be mean! He is too sick anyway.'

'He will not be tomorrow. We will make him undergo a liver biopsy and see what's killing his liver. The tumours or something else,' he said. 'For now—no more pain medication. How does that sound as payback?'

'You're not doing that!' she exclaimed even as her lips curved into an impish smile.

'Watch me.' He winked, got up and pulled the curtain away. He was about to reach out to the drips but stopped when he noticed Dushyant reach out to his table for a glass of water. Startled to see Arman appear from behind the curtain, he panicked and rolled off the bed. With a loud thud, he fell face-first on the ground. Before Arman could react, Dushyant shrieked out loud, rolled over and clutched his hand.

'FUCK ME!' he shouted as he clenched his fist and banged

it on the floor. Arman saw him wince in pain and rushed to his side. Dushyant wouldn't let his hand go, even as Arman bent over to get a better look. He was sweating now, his face was flushed red, and his whole body was trembling in pain as he kicked wildly.

'LET ME HAVE A LOOK,' Arman said sternly, but Dushyant kept rolling from side to side, frothing at the mouth.

Overhearing the commotion, Pihu got down from her bed. 'Let him see it,' she implored and Dushyant let his hand free.

Arman took a cursory look and said, 'I think it's broken.'

'But I didn't FUCK FUCK FUCK fall that hard,' Dushyant said, his face wet with tears and sweat. 'Arghhhhh. It's hurting!' he shouted.

'Your bones seem to be a mush,' Arman noticed.

'I think I know what it is,' Pihu reasoned and added, 'It's cadmium poisoning which is killing his liver.'

Even as Dushyant watched Pihu in disgust, Arman's brain cells tingled and he was stunned. It made perfect sense. She was right. *How could I not see it?* Dushyant whined in pain as Arman smiled at Pihu. *YES!* Pihu seemed to say with her eyes.

~

Later that night, Dushyant was scheduled for surgery to get the bone in his left hand fixed. Arman went over all his reports again. Cadmium poisoning fitted and all the vital symptoms could be accounted for. His other problems wouldn't have been so hard on his liver, if acting alone. Finally, after days of groping in the dark, they had an approach that could get Dushyant better.

It took Arman a long time to get Pihu to sleep. She had beeen smiling from ear to ear ever since she got the diagnosis right. For the last three hours, he had been making constant trips to her room to keep a check on her. A strange feeling of being dependent—even if it was in a small way—disgusted him a little. But the contentment of seeing her sleep calmly stirred something much more human in him. With time, he had come to see only patients, not people, not problems but diseases, not emotions but weaknesses, and fallible human character. Something had changed in him; something that reminded him of a life he had left behind.

The operation was to last two and a half hours and the treatment for cadmium poisoning wouldn't start until the next day. Arman felt like he had just closed his eyes when someone knocked on his door. It was Zarah. *Isn't she early?* He looked at his watch and found that it was already eight. He had been sleeping like a baby for four hours, with his legs sprawled on his table, dreaming of Pihu in a doctor's coat, like a hopeless romantic.

He staggered to his feet and asked Zarah to come in. After excusing himself for a moment, he trudged to the washroom, washed his face, brushed and came back. For a change, he picked out a shiny new white shirt (that he had ordered off the Internet) from the locker room, put it on and wondered if Pihu would like it. *It's a white shirt for heaven's sake!* he told himself. A cup of steaming coffee was waiting for him on his table when he got back and Zarah was going over Dushyant's file.

'He had a fracture?' Zarah asked, shocked. 'The operation went well?'

'As if you don't know. You went to his room before you came here, didn't you? And you checked all the charts, too. Clearly, you care about him,' he smirked.

'How do you—?'

'Leave that. I just know,' he said and sipped his coffee. He knew one thing for sure and it was that Zarah was an excellent choice as soon as he took a sip. 'Brilliant coffee, I have to admit that. You're weird, Zarah, and you know that, but I like your coffee.'

Quite often, Arman had noticed her reluctance to hold men's hands to pump in medicines and how she tried to keep her distance from male patients—except Dushyant, of course. There was something eerie about this girl, but Arman had chosen to ignore it.

'Okay,' she said. Arman knew he had put her a little off balance by his rare politeness. Zarah shrugged off the anomaly and asked him, 'What really happened with Dushyant?'

'He fell down, but that didn't break his arm. His bones were soft and withering away. We tested him for cadmium poisoning and he tested positive. That's what is eating his liver. We have to treat him for that first before we can start treating the tumours.'

'That's brilliant!' she exclaimed as she always did whenever Arman came up with an improbable idea like this. 'Keep me around for the coffee, but please do keep me around.'

'I didn't come up with it,' he clarified. 'Pihu did.'

'Pihu? Pihu Malhotra? The patient?'

'Dushyant's ward mate. She was there, too, when it happened. It took her just a split second to realize what was wrong,' he explained with a hint of pride in his voice.

'Umm . . .'

He saw her run out of words and could understand her disbelief. They sipped on their creamy coffees. Finally, she said. 'What were you doing there so late in the night?'

Arman didn't answer for a few seconds and then said, 'I was checking up on Dushyant. And I ask the questions, not you. You make coffee.'

'But—'

'I thought I was pretty clear,' he interrupted to avoid further questions. It wasn't the discomfort he felt when others prodded him about his personal life, it was the uneasiness he felt thinking about his dysfunctional relationship with Pihu. He had been through the same thing before and it distressed him to think he was going down the same road again. A relationship with a patient was always a road spiralling downhill.

Zarah smiled and Arman knew she had assumed what there was to assume on her own. She picked up the files and prepped herself up for the first round of patient check-ups. Arman tried to avoid her eyes.

'Are you starting to see your patients now?' Zarah asked and chuckled.

'I think I have to, since my patients are coming up with better explanations for diseases. I don't know why we hire interns and doctors any more. We should just ask patients to come up with solutions, shouldn't we?' he smirked. Zarah didn't flinch and the smile was still pasted on her face. By now, she was used to the condescending taunts. He left his office and headed to the cafeteria for breakfast. And, more importantly, to avoid Zarah's piercing questions, and some of his own.

He also needed to see how she was doing.

15

Zarah Mirza

Zarah lived fifteen minutes away from the hospital and usually the roads were deserted by the time she got home. That night was no different. She was tired, both mentally and physically, after a long day of injections, tests and complaining patients. She parked her car at her usual place—outside the apartment complex. After six months of fighting and haranguing with neighbours and other flat owners for parking space, she realized it just wasn't worth her time. It was just a car! Parking feuds were common in her neighbourhood and she felt lucky she wasn't a part of them any more.

She dragged herself up the stairs of her apartment—something she did regularly to keep herself in shape—and put the key in. She tried it again. She kept jemmying the keys for the next thirty seconds but the lock didn't budge. *Locked from the inside? Oh no. This can't be happening*. Reluctantly, she rang the bell and waited for the worst. The sound of approaching footsteps made her belch. She wanted to run away. The door was flung open. She could feel the vomit in her mouth.

'Hey, beta!' her mom shrieked and then hugged her. The dupatta wrapped around her nose and mouth indicated that she had been mopping and cleaning the house.

'You come home so late? Every day?' she asked as Zarah walked inside the flat, her shoulders drooping, and threw her bag on the shoe rack. The house was much cleaner, and smelled fresh. She had never been messy—given her cleanliness-obsessed mom—but her mom still made the house look a lot cleaner. She wondered what had happened to all the bottles of alcohol—stacked in neat rows beneath her bed—she had duly collected to empty them into herself—or herself into them.

'There is just so much work,' she said.

'It's not safe at all. And this area is so dangerous. Only yesterday there were reports of a chain-snatching incident in the neighbourhood. I think you should get married. At least then we wouldn't have to worry so much about you.'

'So you would have someone else to worry about me, and not you?' she snapped.

'You know what I mean.'

Her mom's rants went on and on. She told Zarah about the overage girls in their family who were having trouble finding a suitable match, and Zarah chose to ignore her concerns with a brief smile. In the corner of the room, her dad was watching television and had not noticed that she was in the room too.

'And the house is so dirty. Doesn't the maid mop the floor? And the bathroom mirror looks like it has never been cleaned. How much do you pay her? I will talk to her when she comes tomorrow. Why don't you say anything to her? And you leave hundred-rupee notes lying everywhere. I am sure the maid flicks a lot of them. She will take all your money and run away some day!'

'I am busy, Mom. I don't have three hours to look over what the maid is up to,' she argued and lay back flat on the drawing room sofa.

Her dad noticed her. 'Oh, you are here? When did you come? Your mom has been cleaning the house. I asked her not to, but you know your mom.'

And I know you. 'Yes,' she said, met his eyes and looked away. Her mom rolled her eyes. She had always wondered what Zarah's father had done wrong. He was a good man, a good Muslim, but his relationship with Zarah had been strained for as long as she could remember. That one summer long ago, things had been quite all right . . . great, even. And over the course of one day, they had become as bad as they could have been. She had waited for it's to sort out on their own, assuming every father–daughter duo goes through such a phase, but things never looked up.

'I will go and change,' she said and went to her room. She closed the door behind her and bolted it. *Michel de Montaigne once said—'Nothing fixes a thing so intensely in the memory as the wish to forget it.'* She knew this better than anyone else.

If only she could snuggle into her bed and stay there till her parents left the house, the building, the apartment and were *far far far far* away. She wished she could do that. After splashing some water on her face, she sat down with her newly bought and inexplicably expensive MacBook Pro, which she hardly had the time to use. She logged on to Facebook and scrolled down her newsfeed mindlessly. Some friends were getting married. Others were on vacation. A few had pictures in short dresses, partying in glitzy clubs with rich-looking, fat boyfriends.

On the other hand, her life had a sense of overbearing inertia . . . slow and moving at a dreary, constant pace. But she was sure no one else looked at her life like that. After all, she was the lucky one who was interning at a renowned hospital known for its unparalleled research facilities and labs wielding the most cutting-edge technology. She was the one who had

got a chance to work with one of the best doctors one could
have asked for. A few years in the US and her success would
be a coffee-table conversation topic amongst her peers for
years to come. Disappointed, she switched off the laptop and
cursed her wretched life. She desperately wanted a smoke, but
her mom was persistently banging on her door. She thought
of Dushyant and how he had managed to shed his family and
move ahead.

After changing into her night clothes, she joined her
mom in the kitchen and helped her out a little. Her mom had
managed quite a spread in the little time she had. Dal makhani,
paneer kofta, butter chicken, boondi ka raita—the only things
that made her want to go back home and stay with her. They
sat on the table and she tried hard not to meet her father's
searching gaze. She hoped it would be over soon. For her, the
incident that had scarred her for life was her father's fault and
she had accepted it as God's honest truth.

'How's the doctor you are working under? I heard he is
pretty good,' her dad said.

'Yes, he is.'

'Tell your dad more about him,' her mom nudged to
encourage conversation between the two. She had been the
silent sufferer all these years.

'There is nothing more to it. He is a great doctor and a
brilliant teacher.'

There was silence again. Her mom tried to bring up topics
like when she planned to get married, and whether she was
in love with someone, and she shot everything down with
disdain. Her parents had stunned expressions on their faces,
wondering what they had done wrong to deserve such hostile
treatment from their daughter. *What do they know?* She, on
the other hand, felt nauseated sitting next to her father. After
dinner, her father opened up a bottle of whisky he had got

and invited Zarah to join him. She refused, even though she really wanted that drink.

It took her three hours and two potent joints to fall asleep. Stoned, she even dialled Dushyant's number, but couldn't get through. The network in the hospital had always been suspect. Her eyes were sore and the pillow was wet by the time her eyelids swept down. She wished her dad had understood her when she really wanted it . . . No, needed it. At times, she wondered if he still remembered that day when she had mentioned the incident to him. Did he really not know that their discord had stemmed from the moment when he had not believed his own daughter? Was he such a coward that he couldn't stand up to his seniors?

Every time she thought about forgiving her father, horrifying images of a young Zarah dragging herself through the washroom, blood trickling down her thighs, crying soundlessly, waiting for her hero—her father—to save her flooded her mind. If her dad had not been there to support her through that *then*, she certainly didn't need him *now*.

16

Pihu Malhotra

Pihu's condition had started to worsen. The first signs of the relapse of ALS were beginning to show in her body. The nerve conduction tests showed that there was a significant loss of sensation in her legs. That morning, she had bumped into the door when she had gone to the bathroom. Her hands were starting to betray her again. She had started to drop things and had become clumsier. The horror of being an ALS patient was back. The loss of sensation and control didn't bother her as much as it bothered Arman, who was the first to go through the reports.

'Maa, I will be okay,' she reassured her mother who was inconsolable on seeing her daughter struggle to do the simplest things again. The disease was *back* and it was worse than ever.

'No, you won't be. It's our fault,' she said. 'We must have done something wrong,' and she burst into tears. Her dad stood over her mom's shoulder and smiled at his daughter. That's the only thing he did. Someone had to be strong, hold the pieces of their lives together and remind them that there was still hope, that all was not lost. Yet. It was a little unfair to expect it from Pihu.

'When is he scheduling the treatment?' her dad asked.

'Soon,' she said.

They had discussed the treatment before. It was illegal and highly dangerous but Pihu saw it as a win-win. It was no secret that there were just two possible outcomes of the radical stem cell treatment. Either die a quick, painless death or be cured. It made perfect sense for her. Having seen herself rot and almost die, she knew what it took for her to plod through that time. Behind the smile and the emotional strength she portrayed, inside she was still a little girl scared to death. Either the *disease* would kill her or the *treatment*—she preferred the latter.

Her sobbing mom excused herself for a bit and her dad sat near her.

'Do you think we should do this, beta?'

'Dad, it's our only option. And Dr Arman is a brilliant doctor. He is putting himself on the line to try this out. I am sure he has something in mind,' she assured him.

'But what if—'

'Don't worry. I am in good hands,' she said and her dad snickered like a child.

'What?'

'You know what I think about sometimes?' her dad said. She looked at him and encouraged him to continue. 'Every time that Arman comes in to check on you, I think what if you two were to be together. As in, be married. You know. I know it's stupid but I can't help it. All the jewellery your mother bought for you . . . and her . . . her . . . dreams . . .' His voice trailed off.

'Aw. That's sweet, Dad. But isn't he a little too old for me? And you forget—he is trying to kill me with his scientific experiment. You wouldn't want your daughter in the hands of a guy who uses girls as his guinea pigs.'

'That's funny,' he said. 'By the way, I have something planned for you. I really hope you like it.'

'For me? A birthday gift? I am not dying in fifteen days, Dad,' she said and wondered if it was a possibility. Her birthday was in thirteen days and she wondered if she would see another one after this. She had never really been a birthday person, but every year her parents put together a family-only birthday party with a butterscotch cake, trick candles, heart-shaped balloons and birthday hats to top it off! Oh well, maybe she had *always* been a birthday person because she loved these parties, and pitied other friends who spent theirs in clubs, decked up in newly bought shiny dresses and claiming to have brought the house down.

'I know you're not going anywhere,' her dad responded. The smile had vanished for a bit but now it returned. 'It's just something I wanted to do for you.'

She listened closely, waiting for her father to give more away.

'I will tell you more about it later. I think you should go sleep now before my son-in-law comes in!' her dad joked.

'Yeah, he can be a pain in the butt,' she smirked and closed her eyes. Her mind started to concoct images of her getting married to Arman in a huge marriage banquet hall with all her friends and relatives lit up like Diwali in their sequined saris, mixer-juicers and enveloped money in hand. In a red-and-gold saree, she thought she looked resplendent while Arman looked his dapper self in a white *bandgala*, tailored with golden thread. She wished. Oh, how she wished! With dreams of a lovely, romantic honeymoon in the bluish-green waters of Malé, which she remembered from the holiday-package pamphlets, she went to sleep. For the first time, she fantasized about kissing a boy and clutched her pillow tighter.

When she got up a few hours later, she saw her father pacing in the room excitedly. *The surprise?*

'What's wrong?' she asked groggily.

'Nothing, nothing,' he answered and smiled broadly. On the next bed, Dushyant, who had been heavily sedated since he broke his arm, was grunting in his half-asleep state. She couldn't wait to tell Dushyant it was she who had found out about his cadmium poisoning. After all, it was her first diagnosis. After her own, of course.

Just as her father sat down, tired, the door of the ward opened and ten familiar faces with big smiles came in, and crowded the tiny room. They shouted Pihu's name in unison and hurrayed. Seeing her friends from the medical college again opened the floodgates of the happiness hormone in her and she felt her heart would pump out of her chest. She hugged them one after the other, Venugopal being the last one. He had the biggest smile, and the most crushing grief behind the misleading eyes. They had not come empty-handed. Similar rectangular boxes wrapped in yellow Pikachu wrapping paper. Some of them carried helium-filled balloons which were now kissing the ceiling and she wondered when they would come down again. Would it be when she was sleeping and would it scare the shit out of her?

All of them sat around her bed and asked her if she was doing okay. She pulled out one of her 'I am going to be dead' jokes and everyone laughed out loud. They told her how proud they were and how strong she was. A couple of girls broke down.

'Who's he?' a girl asked about Dushyant lying on the next bed. 'He's hot, isn't he?' the girl winked at her.

'He has AIDS, so you should probably leave him alone,' she said.

'You are kidding me, right?' the girl said, duly horrified.

'Obviously. He is a poisoning case. Though he is really rude and we don't talk,' she said and smiled. The girl's eyes were still on Dushyant. 'It's so sweet of all of you guys to come here. I am so happy! Can I open these? Please?' She flitted like a small child amongst all the boxes, touching them, guessing what they were. She knew. It was one of those things when you know what the gift is but you don't want to believe it till the time you unwrap it, just to prevent disappointment.

Everyone looked at her and smiled. Her dad, standing in the corner, radiated happiness and her mother was choked with tears. She ripped open the presents one by one. They were books. Big books. Mean and thick. Books on medicines. *Holy shit.*

'What is this?' she said, her eyes a barge of tears, threatening to flood.

Her classmates were bewildered. They knew she would *love* them, but her smashing, teared-up smile exceeded their expectations. Venugopal said, 'We all know what you want the most. You're a freak. A junkie. So we are giving you what you want. That is the whole course for the next two years. And some old notes from a few seniors. Potent stuff.'

After taking time to compose herself, feeling like all the happiness in the world was concentrated in that tiny moment, like a hundred Christmases coming together on one single day, she said, 'I have to say I am a little disappointed. I thought you guys knew me better. I have already read half these books, you know?' Their shoulders drooped, defeated. 'Obviously, I am joking! This is the best I could have ever asked for! You have no idea what it means to me. If you think you do, I feel about a millionfold better than that!' she shouted and everyone laughed. The two girls who had cried hugged her and cried a bit more. 'Though I wasn't joking completely. I have finished a bit of it.'

There was a fresh round of banter, after which the room slowly transformed into a college hostel room after the last exam for which no one had studied, everyone thankful that it was over. Pihu's parents left. Soon, the room was what teachers in school describe as a fish market! They shouted, joked, laughed, cursed and fell all over each other. Pihu saw Dushyant grumble and mumble irritably in his sleep, but no one was in any mood to mellow down. They started to discuss their various professors, their quirks, the dissections, other medical-college stuff and uninteresting college gossip about who got caught making out and who was cheating on whom. In the middle of the conversation, she would close her eyes for a split second and imagine herself amongst frozen corpses, driving a knife through them, studying their slimy insides and taking elaborate notes. In those moments, she felt like she had lived a lifetime. Venugopal ordered pizzas, stuffed with molten cheese of three delightful kinds, for all of them and they ate like hungry cavemen. Pihu could really get people to talk and people loved talking to her. Except the guy on the other bed.

'Can you guys just KEEP IT DOWN? FOR FUCKING HEAVEN'S SAKE!' Dushyant shouted from the other side.

'What the hell—?' Venugopal replied.

'If you don't fucking leave this ward this very moment, I am going to kick you out. All of you,' Dushyant warned.

'Try it,' one of them snapped.

'Yeah, fuck you,' added one of the girls who had cried earlier.

Dushyant had blood in his eyes, like when those invisible veins in your eyes fill up and make their presence felt. 'Fuck you,' he sneered and ripped out the tubes from his hands. His forehead popped a vein as a stunned Pihu watched in horror. Before she could react, Dushyant had jumped at Venugopal and hit him with a left hook that landed squarely on his chin. Venugopal lay on the floor in evident agony. He moved swiftly to the next guy, filtering out the girls and charged with an open hand. It landed on the other guy's head and he tumbled to the ground.

'Anyone else?' he yelled as he stood there, breathing heavily.

'Such a dick,' a girl finally murmured as everyone looked at him, dazed.

As soon as he had hit Venugopal, Pihu had pushed the emergency button and two ward boys came barging into the room now. Along with them came Arman who was in the vicinity and had followed the ward boys inside. The ward boys instinctively grabbed at Dushyant, who hit them and they went crashing against the door. The other boys helped up Pihu's friends who were sprawled across the floor, still overcome with fear and shock. Finally, after smashing the two ward boys to a pulp, Dushyant let them go and slumped on his bed. Arman, like the others, was too shocked to react.

'What on earth is happening here?' Arman grumbled as he looked at Dushyant and demanded an explanation. His fists were clenched and Pihu could tell he was restraining himself from boxing Dushyant's face in.

'They were fucking with me. I gave it back to them in equal measure,' Dushyant replied, with fire in his eyes.

'Take this bastard away and put him in the pathology test section,' Arman ordered the three ward boys who were still reasonably scared of Dushyant. They grabbed his wrists. 'I will deal with him later.'

'I will go on my own,' Dushyant snapped and broke free. 'Assholes. All of you.' He turned his back and headed to the door.

'Hey, you, smart-ass,' Arman called out. 'The girl who you are calling an asshole saved your worthless life. Cadmium poisoning. No one else got it, she did. I wish she hadn't and you had died on this bed.' Dushyant looked back, surprised. The excruciating pain from his fall that day had numbed his brain—the fact that it was Pihu who had finally diagnosed him had not registered in his mind. Arman added, 'Yeah, now fuck off before I throw you out of here.'

Dushyant left the room without a single word. Pihu blushed as everyone looked at her in amazement.

'Yes, she did,' Arman proclaimed. 'She is better than a few doctors here, I am sure.'

'He is just sweet to a dying girl,' Pihu purred.

'Can you stop with that? Dying girl and bullshit like that. No one is dying here,' Venugopal added.

'YES,' the others joined in.

'Oh, by the way, I am Dr Arman Kashyap,' Arman said and waved.

There were appreciative smiles all around as most of them had heard of him somewhere or the other. For those who hadn't, Pihu had told them in the last hour about the hot doctor in the hospital.

'Pihu thinks you're cute,' one of the girls chuckled. The girl who had cried.

Arman smiled at her and responded, 'I think she is quite stunning too. Isn't she?'

No one replied, though the girls stared at him with unwavering eyes and batted their eyelashes. Pihu wasn't really at ease seeing the other girls stare at him and flash their best smiles. He was all hers, she was the one who was dying, she deserved the searing-hot doctor who saved lives for a living. Oh wait, what, did he just call her stunning?

'I think I should take your leave now,' Arman said and picked up one of the books lying on her bed. 'You're feeding an addiction, I hope you know that.'

'An addiction that you have too, don't you?' Pihu replied.

'But you should be resting and not reading medical—'

'And you shouldn't be? When was the last time you slept?'

'I don't need sleep. I am too busy helping your kind,' he argued.

'And that's not addiction?'

'You should sleep,' he said and put the book back down. 'I will check on you later. Goodbye, guys. And really, if anything, you should have got her jewellery or something. Not that she needs anything to look prettier.'

He turned and left the room. For the past few seconds, it was as if no one else existed. Slowly, conversation returned to the room and the topic hovered around the charismatic doctor who clearly had a thing for Pihu.

'I think he is into you,' one of the girls said.

'He is a doctor, he is supposed to be nice to everyone!' Pihu retorted.

'Oh, c'mon. Did you see the way he looked at you? He is clearly into you. It was as if we didn't exist!' another girl added, disappointedly.

'Whatever.' Pihu shrugged and they moved on to other areas of discussion, even though she couldn't really think about anything else but him. *Pretty. Stunning.* All in the same conversation. It really did feel like her birthday after all.

They left after a little while. Everyone wished her luck, some for life, and others for her non-existent relationship with her doctor, Arman. They had come scared, thinking they would find a girl devoid of hope, but what they had found was a girl throbbing with more life than all of them combined. Venugopal hugged her the longest and told her that he had started to date. It was the girl who had cried. Pihu nodded approvingly.

Alone in the room, she started to daydream again. This time Arman was the visiting professor and she was the bubbly, enthusiastic student in the front row who would do anything to get a good grade. *Anything.* She blushed in her sleep as she fantasized about kissing him in the staffroom. Slowly, she drifted off before things got nastier.

~

It was late evening when she woke up to an empty room. She hadn't slept that well with all the books around her distracting her, begging for undivided attention. Throughout her sleep, she had been tossing and turning, thinking about the time she would wake up and write her name in blue ink on each of the books she had been given. She really wanted to use the fountain pen Venugopal had gifted her too. And she was pleasantly surprised that Venugopal had started dating a *real* girl (after a slew of imaginary ones), a Punjabi at that, and imagined the girl who had cried today laughing at Venugopal's terrible Hindi. She missed him, and she missed her college. At times, she really missed the physical part of studying medicine— cutting open a dead body and seeing what lay inside. Rotten lungs, shrunken pancreases, wasted livers—these were things that really got her skin to tingle and her face to light up. She got up and walked awkwardly to the bathroom, her feet and hands not really strong enough to support her, and washed her face. Her body might be giving up, but her spirit wasn't. Plus, Arman had just called her stunning. She had every reason to be the happiest she had ever been. The warm, fuzzy feeling still tickled her and the shy grin refused to wash off her face.

Once back in the room, she picked up a few of the books from the pile and dumped them on her bed. With the fountain pen she wrote *'Pihu Malhotra, 2nd year, MBBS'* on each one of the books. Once that was done, she picked up a book on cancer and flipped through the pages. It had numerous coloured pictures interspersed with millions of bits of text. She flipped to a random chapter and started reading through it. There would be no exams and this only heightened her pleasure of studying medicine.

She was on the fifth page when the door opened and she saw Dushyant walk in. He headed directly to his bed and clambered up. Two ward boys in white overalls walked in beside him and hooked him up to all the syringes, needles and drips.

Despite what happened earlier that morning, she didn't feel any hatred for him. In all of her nineteen years, she had never felt that emotion for anybody. Though she did have a good laugh when a furious Venugopal had said, 'Had he not been sick, I would have taken him down.' Pihu knew he would do no such thing. Venugopal was a nice guy. Dushyant, on the other hand, was battle hungry and war scarred. If anything, she felt sorry for him, for his anger, his lack of friends and his affliction. He could fight though, and girls love that in a man. Pihu was no different. Tense arms, anger in his eyes, pumped chest. All he was missing was a kind heart.

17

Dushyant Roy

Dushyant winced in pain as a syringe plunged into his vein and a transparent liquid was pumped into his bloodstream. His eyes were stuck to the bed next to him— empty. Zarah overlooked the administering of the medicine and the subsequent blood draw.

'You look distracted,' Zarah noticed.

Dushyant looked away from Pihu's bed and replied, 'Not really. You didn't come in the morning. Why?'

'My parents are living with me. They wanted me to spend some time with them. So I took the day off,' she said and rolled her eyes.

'You look sad.'

'I can't stay at home any longer,' she said. 'It's okay when I go to their place . . . I mean where I used to live, but not when they come over.'

'I can understand.'

'I don't think you can,' she fussed.

'Why don't you make me?' he asked. 'Is it done?' he asked the nurse who was constantly plunging needles into him. The nurse nodded and took her leave.

'You look tolerable today. What's the matter?' she queried with a smirk.

'What do you mean?'

'Usually, it's hard for people to stay around you. You're aggressive and unnecessarily rude, and don't tell me you don't know that.'

'I am not—'

'Oh, please, you are,' she cut him off.

'Whatever. By the way, why didn't you tell me that she diagnosed my illness? Did she really?' he asked. 'Or was Arman just blabbering?'

'First, Arman never blabbers. And she did. She got it within minutes of you breaking your bone. Arman was impressed and he never gets impressed either,' she clarified.

'Fuck,' he grumbled.

'What happened?'

'I think she had her birthday or something. There were a few friends of hers who came here this morning and were making a shitload of noise . . . and . . .'

'And?'

'I might have hit a few of them,' he murmured.

'You WHAT?' she exclaimed.

'You know, I was irritated. I asked them to shut up and they didn't. I punched a guy and hit another one,' he shamefully admitted.

'Are you crazy, Dushyant? What did Arman do?'

'I think he wanted to hit me but he didn't. He shifted me to a different room for a bit and then I was shifted back last evening. I feel so crappy now. Why did that girl have to diagnose me? It's so irritating,' he growled.

'Why? Because if she hadn't, we would have killed you by now. We were treating you for the wrong disease. You should be thankful to her,' she said.

'I think I should. She is a sweet girl after all. Why did she have to choose this room? So annoying,' he squeaked and lay his head back. If he could have made himself disappear for a bit, he would have done that. Dushyant had done a million things he wasn't proud of, but he was never sorry about it. But in those moments, he was. He looked over to Pihu's bed and wanted to thank her. It really didn't matter to him whether he lived or died; he was usually terrified of waking up the next morning and dragging himself through another day. But he felt a little odd about having thrashed the friends of the girl who had saved him.

'I think I need a smoke,' he croaked.

'Are you sure?' she asked and sat on his bed.

'Yes,' he asserted. 'And I need to thank her. What's her name again?'

'Pihu. Don't tell me you don't know!' she squeaked.

'I mean . . . I did, I just forgot. Can we go?'

Zarah unscrewed the drips and helped him down his bed. On their way out, Zarah picked up Pihu's chart hanging on the entrance of the room and said, 'Her birthday isn't until two weeks from now. I think you should get her something.'

'You think I will still be here after two weeks?' he asked, his voice reeking of nervousness.

'There are tumours in every place we see, Dushyant. You're lucky to be alive. I think you will be here for a really long time,' she said.

'I really need that smoke.'

Both of them left the room and walked through the corridor wordlessly and rode the elevator to the sixth floor and then went to the balcony. Zarah had a few joints—perfectly rolled— in her handbag and Dushyant was pleasantly surprised, if not downright impressed.

'That's good,' he said after inspecting the joint carefully between his fingers.

'What? You think I can't roll a joint?' she asked.

'You don't look the type. But anyway, you don't look the type who would risk the life of a patient, too, by unhooking the meds and getting him high,' he chuckled.

'I am not risking your life. It's to soothe your pain. This is medicinal marijuana! It's totally legal,' she claimed.

'It would be legal if you weren't stealing it, which is quite obviously the case here. And I don't think they give it you so that you can pull a patient out of his bed and make him smoke it,' he said and took a long drag. The smoke scraped his foodpipe on the way down and dulled his senses.

'Whatever.'

'Okay, fine. I agree this soothes *my* pain. And it's incredibly strong,' he noticed. 'But what pain are *you* soothing?' He passed the joint to her.

'Nothing.' She shrugged.

'C'mon. You can tell me. I am almost a dead man. Your secrets are going nowhere,' he pressed. 'I am sure you can trust me. A few more days and you won't even see me any more. And if you think I am not worth your trust, you can kill me in my sleep.'

'No, junk it. It's personal,' she sneered.

'I was just trying to help.'

'I know. It's just that I haven't really shared it with anyone. I don't think it makes sense sharing it with you. I don't even know you,' she said, her eyes now glassy and distant. Dushyant knew she was vulnerable and she would spill it out and tell him everything; he just needed to push her over the edge.

'You can. I was reading a book on war soldiers. Experiencing the horrors of war over and over again makes it easier to tolerate the pain. Sharing with me might help,' he pestered.

'I don't know—'

'You know you want to,' he interrupted.

Zarah hesitated and looked away from Dushyant's

inquisitive and piercing gaze. Dushyant wondered what she was hiding behind her glassy eyes and guarded exterior.

'I was raped,' she squeaked and a lone tear streaked down her cheek.

Dushyant stood there, doubting what he had just heard. It reverberated in the space near him and he couldn't bring himself to believe what he thought she had said. *She has got to be kidding . . .* The silence confirmed the matter's seriousness. His throat dried up and he struggled to say something. *What? Why? Who? When? What did you do?* Nothing but a silent sigh escaped his lips as he stared at her, as if he had seen a ghost.

Zarah said, 'My father works in the army. During one of the many army parties, two of his drunken seniors raped me near the washroom. I was fourteen.' All of a sudden, the tears in Zarah's eyes vanished and the glum expression on her face was replaced by a calm, practised, nonchalant look.

'Then what happened?' Dushyant inquired as soon as he got his voice back.

'Then, nothing happened,' Zarah said with an air of finality to end the discussion.

'What nothing? Didn't you tell anyone? Your parents? Your mom? Dad?' he questioned.

Zarah gazed wordlessly at the glittering lights of the city while Dushyant waited for her answers. It felt like he had been violated, not her, and his fists clenched in anger. He stepped closer to her, Zarah's hair brushing against his face. A part of him wanted to turn her around and envelop her in his arms but he didn't know how she would respond.

'You can tell me,' Dushyant pressed again.

'I tried telling my father . . .' Her voice trailed away.

'What did he say? Didn't he do anything?' Dushyant almost bellowed, the Anger Vein in his forehead now far more prominent.

'He didn't believe me.'

'He didn't believe you? That you got raped? Why the fuck? How can that be?' Dushyant clutched her hand and jerked her around, almost as if it was not Zarah in front of him, but the men who had raped her. 'There are tests, aren't there?'

'I didn't tell him I was raped. I told him I was manhandled ... Molested.'

'Why? Umm ... but still ...' Dushyant struggled with his words. He grappled in the dark to come up with an explanation as to why her father didn't believe her and why she had to lie. He also wondered if Kajal had told anybody what had happened that night.

'He refused to believe me and said I was imagining things,' Zarah said, her voice steeled now. 'I didn't know what to tell him.'

'And you have not talked about it to anyone?' Dushyant still pressed on, looking for answers, trying to make sense out of this ridiculous atrocity.

'You're the first person I have told this to,' she confessed.

Why? Dushyant felt burdened by the truth. All of a sudden, he felt accountable for what had happened to Zarah fifteen years ago. He started to imagine a lonely little girl being ravaged by two big army generals as she screamed powerlessly in agony. He felt vomit rising to his throat.

'What about them? The men who . . .' Dushyant asked, hoping for the worst.

'One of them died in action a year later. The other had an accident at home and slipped into a coma. He was taken off the ventilator recently and he died too,' she said with air of triumph.

'I hope it was painful,' Dushyant spluttered.

'You sound angry,' she said.

'Obviously, I am! Who wouldn't be?'

'I have hated men ever since. I am scared in their presence.

I loathe touching them and I wish they never come near me,' Zarah said and shifted in her place.

All men are the same, Dushyant thought, as the memories of the night when he had forced himself on Kajal came rushing forth.

'Your father should have supported you. This is simply unacceptable . . . Oh, is that why you don't get along with your parents?'

'Just my dad,' she corrected.

'Don't you think he has the right to know? Or you have the right to tell him?' he interrogated.

'What good would that do?' she responded, her face contorting to show she didn't care, even if she did.

'You never know. I mean I don't know why your father did what he did, but you need to tell him where he was wrong. He should have been there and he was not,' he said.

'I don't think that will help. I am over it,' she clarified.

'You are over it? You're close to tears, Zarah,' he said.

'I am not—' she said and was reduced to a puddle of tears. Before Dushyant could say anything she wrapped herself around him and started to sob profusely. Dushyant ran his hands on her back in an attempt to soothe her and make it better, all the while wondering if she was repulsed by his touch too. He, too, was a rapist after all.

'I think I need to go,' she whimpered.

'No, you don't,' he said, his hands locking firmly around her. 'I think you should stay here . . . with me.'

'Seriously—'

'I am not letting you go,' he interrupted.

'I need some fresh air. Let's go for a drive?' she suggested, trying hard not to cry any longer.

Dushyant nodded. As they rode the elevator down to the last floor of the hospital, Dushyant felt a throbbing, piercing pain in his lower abdomen. He winced in pain and looked the other way.

'Are you okay?' Zarah asked.

'Shouldn't *I* be asking *you* that?' he said, smiling.

He needed another smoke, he thought. She checked out in the staff register and they walked to the doctors' parking lot.

'Nice car,' he muttered. His abdomen throbbed. He really needed the pain meds.

'If that's a joke, it's not funny,' she said. A smile crept behind the unyielding tears.

They climbed into the car and she put it in gear. As they hit the main road, the tears dried up in the wind sweeping in through the open car windows.

'So are you going to tell him?' he asked. The pain intensified and it reached his lower back. It felt like his insides were being ground in a blender. He started sweating, his hands became clammy and even the cool air didn't help.

'I am not telling him anything,' she replied, 'I don't see the point.'

'But there is one . . . You need to understand that. What's the harm anyway? You say you are over it, right? The people who did it are dead. You don't get along with your dad even now. I think you should tell him,' he grumbled. The pain was piercing and he felt his body getting warmer, trying to fight the pain off. Blood rushed to his face and he felt like his eyes would pop out. It felt like someone had got hold of his body and was scrunching and twisting it over and over again.

'Dushyant?' Zarah said. 'Are you okay? You look flushed . . .'

'I am fine,' he replied. He felt like he would pass out any moment.

'You don't look fine,' she said and put her hand on his forehead. 'You are burning up!'

He opened his mouth to say something but a flood of his insides filled his oesophagus and he vomited furiously. He opened the door of the car and slumped on the pavement. His back shook uncontrollably and he started to puke blood and half-digested food all over. Zarah bent over and patted his back to give him some relief but his body still shook hysterically. There was blood all over. After he was done and his eyes rolled over as if he was dead, Zarah somehow got him back inside the car and drove back to the hospital as fast as she could. Three ward boys were waiting with a stretcher at the main door of the hospital. They rushed him to the ICU while Zarah frantically checked in and put on her doctor's coat. She ran to the operation room where she noticed that Dushyant had already undergone a seizure and the doctors were cutting a hole in his throat to help him breathe. Dushyant's body fought involuntarily against the knife which pierced his throat. Zarah stood there, stunned and traumatized, as the doctors pushed a breathing pipe inside his throat. Not able to take it any more, she slipped out of the room and almost fainted on the bench outside.

Dushyant, though half dead, could see her leave the room before he passed out from the pain.

18

Arman Kashyap

Arman kicked in his sleep when his phone rang. It was the first time in weeks that he was back in his apartment and an uninvited phone call was the last thing he wanted. It rang for the fifth time and he had to pick it up. The patient from room no. 509 had had a seizure and his kidneys were failing. He had puked blood and a hole had had to be punched through his throat to keep him from choking to death. *Fuck.*

After what had happened in that room with Pihu's friends and Dushyant, he wouldn't have cared if Dushyant lived or died. He was a burning pain in the ass anyway. Mindlessly, he stepped into the shower and washed up. As the water ran down his body, he realized he had gained considerable weight over the last few years. He wasn't the young, athletic charmer any more. His body, once as hard as granite, was now slowly withering away, his eyes were sunken and fine lines of tiredness from long hours in the hospital showed on his face. He stood in front of the mirror and wondered how his parents still looked so young. The answer was clear as it was always—making money as a doctor was easier than going out there and making a difference.

He sat in his gleaming blue BMW—one of the few gifts he was showered with on his last birthday—and zipped through the early-morning traffic, reaching the hospital in fifteen minutes. He noticed Zarah's car parked rather awkwardly in the parking lot. He checked in at the reception and headed straight for his office. On his way, he crossed the surgery room Dushyant was in and stepped in for a bit to see what had gone wrong. His eyebrows knitted. He put two and two together.

'What the hell were you thinking?' he bellowed as soon he stepped into his office. Zarah was startled out of her slumber, the pattern of the table mat imprinted on her face.

'What?'

'Do I need to tell you what? You almost killed him. First you make him smoke, then you take him out on a drive? WHAT were you thinking, trying to pull off something like that?' he interrogated.

'I am—'

'If it were not me, you would have lost your job! You almost killed somebody last night,' he snarled. 'I don't even know if you are capable of grasping the concept of being a doctor and not making patients bleed to death. Do you get that? There are rules and regulations that you need to follow. How hard is that to understand for you? I don't know what you fucking share with a useless, half-dead man, but whatever it is, it shouldn't mess up his treatment. I will NOT have his blood on my hands!'

'I am sorry.'

'But what the hell were you thinking? A patient has to stay in the hospital till he or she is discharged—how hard is that to understand?' he said, banging his fist on the table.

Zarah's lips quivered and Arman could see her hands shaking in fear. Though Arman never respected rules and regulations himself, the understanding and repercussions of breaking them had to be grasped to the full. Something that the young doctor,

Zarah, didn't understand. The girl in front of him just looked down at her knees and mumbled something indecipherable.

'Can you speak up?' he asked.

'As if you follow all the rules . . .' she muttered.

'What do you mean?'

'I know you're about to run an experimental treatment on Pihu, aren't you?'

The blood from Arman's face drained away and he stared at Zarah in horror. *How does she know?*

'Who told you?' Arman queried.

'No one did,' the girl looked straight into his eyes and answered. 'I am not stupid. I saw the reports and the frequent tests you have been doing on the girl. Don't worry; your secret is safe with me, sir. I am sure you have something in mind.' Her voice was now strong and resolute. 'Yes, I did something unasked for last night and I am really sorry about it. I will make sure it never happens again. And that patient means a lot to me, just like Pihu does to you. I will do anything to make him live. I am sorry to have let you down.'

'I don't think he has much time left,' Arman mumbled.

'He doesn't? What makes you say that?' Zarah pried like a restless relative. Arman didn't have the heart to tell her, especially since his opinion was based more on experience and instinct than a study of hard facts and test results.

'His whole body is shutting down. His liver has suffered irreversible damage and now it's his kidneys. He is weaker than we thought he was. Just because he doesn't cry out in pain doesn't mean there isn't any. He might need a transplant which he won't get due to his alcohol and drug-ridden past. I don't see him getting out of here alive,' he explained.

'But he was getting better—'

'We just treated the symptoms. His body is a battlefield of diseases and tumours, and we can't treat everything.

Any drastic treatments will kill him sooner than you can imagine. And we can't really transplant every living cell in his body,' he said. 'It's too late to save him, though I have been wrong before.'

Arman, even with his tough exterior, never quite got used to delivering bad news to anybody. Not even fellow doctors. He knew about the bond Zarah and Dushyant had grown to share and it crushed him to tell her this. Also, the fact that Dushyant had been recovering steadily over the last few days gave everyone—Arman, Zarah and Pihu—hope that it was just a matter of time before he would swagger out of the hospital with a joint on his lips.

'We can't remove the tumours?' she posed.

'From a kidney that's already dying out?'

'What are our options?' she pressed on.

'We can apply for transplants for a new kidney and possibly a liver if it deteriorates further but given the time that he has left, I don't think we can get any,' he explained.

'I will fill out the application,' she said. 'How much time do we have left?'

'Not more than three to four weeks,' Arman replied. He had no words to soothe the pain of the young doctor who he knew would take this death seriously. Doctors never forget the first deaths they encounter. They stay with them, reminding them of their responsibility and fallibility.

Conversation died out after a while and he left the room. He had Pihu's test results on his mind. His steps quickened as he hastily headed to the research facility of the hospital to chart out a medicinal routine for the dying girl. She had less time than Dushyant did.

19

Pihu Malhotra

Pihu's eyes were immovably set on the other bed in her room, partly because she was in denial and partly because she felt sorry for Dushyant's pitiable state. The number of drips and the monitors monitoring his vital stats had increased. He wasn't breathing on his own but through a pipe that fit into a nozzle in his throat. His body struggled and writhed in pain with every breath and he looked tormented. It had been almost two weeks since the incident—when he puked blood—and he had hardly been awake after that. Now, he got up, took the medicines, whined and moaned and went back to sleep. Sometimes she noticed Dushyant looking at her, trying to say something but nothing ever made sense. His speech was reduced to long-drawn-out mumbles and painful groans.

Only yesterday, she had mustered up the courage to ask Arman if Dushyant was going to be all right. She was stunned to learn he was dying. *He was just fine, wasn't he?* Her gaze shifted to her own legs which were being examined by Dr Zarah and a couple of more people she had seen for the first time. The medicinal routine had started and she was sick of swallowing twenty pills a day. It had been easy at first but slowly it was becoming tougher. The pills started to depress her and every time she had to take one, the bad aftertaste at the back of her tongue served as a reminder of what she had.

'Can you feel them?' one of them asked.

'Pihu?' Zarah said to catch her attention.

'I can't,' she mumbled as they kept creeping up her leg. She could see their hands mould, prick and knead her legs but she couldn't feel them in the way she used to. Now, her legs were just extensions of her body that she could neither move nor feel any sensation in. She felt helpless, defeated, as she saw the shock and horror in her mother's eyes. The disease was progressing faster than it should have.

Later that day, she tried walking to the bathroom and found it hard to do so, even with the crutches. Her strength was draining out. Since her every need was catered to in the hospital, she had not realized how tough daily chores had become for her. Walking was a problem, getting in and out of clothes was a real pain, and she was a lot slower at eating her meals. To prevent exhaustion from chewing, her meals now consisted of mashed food that had to be reheated at least twice in the course of every meal. Her jaws hurt like crap after every meal.

Pihu knew that she would soon start to choke on her food and require help to bathe and to relieve herself and to even pick up a book. Given the special condition, she knew it could come sooner than expected. She kept the book on cancer aside and picked up *Tuesdays with Morrie*, the book on the real-life account of someone who had died of ALS. It wasn't the first time she was reading the book and she knew it wouldn't be the last. The book gave her the strength to carry on and to keep the spirit to fight alive in her.

Later that night, Arman came to visit Pihu. Her mother was sleeping and her father had gone home for the day. Arman woke her up and she smiled groggily at him. His presence in the room always shook something deep inside her, a feeling that she had never encountered before, a warm, fuzzy feeling that smelled of chocolate . . . and home. It was as if every cell in her body responded to his being in the vicinity. He sat on the edge of her bed and took her hand in his. As he clutched it, Pihu felt the loss of power in her hands. She couldn't clutch it as hard as she would have liked to.

'How are you feeling today?' Arman asked.

'Pretty shitty,' she answered shyly. 'I am slowly losing all my strength.'

'Tell me more,' he replied.

'My bench press is down to 200 pounds and I don't think I can compete in the Delhi marathon this year,' she said in all seriousness. Arman chuckled. She laughed.

Pihu told him about her loss of strength and coordination, about how she could no longer use the fork or the knife to pierce or cut through food, about how she felt that she would not be able to walk, even with a crutch, for long and how sometimes she had trouble breathing. Most ALS patients die because their diaphragm muscles are too weak to support breathing and they suffocate to death. She asked Arman if that was the way she would die. Arman comforted her and told her whatever he knew about the disease—which was everything there was to know.

All of a sudden, Pihu started to cry a little. Arman put his hands around her and comforted her and she kept sobbing softly in his arms. The crying went on for an inordinately long period of time. When she looked at the clock that hung on the wall just opposite to her bed, she noticed that she had been crying for the past thirty minutes, twenty-five of which had been in Arman's warm embrace. She tried to stop but couldn't.

Thinking of the horrors that were yet to come, she did not want to live any longer. If she were to die sleeping, her lungs screaming for a few last breaths, she would rather die now.

'Are you okay now?' Arman inquired as she stopped crying.

She felt embarrassed and said, 'I am sorry.'

'You don't have to be. I thought you knew that heightened emotions are a symptom of this disease. Patients continue to laugh or cry for longer periods of time because of the degeneration of brain cells which control these emotions,' he clarified.

'I think I read it somewhere,' she mumbled. 'Very nice to know that my brain is getting smaller. It makes sense though. My brain's too big for my cuteness.'

'I can second that.'

She chuckled and stopped. 'I am just afraid if I laugh for too long, I might not be able to stop,' she said. They both laughed and high-fived and Pihu wanted to hug him again but thought it would get awkward.

'Anyway,' he continued, 'we can schedule the first surgery whenever you are ready.'

'I am ready,' she said.

'Tomorrow?' he asked.

'That soon?'

'I think it's time. Also, I need to ask you a few questions before the surgery,' he added, his voice grim and stern. 'I want you to talk to your parents before you answer the questions.'

'What are they about? You're scaring me,' she replied.

'It's nothing to be scared of, just the usual questions. It's something you should discuss with your parents,' he said solemnly. Arman's voice quivered, which was a first.

'What are they about?' she queried again.

'Umm . . . It's about whether you are in favour of us keeping you alive with external support if and when anything goes wrong. Do you want us to revive you in case you lose your pulse . . . that sort of stuff,' he whimpered. The weight of the questions clearly wore Arman's voice and spirit down. More than anything else, Pihu was bothered by the look on the doctor's face.

'I have already made that decision,' she said.

'You have?' he asked nervously.

'I want to live for as long as my body allows me to, even if it means keeping me alive artificially,' she explained. She knew she wouldn't have cried if the look on Arman's face hadn't changed from one of limitless grief to one of relief. As she found herself in Arman's embrace again, she felt the warmth of Arman's chest and rapid short breaths and felt something she had been yearning to feel ever since she read the sexually charged Mills & Boon collection of her mother. She felt close to someone in a way she hadn't felt before. The sense of it being forbidden, *wrong* even, heightened her excitement. Maybe Arman was crying . . . she wasn't sure. But the very likelihood made her smile even though she couldn't keep the thought of being kept alive using by a machine out of her head. Back in medical school, she had come across numerous cases of people hooked on to life support and she had always wished to relieve them of their pain.

'Are you sure?' Arman asked again as he let her go.

'More than anything.' She smiled at him and added, 'I am ready for tomorrow. But you've got to tell me what you will do to me. Like the exact procedure down to the tiniest details.'

'I sure will. You're probably the most self-aware patient I have ever treated! If everyone were like you, life would be hell for us doctors,' he mocked.

'Can I ask you something?' she asked.

'Sure.'

'Aren't you afraid you might lose your job? Your licence?' she asked. 'And don't give me the old reasons. You know that even if I am cured, you can't put me up as an example to further research on this procedure. It would still be illegal.'

There was silence.

'I want you to live and that's my reason,' he said.

Her eyes didn't leave his face and he looked away. Finally, he said, 'Can we not talk about this?'

'Why not?'

'I just don't want to imagine you dying soon,' he said. Unnoticed, his hand crept up to hers and he held it. The touch of his hand against hers made her feel like she had never felt before. It was the way he held it. She felt special, she felt loved. The unsaid words between them were beautiful and fulfilling. The creases on Arman's strikingly gorgeous face reminded her of the age difference between them. But anyone would pine for someone like Arman. What perplexed her was why he took special care of her. Why was she more than just a guinea pig for his research? He deserved better, didn't he? She was young and she was stupid. And she was no match for the gorgeous, phenomenal doctor. Was everything in her head? No, it wasn't. The tenderness of his touch, the fondness in his eyes and the unmistakable look on his face hinted at more than just concern. She was sure of that. Or was she?

'I don't want to die soon either,' she said.

Arman could just beam like a schoolboy.

'You know what?' she purred.

'What?' he responded.

'You will laugh at me,' she whimpered and her face flushed, her insides all warm and fuzzy.

'I will not,' he assured her. 'What is it?'

'I have never had a boyfriend,' she said and paused, 'and . . . I have never been kissed.'

Almost as soon as her words left her lips, she regretted it. Seeing Arman not react only made it worse. His face was stoic and his eyes were stuck on her, unmoving. Every passing moment was worse than the one preceding it.

'You should have been,' he disagreed and wrapped his hand tighter against her soft, fragile fingers. His body leant into hers as she found hers leaning into him. Her eyes closed midway as the stretch between them closed further. Arman's hands left hers and reached for her face which was now feverish in anticipation and exhilaration. Little by little, he pulled her towards himself and their lips touched. She convulsed as his lips wrapped hers in a torrid, passionate embrace. The dampness of his lips was like her life's elixir. In those moments, as Arman's fingers lingered on her neck and her face, slowly caressing them, she felt she was cured of every ill. She lost herself, her body went limp as his body met hers and she found herself in a magical daydream. Her tongue played around involuntarily with his, while even there Arman commanded respect and guided her through the motions. His tongue played around with hers, hers played around with his and there was no telling apart their tongues. Arman's short and heavy breaths and his frenzied moans only heightened her contentment. A few seconds later, Arman let go of her. Pihu dropped back on to her bed like a sack, helpless and weak, still lost in the Just Been Kissed moment.

A precious few minutes went by before she opened her eyes and saw his stunning eyes looking at her with unwavering focus. She couldn't face him, feeling enormously shy about looking directly at him. She fidgeted with her fingers.

'For someone kissing for the first time, you're damn good,' he chortled. 'We should have done this long ago.'

Pihu had never felt more uncomfortable. Her fingers were still trembling and she had no idea what she should say next. The moments just gone by had seared themselves in her brain and she knew there was no forgetting them.

'Thank you,' she whishpered.

No one said a word as slowly they slipped into each other's arms again. She rested her head on Arman's strongly built chest and heard his heartbeat rise and fall periodically. Sometimes she felt his fingers on her face, brushing away the strands of hair that hovered over her eyes.

'Are you scared about tomorrow?' he asked.

'Not any more,' she replied and looked at him adoringly.

'I am scared,' he said, the mother of all fears in his eyes. 'I don't want to lose you.'

'You're doing your best not to lose me,' she assured him. 'And think about it, had I not been inflicted with this disease, I would have never met you. This is destiny, isn't it?'

'That doesn't make this any better,' he said, his heart now a twisted heap of emotions. It showed on his face and Pihu didn't know how to make it better. It was ironical because she couldn't remember herself being more satisfied with how things were.

Pihu didn't let go of Arman's hand till late in the night and only unclasped it when she realized that it was late and he had other things to do. She pretended to drift off and smiled when he tucked her in and kissed her forehead.

Of the nineteen years that had gone by, she was convinced that there was never a night more gratifying than the one she had just lived.

20

Kajal Khurana

Kajal had always found herself in the midst of confusion and mental strife. Decisions never came easy to her and even if they did, she always wallowed in doubt and reservation after making them. That day, surrounded by her technical books on Fourier transforms and traction devices, she played out her life in her head in technicolour. It seemed everything had gone wrong, though the worst part of it was that she didn't have anyone to talk about it with. She was a rich kid, and it was unfathomable for people around her to comprehend that she could have any grief to lose sleep over, beyond the trouble of picking out what new to wear.

It had been a few days since she had decided to snap all ties with Varun, and despite repeated efforts by him to talk to her, she stood her ground. A part of her wanted Varun to try harder, to call her and drop by at her college hostel, insist on dinner, send her flowers, but all she got were a few persistent calls and texts pleading her to give their relationship another shot. Sometimes, she knew she was being unreasonable and irrational, but she had been the understanding person in the relationship for a little too long now.

She wasn't sure if she wanted to run away now or if it was something she should have done a very long time ago. But the thought of staying at the Delhi College of Engineering any more seemed like a pain she couldn't endure any longer. It wasn't what she loved. A little voice in her head told her she should have listened to her parents—who were never wrong—and applied for a course in journalism or literature in London.

Her decision was made; it was just a matter of time—she knew—before she would commit to it and tell her parents about it. Her mom, a rich but responsible socialite, wouldn't mind. She had always found it bizarre to tell her friends that her daughter was doing engineering from a premier institute. Kajal knew her mom's friends thought they had paid for her daughter's admission into an engineering college. The day she had cleared the entrance examination was a day of rampant gossip in her mom's circle. The news of her daughter applying to a college that taught liberal arts and not switchgear mechanics would certainly gladden her.

Only yesterday she had talked to her sisters and they seemed enthusiastic about their sister's career move. But they seldom opposed her choices in life. She was the spirited little girl who was loved to bits by her family. She wondered how much of her decision was influenced by her recent break-up with Varun and Dushyant's behaviour towards her. Was she running away from things which had the capacity to hurt her? Or did she realize there was nothing left in Delhi for her to stay back? For she knew she had a perfect life apart from a few speed bumps—Dushyant, Varun and Fourier transforms—that upset her rhythm here and there. Impulsively, she left her hostel room, her hair still in disarray and her clothes crumpled and untidy. She waved frantically for an auto to stop and asked the driver to take her to GKL Hospital.

As the wind hit her face, pulling her back from her own
dreamlike world, she started to grapple with the reality of
facing Dushyant again. Dushyant had always struck her
as someone who loved once, and never again, so she knew
Dushyant was intentionally pushing her away. The rage in
his eyes, the Angry Vein on his temple and the clenched fists
were just a physical manifestation of how Dushyant still felt
about her. She had seen and faced his ire before, the day they
had kissed their last.

The autorickshaw driver dropped her at the entrance of the
hospital and Kajal nervously clutched her handbag. She was
sweating now even though there was a slight nip in the air.
Her heart was pumping furiously and her mind argued the
futility of such an exercise. Reluctantly, she trudged towards
the receptionist and asked if the patient was still in the same
room as before. The receptionist checked the database and
confirmed this.

'Are you a relative?' the receptionist queried. She nodded
and walked away from her, wondering if she meant anything
at all to him. Her steps became smaller and her walk more
uncertain as she stepped out of the elevator and went towards
the room she had been admonished out of. A deep breath. Two
deep breaths. She knocked on the door and waited for someone
to respond. No answer. She knocked again and heard a feeble
voice from the other side asking her to come in.

She entered the room which reeked of the peculiar hospital
smell of sterilizers, phenyls and disinfectants. And of almost-
dead people. Before her senses could acclimatize to the foreign
surroundings of the room, she saw Dushyant lying almost
lifeless on the bed and her face fell. Her throat collapsed as
she tried to say something. Tears formed tiny puddles just
below her eyelashes and were on the verge of streaking down
her now-pale face.

'Dushyant . . .' she choked on her own words. Dushyant's chest rose and fell periodically and made a horrible whooshing sound every time that happened. It sounded like his life force was leaving him with every laborious breath he took. His eyes were closed and he seemed under influence. Slowly, she walked up to the side of his bed and sat down. Dushyant's face looked a lot different from the last time; it was sunken and it seemed he had lost a lot of weight. There were blotches on his cheek where the flesh had retreated towards his jawbones. Kajal placed her hand on his chest and ran her fingers on it. She knew Dushyant couldn't feel a thing.

'A friend?' a voice from the other side asked.

Kajal looked up to see a smiling face staring at her, waiting for an answer.

'Yes,' she replied, finding her voice momentarily.

'I am Pihu. He is sleeping, I am afraid,' the girl said.

'I am Kajal,' she responded. 'Will he be okay?'

'I don't know. Arman said his condition is critical. A lot of his organs are failing and he might . . .' She stopped.

'He might?'

'There is a slight chance that he might not make it,' Pihu said solemnly.

Kajal couldn't say anything beyond that. She felt the walls of the room close down on her, locking her in and making her claustrophobic, suffocating her. She sat there with her hand wrapped around his and trying hard to stifle her sobs. Pihu's eyes were still on her. As Kajal's eyes surveyed the multitude of tubes, monitors and drips around her, she blamed herself for Dushyant's pitiable state. She imagined a situation where they would be together and happy, no one would be hooked to life support and no one would be browsing through colleges in London.

'If it makes you feel any better, I am dying too!' the girl on the other bed said with a big smile pasted on her face.

'It doesn't,' she snapped. And later added, 'I am sorry. I didn't mean to—'

'It's okay, I didn't take offence,' Pihu replied.

'But you look healthy . . .' Kajal said out of curiosity and shock.

'I know I do. I am dying of progressive paralysis. It's creeping up from my limbs and spreading to other parts of my body. One day it will reach my chest and I won't be able to breathe and end up dead!'

How could she be so nonchalant about something so *deathly* serious? Kajal wasn't sure whether to be shocked or be in awe.

'How do you know Dushyant?' Pihu asked.

'We are friends,' she answered, not wanting to go beyond that.

'Wait! You were that girl? Who came that day?'

She froze. Now, she was embarrassed. It hadn't occurred to her that someone had listened to her humiliating conversation with Dushyant from that day.

'Yes,' she agreed. 'Actually, we used to date.'

'You were *his* girlfriend?' she asked to confirm. She could spot a sense of pity in the way Pihu asked it, as if she was apologetic that Kajal had a boyfriend like Dushyant. It wasn't the first time, though. Kajal's friends were always disapproving of her relationship with Dushyant which they believed— though torrid and passionate—was a catastrophe waiting to happen.

'Yes, I was,' she replied. 'It's been years now.'

'What brings you back?' Pihu asked earnestly.

Kajal, although in no mood to talk, was compelled to answer her. 'I had never stopped worrying about him. He is majorly self-destructive by nature,' she said and her eyes roved back to where Dushyant lay—weak and dying.

'I have seen that,' Pihu added.

'You have?'

'Yes, I have. He has been a pain in the butt,' she chuckled.

Kajal knew exactly what she meant. Every passing second Kajal spent sitting next to Dushyant made her want to stay there longer. As Pihu explained to her how he had charged at her friends, Kajal thought about how different life would have been had they still been together. Maybe she would have convinced him to give up his addictions. Maybe he would have eventually emerged as a better man, and she knew he was capable of that. Dushyant, in his very core, was a nice person, but one had to flail blindly through the haze of tobacco and weed in which he had lost himself to get to that *nice* person inside of him. Maybe that resounding slap on her face was a one-off incident; maybe it was not. Maybe that forced intercourse was a one-off incident; maybe it was not. Maybe it was the start of an abusive relationship; maybe it was not.

'He hit your friends?' Kajal wanted to confirm, as she had drifted away on her own thought train.

'Yes,' she clarified. 'Yes, they were making a little noise, but nothing that would make anyone hit them. He is a little, well, you know, self-destructive. Do you still love him?'

'No, I don't.'

'Then why are you here?' Pihu probed.

'I just worry about him,' she answered, a little uncomfortable about the concern Pihu had for him. After all, she spent almost all her time next to him. 'Why are you so bothered?' Kajal asked, almost envious now.

'I just want to know who can love him. I mean, he is a little rude, isn't he?' Pihu chuckled and added, 'But I still like him. He is a little misunderstood, I think.'

'You like him?' Kajal asked.

'Like, as in *like*? No, no! Not at all. Yes, he is cute. But I don't like him *in that way*. In fact, the way he talks to me, it's a surprise I don't hate him,' she responded.

'Why don't you hate him?' Kajal asked, because in spite of everything, neither did she. For all the times that Dushyant had been needlessly oppressive and possessive, she had never managed to hate him. There was a growing discomfort in their relationship, but not once did her feelings towards him waver.

'As I told you, he is misunderstood! And you don't have to worry about me. I have my eyes on someone else!' she smiled and winked, and Kajal was caught off guard by an unnaturally excited Pihu.

'Truly?' Kajal responded, not knowing what to say.

'Yes, I know it's crazy and I know I am dying … Well, that's a problem. But he is so great and enormously gorgeous,' she ranted in front of a confused Kajal.

'Oh. That's nice.'

'He is a doctor, and you wouldn't guess who he is!' she continued.

'Who?'

'Dr Arman!' Pihu screeched and waited for Kajal to react.

Kajal looked at her dumbfounded, and said, 'I don't know him.'

'Oh. Okay,' she whimpered disappointedly and added, 'He is my doctor, and he is treating him, too.'

Although Kajal thought of Pihu as a little bit loony, she noted that her tears had dried up and she felt a little better. She almost felt guilty for feeling better because Dushyant wasn't getting any better. The thin thread of hope he was hanging on to was burning up fast.

'And you like your doctor?' Kajal asked.

Pihu's mom turned restlessly on the couch and they realized they were talking a little too loudly. Pihu asked her if she could come and sit closer. Kajal nodded and sat on the other side of the bed, and took Dushyant's hand in hers again. *He is in no pain*, she thought to herself.

'We just kissed yesterday!' she exclaimed. 'He got really scared of losing me and kissed me. I think it was out of pity, though. He didn't want to let me die un-kissed. Have you ever been kissed?'

Kajal chuckled as she heard Pihu blabber enthusiastically like a child. *Have you kissed someone? Who talks like that?*

'Yes, Pihu, right?' she asked and Pihu nodded. 'I have kissed a few guys.' She still couldn't suppress her smile.

'Oh. A few? What's that like? I mean, how many? Is there a difference?' she asked fervently. 'Am I asking too much? Actually it was my first kiss and I don't know if I was any good and I don't know whether it will happen again.'

'Of course it will happen again,' Kajal assured her.

'I hope so,' she purred. 'So, have you kissed Dushyant?'

'Obviously, I have,' she replied and added, 'And he was a good kisser as far as I remember.'

'As far as you remember? I will never forget my kiss! Although I don't have much time to live, but still.'

'Will you stop saying that?' Kajal begged. The constant allusion to her dying made her think about Dushyant's fatal condition and it wasn't pleasant.

'I am sorry, it's just that the more I say it, the more acceptable it becomes for me.'

'I am sorry. I have no idea what you're going through. The very thought of death and dying makes me uneasy. Only a few days back he was healthy and everything and now he is like this. It's ridiculous,' she said and choked on her words. 'And you're dying? Who would believe that?'

Pihu didn't say anything. Kajal's eyes welled up and she didn't know how to react. It was as if the time after Dushyant and she had parted ways didn't exist.

'Tell me about him?' Pihu asked as she rested her chin on her knuckles and bent forward.

'Umm . . . I am not sure.'

'Oh, c'mon. He is not waking up until morning and you have plenty of time,' she implored. More like begged.

'Fine,' she said and continued, 'It wasn't a perfect relationship. Nothing about it was how they describe it in the books or the movies. He wasn't my knight in shining armour but he was all I needed. He never said the right things, he never regaled me with gifts and such, but he was always there for me when I needed him the most. We fulfilled the darkest desires and the silliest pleas of each other.

'Every time he looked at me, it was as if he was looking at me for the first time. The adoration in his eyes and the tenderness of his touch made me feel like I had never felt before. There were problems, but love is like that. You fall and break and then you get up again and life goes on. I had heard about perfect relationships and mine was nothing like that. It was better. We owned each other and we loved each other and we hated each other. We reserved every pure emotion for each other.

'I don't know where life will take me and what kind of person I will be, but I know I am a better person because of him.'

A solitary tear escaped her eyes, streaked down her cheek and wet the hospital bedsheet. She had lied; she still loved Dushyant. As she closed her eyes, she felt Dushyant's hand tenderly move and grip her hand. She looked at his face and he was still sleeping peacefully.

21

Dushyant Roy

Dushyant had not woken up for more than a few hours every day ever since he bled out in Zarah's car. He had been under constant observation and his condition was deteriorating rapidly. His liver and kidneys were totally shot and he was under a multitude of different medications. His days had reduced to just lying in bed and writhing in pain. Even though he felt a lot better today, he woke up with an intense pain in his abdomen. He tried to call someone to give him something to get rid of the pain, but nothing more than a little yelp escaped his lips.

'Is there a problem?' Pihu asked and looked up from the book she was reading.

She waited for him to say something; instead, his face contorted in pain and he held his stomach and rolled over.

'Fine, I will call someone,' she said and shouted for help.

Minutes later, a nurse came rushing in and checked Dushyant's drip. She asked a few questions, which Dushyant answered in inaudible mumbles. She pushed an injection into his drip and assured him that it would take away his pain. The nurse walked away from him even as he cringed and clutched the bedsheet, as the pain reached his chest. It felt as if his insides were exploding and turning into mush. He wondered if these were his last moments. It certainly felt like it. His thoughts took him to the morgue where they would cut him open and find nothing but a tangled mesh of human intestines ravaged with tumours and other afflictions. He imagined the morticians judging him even after death. Frankly, it made him a little uncomfortable to imagine someone probing inside his naked body. The pain was gone. And he was awake.

He looked around and was equally disgusted as he had been on the first day when he found himself confined to a bed that a thousand others had used before him. On his left, Pihu was staring at him and like always, she was ready to spring into a conversation that would drive him to kill himself. But he didn't really mind that day. He owed his life to her, or whatever was left of it.

'Hi,' he mumbled.

Pihu looked at him and showed no signs of anger or irritation, despite all that he had done to her. 'Hi!' she answered excitedly as if she had been waiting for him to take the initiative. 'How are you feeling?'

'The best in quite a few days, I think. I am not being torn apart and I am awake, so that's good I guess,' he said.

'Good for you!' she shrieked and flashed a thumbs-up sign.

'Why are you always so happy?' he asked.

'What's not to be happy about?' she responded.

'The fact that I am dying? The fact that every time I try to get up, it feels like I'm going to pass out because of the pain. The fact that it feels like someone has reached down my guts and pulled out everything?'

'At least you're living,' she reasoned.

'Is this what you call living?'

'I would happily switch places with you,' she answered.

'That's because you're crazy,' he said and was perplexed. *Why would a girl who looks healthy and gets fancy tests done on herself all day long switch lives with me?* She never seemed in any pain nor did she ever bleed herself to death or get herself strapped to a bed for days on end. Confused and curious, he asked, 'What's wrong with you?'

The girl paused for a bit and then said, 'Nothing serious, I am just losing a little sensation in my limbs.'

For the first time, her voice quavered and she didn't look into his eyes with her own big, doe-like eyes brimming to the edge with hope and happiness. He felt a little strange but didn't want to probe. The last thing he wanted was an annoying, crying girl on his shoulder. The next few words came with a great deal of difficulty to him, but he knew he had to say them.

'Thank you,' he said, 'for saving me. Had it not been for you, I might have been dead.'

'See! I told you, what's not to be happy? And thank you. By the way, that's what room-mates do! They have each other's back!' The excitement and the effervescence in her voice were back.

'We aren't room-mates. We are in a hospital ward. And no, we are *not* supposed to have each other's backs. If the doctors were good enough here, which they are clearly not, we wouldn't need each other. How could they not get it . . . And you did? That smart-ass Dr Arman—'

'Hey!' she interrupted. 'Dare you say anything against Arman! He is a good doctor! And my diagnosis was just a guess. I was lucky.'

'Why are you defending them? Had they been smart enough, they would have got it! And luck? How can you leave a patient's life to luck? Isn't that why they spend seven years in medical school? To not rely on luck and learn something?!'

'Listen, you're going too far,' she said angrily. 'I told you, it was hard to diagnose. It doesn't come out in any test and it's a one-in-a-million case! And with you, who has abused his body to the limit, it was even harder!'

Her sudden change in voice almost caught him off guard but he was in no mood to relent.

'Don't put it on me now. Just because I have a body which is dying doesn't mean the doctors will try and do everything else to kill me sooner!'

'They were not trying to kill you!' she argued.

'All the evidence points to the contrary. I broke my arm, my kidneys are shot, and so is my liver. I bled out like I was pissing after getting drunk! I think they did everything possible to make sure I died,' he said and he saw his words work their magic. She looked angrier; her hands had gripped the railing of the bed like she was trying to snap it into half. 'Frankly, that Arman guy is just a rude bastard who doesn't know the first thing about medicine!'

'Fuck you!' she shrieked. 'He knows EVERYTHING! Maybe he *was* trying to kill you! He should have! You have no right to live. Anyway, he is a much better person than you are. At least he knows how to treat girls and not hit his own girlfriend after getting drunk!'

She looked away from him and picked up a book. He saw her chest rising and falling rapidly with every breath. For a few seconds, he couldn't absorb fully what she had just said. It didn't take him long to realize what she was talking about, but he was infinitely shocked. *How could she know?* He was embarrassed, intrigued and angry—all at the same time! His heart shrank to the size of a raisin as he thought about what he had done. Slowly, as his own breathing stabilized, he wondered if Kajal had been visiting Pihu to ask her about him. He smiled beneath his furrowed eyebrows—his face fuming.

'How do you know?' he grumbled. Pihu didn't budge and pretended to read. 'I asked you something—how do you know?!'

'I don't want to talk to you,' she replied and pulled the curtain between them.

He pulled the curtain back to its original position. 'Can you tell me? Please?' he begged, half-heartedly.

'I need to go to the washroom,' she said and grabbed at her crutches. Awkwardly, she pushed her lifeless legs to the edge of the bed and let them hang from it. The crutches were a little out of reach for her outstretched hands. 'Do you mind?' she looked at Dushyant and pointed in the direction of the crutches.

Dushyant nodded and stepped out of his bed. He dragged the hanger with the drips along with him, moved to her side and handed over the crutches to her. Pihu walked gawkily to the washroom, falling over twice, only to be helped up by Dushyant, who walked right beside her.

'See, I told you we would have each other's backs,' Pihu said. 'Now we are even. We are 1–1!' She closed the door and Dushyant waited for her to finish inside.

'I'm done,' she said as she opened the door. Dushyant helped her walk back to her bed and climb up. Then he returned to his. She opened her book and started to read.

'You can read later. Can you please tell me how you know about me?'

'I know you helped me and everything right now, but I think you need to apologize before I tell you anything.'

'Okay. Fine. I am sorry. I will not be rude to you.'

'And Dr Arman?'

'Arman, what the—'

'Just do it!' she exclaimed.

'Fine. Dr Arman is a great doctor. The best. He knows everything!'

'You were sarcastic, but I accept it,' she said.

'Now, tell me? How did you know? Does she come here? To ask about me?' he asked impatiently. Even though the very mention of Kajal evoked anger and disappointment, he wanted her to say yes to every question he had just posed.

'She was here yesterday. You were sleeping and she told me about the two of you. She waited for you to wake up but you didn't,' she said. 'We talked for a few hours and . . .'

'And?'

'I think she still has feelings for you. She never let go of your hand last night. When I asked, she said she was just worried about you because you always seemed in a mad rush to destroy yourself,' she said.

'I am sure she doesn't have *any* feelings for me. She has a boyfriend and they have been going steady for quite some time now,' he said, his head hung low and his voice dry.

'She broke up with him. She told me she is going to London in a few days for a course in liberal arts. Literature or journalism . . . something of that sort.'

'What?'

'You don't know? I thought you did,' she said. 'Oh yes, she told me you guys haven't talked for the last couple of years. I wonder why you didn't pursue her. She is certainly a keeper. Tall, beautiful and very nice—you guys would look so cute together.'

'I tried . . .' he said and his voice trailed off. He didn't know what else to say and Pihu didn't think she should say anything. She got back to her book.

'I think I need to sleep for a bit now. Thank you,' he said.

'My pleasure,' she said and smiled.

She held my hand? He rubbed his hands together and looked at them and even smelled them to find traces of her. Dushyant rolled over to the other side and imagined what last night would have felt like had he been awake and not been an asshole like the last time. He would have got to hold her . . . maybe she would have cried, maybe not . . . Maybe she would have told him she loved him, maybe not . . . Maybe she would have told him that everything would be all right, maybe not. He scolded himself for thinking the way he was. The only reason she had come back was because he was dying. If not, then what had changed after two years of ignoring him and acting like he didn't exist? Two years of treating him like an outsider? Maybe he deserved it, he thought.

He was absorbed in the concocted scenarios where the two of them would be together, when the door was pushed ajar and three ward boys walked in. He thought they were coming for him but they walked to the other side and swiftly wheeled Pihu away. The knitted brows of the ward boys and the stiff face of Arman who stood at the door made him anxious. He wanted to say something, a part of him almost reached out to stop the ward boys from taking her away but he couldn't move. A terrifying feeling gripped him; it felt as if he would never see her again. Pihu had just smiled as they took her away. Restless, he looked around and fidgeted with the tubes and the drips. Were they discharging her?

He tried to sleep to dull the pain in his body but it wouldn't come to him. The tense, edgy faces he had seen were still fresh in his head. He rolled restlessly on his bed from side to side. He got up and, leaning against her bed, started to sift through the books that Pihu had been reading. They were stacked neatly on all the tables the small ward had to offer. Most of them were as thick as his wrist and repulsed him. In the corner he saw a book, a rather thin one, named *Tuesdays with Morrie*. With nothing else to do, he picked it up and got back into his own bed. He was feeling better that day. He could move around without passing out from the pain. The book was hardly 190 pages and he knew it wouldn't take him more than an hour to read it cover to cover. Always a quick reader, he had an advantage in all the examinations he took for hopeful CAT aspirants. Questions on long essays were his strength.

He started reading the book. Just after the first few pages, he saw the book was heavily underlined, sometimes with more than a single fluorescent stroke. It was a book written by a seventy-year-old man's student who was seeing his teacher slowly dying of ALS or Lou Gehrig's disease, on how he coped with the affliction as slowly, every bit of his body became paralysed, shrivelled and useless. ALS stands for amyotrophic lateral sclerosis, but she had cut those words out and replaced them with her own version— Always Live Strong, followed by a smiley. With the flip of every page, he got more anxious and started to put the pieces in place. Pihu had told him she was losing sensation and that it was nothing serious. She was lying! Instead, she was dying. He wiped the beads of sweat from his brow as the old man in the book got weaker, now not even able to eat on his own. He had a pipe inserted into his abdomen and his legs had shrunk to the size of a kid's. The last days of the old man were painful—his muscles were wasted, he had bedsores, he had pipes for food, for excreting and for breathing. One day, he slipped into a coma and two days later, he died. Dushyant's heart sank. His eyes glazed over and the guilt of being rude to a dying girl came crashing down on him.

The book couldn't have been a coincidence! It was underlined and there were tiny coloured slips on pages where the disease of the old man had progressed. What did they take her away for? Maybe there was a treatment now. After all, the book was written years ago and a lot had changed since then. Surely, there was a cure now. Frantically, he seized his cell phone and searched for any information he could google about the disease. Blood was sapped out of his face as he read more about ALS and he was aghast at the unfairness of the whole deal. How could she die? She looked just fine. He forgot about his own pain and felt terrible for her.

All of a sudden, everything that had happened between them played out in a slow, excruciating replay and he felt crushed for having treated her the way he had. He had chastised, been rude to, disparaged and insulted a dying girl. *A dying girl!* Can anyone be worse? He dug his face into his palms and felt the worst he ever had . . . and that was saying a lot, considering he had been through some serious shit in life. Reading the underlined portions in the book over and over again, he felt like throwing up.

Anxious and beaten down, he found himself dialling Kajal's number. The phone rang a few times, but there was no answer from the other side. Of course, having changed his number more than a few times in the past, he didn't expect her to have his number. After a few more calls went unattended, he called Zarah. Zarah wanted to know why he wanted to meet her so urgently and Dushyant said he would let her know when she reached there. Minutes later, Zarah walked into his ward and Dushyant was still in shock.

'What's the problem?' Zarah asked. 'Are you okay?' Instinctively, she put a hand across his forehead and checked his temperature.

'I am fine,' he answered and pushed her hand away. 'Why didn't you tell me about Pihu?'

'What about her?'

'That she is DYING! She is dying, isn't she? I saw her reading this book a few days back and read it today. She is dying, right?'

'Which book?'

'How the fuck does that matter? Just tell me. Is she dying?'

'Yes,' she mumbled.

'Why didn't you tell me?'

'I thought you knew! Everyone knows. You spend hours together sitting in the same room. I just assumed you knew about her condition,' she responded.

Though it made sense, Dushyant was not looking for a sane explanation. Instead, he was busy struggling with the truth.

'I didn't know! Had I known I wouldn't have been so harsh on her. She was always smiling and laughing, so I thought she had some minor problem like appendicitis or such. But ALS? She is not even old! The guy from the book was seventy!' he protested as beads of sweat slowly trickled down his forehead. He was still far from being at ease.

'Dushyant, you need to calm down,' Zarah said and sat beside him. 'How's the pain today?'

'I am not in any fucking pain! Why didn't I know?' He dug his face again into his palms.

'I am sorry I didn't tell you and also for having assumed you knew. Did she tell you about it?'

'When I asked, she just told me that she had some problem with sensation in her limbs and that it was nothing serious,' he told her.

'You talked to her? That's new. It will be fine. She doesn't hate you for the way you were to her. In fact, she never hates anybody,' she clarified.

'I feel like such an asshole right now,' he said, shaking his head.

'Feel? You're an asshole, aren't you? In fact, you pride yourself on being one,' she chortled.

'Now that's mean,' he said.

The more they talked about it, the more the situation sank in and the pieces fell in place. It explained all the nights he had seen her mother cry and bicker. All the times she had looked at him in envy. It all fit in now because her daughter was dying and he wasn't. As he sat there, he wondered if her mother had wanted him dead in lieu of her daughter living a few moments extra. Guilt kept wearing him down as he thought about the day her friends had come to meet him.

Zarah probed him more about what they had talked about and Dushyant told her about Kajal, his unconsciousness, the hand holding and other details. He thought he saw Zarah's face droop as he narrated Kajal's rendezvous with Pihu. As he further shared his apprehensions about being in touch with Kajal again, he certainly noticed a distant look in her eyes. With so much going on in his head, he chose to ignore it. A little later, the crippling pain reared its ugly head again and Zarah had to inject him with sedatives to mute his screaming, dying organs.

Soon, he drifted off as Zarah left the room without a smile on her face.

22

Zarah Mirza

It was her sixth cup of coffee that morning, each one stronger than the last. Had her system not been used to the regular caffeine intake, her heart would have pumped itself out of her chest. She needed it. Her senior doctor was performing an experimental surgery on his patient and if he were to get caught, there were chances of her being in trouble too. She could lose her licence as well, and not by too long a shot at that. If that wasn't enough, there was the news of Dushyant's ex-girlfriend—the one that got away—hanging around Dushyant's room, holding his hand, and trying to evoke feelings of lost love. *That bitch!*

What really peeved her was the cloud of uncertainty on Dushyant's face when he talked about Kajal and whether he should talk to her. Kajal wasn't the one who was with him when he had almost died or when he was admitted and everyone thought he was an asshole. It was her! On certain levels, she felt betrayed. Cheated. On others, she felt extremely stupid for he was just another patient. If that wasn't enough, it was a patient who might not see the next dawn. *I can't possibly like him, it's stupid! This is insane!*

188

The words, the diseases, and the insurance forms she had to fill up blurred and she couldn't think of anything else but Dushyant. Every passing moment became a mockery of her good sense and her pedigree. But it happens, right? Even Arman, a doctor far more experienced, clearly harboured feelings which were more than just concern for a patient he could potentially save. Irritated, she gulped down the hot coffee, singeing her tongue, and tried harder to concentrate. After the first few treacherous minutes, she managed to boot out the thoughts of Dushyant from her head and picked up speed. Throughout the day, she avoided *the* corridor intentionally. Although she knew Dushyant would be sleeping, she would still have found herself at his bedside.

Why? He is just an insolent bastard!

To distract herself, she went to check how Pihu's surgery was going. Arman had planned everything to the last detail. He didn't want to use any hospital staff, knowing well that if he were to get caught, it would land the others in trouble too. Days before the scheduled surgery, he had complained of fungus growing in the ventilation vents of the surgery room. The surgery room was closed down for a few days till further notice. Arman was put in charge to see it was taken care of, and that it didn't spread to the other rooms. Arman's boss, the Chief of Operations, was surprised to see Arman take the initiative.

The room was used that day to operate on Pihu. The surgery was supposed to be long and dreary and considering that Zarah had not seen Arman since the morning, it seemed like it was. Zarah knew Arman had sought external help—some surgeon buddy from his medical school—but he didn't want her to know. The less she knew, the better it was for her.

How much worse can the day get? With that in mind, she walked towards the surgery room. When she reached there, she found that it was sealed. She ran towards the elevators and saw Arman shaking hands with a guy almost of the same age. At a distance, she waited for the guy to leave and then walked up to Arman to ask how it went.

'Hi,' she said.

'Hi,' Arman replied.

'How did it go?' she asked in hushed tones. There were others in the elevator too, some of whom were doctors. Arman kept mum till the time the elevator reached the floor of their office.

'It went well. It was tougher than we initially thought it was. It's a very, *very* difficult surgery. Thank God I had—' he stopped.

'Do you think she will be okay?' she queried as they walked to his office.

'I don't know. I think we did everything right. We need to keep her under constant observation to test the progress. We aren't sure of anything yet. The stem cells—'

'She will be okay,' Zarah interrupted. Arman clearly looked exhausted. The dark circles under his eyes and the slouch of his shoulders were screaming indicators.

'I hope so.' He lay back in his chair and sighed. *It must have been a really long day for him*, she thought.

'You want me to get you something?' she asked.

'Coffee would be nice,' he answered.

'I don't think you need coffee. You need sleep. I will close the door and switch off the lights,' she said and reached for the lights of the room.

'I don't think I will get any sleep today. Will you do a favour for me and check on Pihu? If you don't mind, that is. We need to keep her under observation and I can't really explain why to the hospital administration. It will be nice if you can help.'

'I will do that,' Zarah nodded. Seeing Arman tired and uncharacteristically flustered, she felt a little bad for him. Having taken just three steps, she heard Arman call out from behind her.

'I never thought it would be this hard,' he mumbled. 'Seven years, thousands of patients . . . seen many of them die too. This one, I don't know. Every cut I make on her body makes me feel worse, even though I know she can't feel the pain. Every time she loses some function of her limbs, I feel responsible. I never thought it would happen again. It's horrifying.'

Wait? Again?

'Arman? Happen *again*? What do you mean?' she asked, taking care not to probe him too much.

Arman didn't answer. Instead, he closed his eyes and lay down flat on his recliner. Zarah pulled a chair from his desk and sat beside him. Of all the sides she had seen of the eccentric doctor, not one of them was as vulnerable as this one.

'It was in my father's hospital,' he started. 'A woman, six years older than me, came in with severe abdominal pain. I was just starting out and I thought I knew it all. All the years that I had studied medicine, I had disparaged mediocre doctors and treated them like parasites. I knew I could cure the woman. Days passed and she only got worse. She was beautiful . . . and alone. I used to sit next to her, talking through those terrifying nights. My father, who was no longer involved medically with the hospital and oversaw administration, thought it was unhealthy. A month passed and my obsession with her long hair, her fair, drained-out face, her always parted pink lips, her sharp cheekbones and her protruding collar bones grew.

'My failures kept piling up, but the woman had faith in me. She told me that even if she died, she wouldn't feel bad because she had got the chance to see me every day before her last. We never confessed it in clear, lucid terms, but our relationship was far beyond that. Her pain soon became mine. Frustrated at my inability to cure her, I kept trying out one implausible treatment after another. Since my father owned the hospital, none of the senior doctors objected, more so because they didn't know what to do either. Even if they would have come up with something, I would have written them off. She was mine to cure.

'After two months of suffering at the hands of an incompetent, arrogant doctor, she died. The autopsy revealed she had a rare cancer, which was very hard to detect. No one blamed me; even cancer specialists would have missed it seven out of ten times. She had no family, so there were no lawsuits against me. She died at my hands. I could have saved her if I hadn't been so pompous and pig-headed. I watched her die . . . slowly . . .'

When he finished, Zarah found herself at a loss for words. Her throat dried up. She had only imagined Arman as a clinical, heartless doctor who had never gone wrong. *Is this why he never works at his father's hospital? Is that why his relationship is strained with his family?* She wanted the answers to these questions but was unsure whether she should pry into his life.

Before she could string her incoherent thoughts into a single sentence, he continued, 'I left the hospital. I think my father would have wanted me to. I thought it would be best to leave and learn what it is to be responsible. I never had the confidence to go back to that. It took me years to get over it and not be emotional about the patients I treat. After all, it's the first fucking rule of being a doctor.'

And again, she was lost in his words. The last thing she had expected was to see a doctor like him buckle down and spill out skeletons from his past. The first rule is not *'not to be emotional'*, it's to *'move on'*. From one patient to another, from one disease to another, from one set of grieving moms and crying dads to another.

'I don't think you can blame yourself for that woman. Or for Pihu. You're doing your best and that's what we are supposed to do.'

'I know that, Zarah. I just feel . . . sorry for her.'

'We all do,' she answered.

'I just hope it works,' he said and dug his face into his palms.

'Same here.' She patted his back.

'How's Dushyant doing?'

She felt strange because of all the patients that she attended to, he always asked only about Dushyant.

'He is fine. Let's see. He is under observation and I hope he pulls through,' she said.

'Don't make the mistake I did,' he croaked and closed his eyes.

Zarah switched off the light and left the room knowing she had already made the mistake.

23

Pihu Malhotra

It had been thirteen hours and she was lying unconscious in her bed in a dreamless sleep. As she opened her eyes, the first hazy images that registered on her retina were six pairs of curious eyes trained anxiously on her. Immediately, her head started to echo with voices.

Are you okay?

How are you feeling now?

Is there any pain?

Can you see us?

She closed her eyes again to escape those questions and to process what she felt at that point in time. *There is no pain. I could see them. I still have some strength. I think I can get up.* After taking a few long breaths, she opened her eyes and looked around. Mom. Dad. Dr Zarah. A previously unseen ward boy. Dr Arman. *Sigh*. Dushyant.

'I am okay,' she purred groggily as she opened her eyes again.

'I need to ask her some questions; can I?' Arman asked the others and everyone retreated except him.

Arman sat next to her and breathed deeply. For a while,

he just kept looking at her as if he had seen her after months. The sheer fragility of Arman's demeanour, like he would break down if he looked at her for too long, made her feel alive. It wasn't the brazen charm, or the brilliance, or the eccentricity that drew her to Arman; it was the frailty and the humanness behind the facade of arrogance that he so meticulously maintained.

'Why are you looking at me like that?' she said, and reflected on the words that she had just said. Straight out of an old '80s movie with a bad scriptwriter.

'I was just wondering how you could look so at peace even as you went through one of the most difficult surgeries ever performed on anyone.'

'I was in the hands of a very good doctor.' She blushed.

'Okay, before you enthral me with your kind words, I need to run some checks,' he said and checked her pulse. 'Do you have any pain?'

'Not any more,' she teased him and looked him straight in the eye.

'Can you stop doing that?' he grumbled.

Her parents witnessed the whole conversation and Pihu could sense their bewilderment at the rosy atmosphere between her and the doctor.

'Fine, I will be serious on one condition—you will take me out on a date. I have never been on one and who knows . . . I might never go on one ever. I want you to be my *first*,' she purred sweetly.

'For a little girl, you use your *death* card very smartly. On a serious note, it never feels good when you say that,' he said.

'I wouldn't have to use it if you start behaving like a gentleman and treat me like you should,' she chortled.

'Fine.'

'What fine?'

'Tonight. It's a date. I will try to be a gentleman. But I have a condition, too.'

'That is?' she queried.

'You have to get better soon,' he mumbled.

Pihu smiled. Next, she answered all the questions he had for her and couldn't believe her luck that the most gorgeous doctor she had ever seen was taking her out on a date. Wouldn't her dad be proud? *Tonight!* Fairy tales are made of these. Later, she asked herself the question that she never thought she would ask. *What should I wear?* She looked down at her hospital robe and felt sorry for herself. But only for a bit. After all, it was her first date with a guy other girls would kill for. Brilliant. Millionaire. Stunning. Doctor.

~

Her body was aching by the time it was evening. There was a huge scar that ran down her spine where they had opened her and stitched her back up. It pained. Throughout the day, she used the pain as an excuse to avoid having conversations with anyone around. It was strange that even Dushyant wanted to talk to her that day and was in fact very persistent in his endeavour. *Why today?* Restless and anxious, a million questions bounced back and forth in her head. A date in a hospital robe? She tried not to think about it and the more she tried, the more she ended up thinking about the same. There was a small cursory nerve conduction test she was made to undergo during the day and though it had not shown any signs of improvement, she hadn't worsened either. A few times, she got down from her bed and checked if she could walk on her own.

She couldn't.

Her legs were nothing but useless rubber-like extensions to her body which served no purpose whatsoever. A few laboured steps and she was panting as if she had been running. With her legs worthless, other parts of her body were following suit. The operation was still to show any effects. Inside her heart, she had just one prayer—let today be great and I will happily die. After trying a little more to walk with the crutches, she gave up. Once back in the comfort of her bed, she realized she had nothing to hide from Arman. If there was anyone who knew how far the disease had progressed, it was him. They were in this together.

They were supposed to meet at eleven in the night, when everyone else would have slept. Time had slowed down. From eight in the evening, she had glanced at her watch every few minutes, hoping time would move along faster. *9. 10. 10.30. 10.45.* The closer it got, the farther it seemed. In the last ten minutes, she sprayed perfume over herself and brushed her hair the best she could. There was a limit to things she could do and in all honesty, she liked that. It was simple.

Her eyes never left the door, waiting for her knight in shining armour—in her case, a knight with a stethoscope around his neck—to take her away. Her heart was literally throbbing and it was no longer just an expression. The electrodes and the monitors that measured the beating of her heart showed a huge spike and the graph looked as if she had just run a marathon. It became worse with every passing second. Sometimes, she felt she would pass out. Moments later, the door was pushed open and Arman walked in. Almost instantly, she felt dwarfed in front of his imposing personality, now dressed in a dark-blue shirt—a first—and a pair of fitted trousers. His short hair was neatly parted, his face shaved clean of any stubble and he smelled heavenly. The neatness of his face brought out his eyes, big and twinkling, and his teeth, sparkling white. *Oh my God! I hope my jaw hasn't unhinged and fallen off my face! He is gorgeous!*

Finding her voice again, she muttered, 'You look fabulous!'

'Thank you,' he said, softly. Seemed like he had forgotten the rude, abrasive doctor side of him home, and kept the gentlemen part. 'And you always look great.'

'Yes, why not? Every girl dreams of being in a hospital robe on her first date, doesn't she?' she mocked playfully.

'I don't know about other girls, but I know what you want. Your first date in a hospital. It's perfect, right? And not in a hospital robe, but a doctor's coat,' he said and put forward with his right hand a white coat, neatly folded, and along with it, a stethoscope.

'*What?*'

She took it from his hands and memories of medical school came flashing to her mind. It was lame but it was not lame. It was by far the most romantic thing anyone had ever done for her. She spread open the coat and was in for the second shock of the evening when she noticed a badge attached to the coat. It spelled 'Dr Pihu Malhotra'. Below it was the hospital's logo and the name of the hospital. *I wish I could marry him!*

'This is the sweetest thing anyone has ever done for me!' she shrieked.

'It's nothing.' The arrogant doctor blushed and shifted nervously on his feet.

'It's a lot!' she said as she hugged the coat lovingly and smiled at Arman. She put it around her shoulder and slipped her arms in and hung the stethoscope around her neck. It felt like . . . it always felt in her dreams.

'Shall we go?' he asked.

'Sure,' she answered and reached out for her crutches that were on the side of her bed.

'They will not be of any use where I am taking you,' he said and blocked her way.

'Wheelchair?'

'Better,' he answered.

Confused, she looked at him as he swept in and one of his hands went around her neck. She instinctively put hers across his, and his other hand scooped her up from her bed. With one swift motion, she was high up in his arms; Arman's smiling face bore no sign of strain as he headed to the door, carrying her in his strongly built arms. She was beyond words, beyond feelings, beyond senses; she was numb and all she did was stare at him in sheer admiration and heart-wrenching adoration. As he carried her through the corridor, she wished the moment would freeze in time. She wanted to leave her body and see what it looked like—him carrying her in his arms—and then click a mental picture of it and etch it in her mind. *Why wasn't I dying before?* she asked herself.

Arman's long strides were confident and powerful as he walked into the elevator and pressed the button for the top floor. Every step and every sensation of his body against hers took her to a different world altogether. If there was any sensation she wanted to live with as her last, it was the touch of him against her. The elevator reached the top floor and he walked out, his hands still tightly wrapped around her. His warm breath against her hair gave her untold happiness and she had goosebumps on her flesh. The feeling was indescribable as Arman walked to the stairs of the fire exit and climbed a flight of stairs to take her to the roof of the hospital.

It was only after they were up there that she realized she was not in her room any more. The cool breeze against her face broke her out of her trance-like state and she returned to the present. She looked around and it wasn't really how they show it in the movies. The supposedly dreamlike sequence had no tiny red LED lights, or a small round table with candles on it, or a chunky black stereo piping her favourite songs, or glasses of wine, or fancy cutlery with delectable food hidden under steel domes. Instead, there was a small rectangular table and two plastic chairs. On the table were two packed dinners and a couple of bottles of mineral water on the side. A frown appeared on her face momentarily which was creased out as Arman's cologne wafted into her senses again and she found herself smiling.

Finally, he put her down on the chair and sat down next to her. For a few seconds, no one spoke. Okay, so this was strange. No candles? No lights? No music? Bad plastic-bound food? Would her last date be like this?

'So . . .' she said, as she tried to explain herself and ask him for an explanation too, all at the same time.

'I know what you are thinking. Why this, right?' he asked. One of his eyebrows was arched as if he was about to unfurl a devious scheme.

'Yes. I am sure you have a logical explanation. I mean, everything is great, but no flowers? No music?' she poked fun at him.

'As a matter of fact, I do have a logical explanation. Imagine us together five years down the line. What would we be doing? Maybe we will go on dates with flowers, candles and whatever you might have thought of in your pretty little head. But that's not going to be our life—is it? Our life will be this—sitting in the hospital cafeteria, eating bad food and discussing patients. Fighting over who's wrong and who's right. Learning from each other. Quarrelling. Laughing. Crying. That's what we would be about. Those will be the big moments of our lives. Those will be the happiest moments of our lives. No one remembers one anniversary from the other. Years down the line our thirteenth or fourteenth or fiftieth anniversary will be the same to us. But we will remember those years, not those anniversaries. Days aren't important, years are. Years aren't important, experiences are. Experiences aren't important, lives are. And this will be our life.'

'I get your point. But can't we do that with flowers?' she chortled. 'Just kidding. I think it's great and I don't think you could have put it better. And you just said "ours", so I am happy. But what's all this?' She pointed out to the file on the table which was almost six inches thick. The papers in the file were frayed at their ends and appeared to have been filed improperly.

'This is the file of the sixty-three most interesting cases I have ever handled. Some of them died, some of them lived. These are the charts of their diseases, the progress, the medications and finally, the results. Some of them are beyond your understanding, but you have proved more than once that you're more than just brilliant,' he said. 'I think we would have fun doing this.'

At that point, she hated to admit it but she was aroused. It was like mental sex with multiple, unending, exploding orgasms, only better. Gingerly she opened the file and started to go through the first patient.

'2004, a fifteen-year-old boy came to the hospital with chest pain and rashes all over his body—'

'You compiled this for me?' she interrupted.

'Let's concentrate on the case,' he said and continued.

For the next one and a half hours, they went through numerous cases, fought over potential diagnosis, ate the cold, tasteless food, looked into each other's eyes and knew nothing would make them happier if this was their routine for the rest of their lives. Somewhere between the heated conversations, Arman had shifted right next to her and taken her hand. They were talking about dead patients, but both of them knew what they were *really* talking about. When both of them were exhausted, Arman took her back to her room and tucked her into her bed. The goodnight kiss lasted an eternity and then Arman left.

Pihu couldn't sleep for the rest of the night. She couldn't stop replaying the night in her head. That and the niggling chest pain and the rising difficulty in breathing kept her awake all night. *Nothing is wrong*, she told herself and closed her eyes. *This is my life*, she told herself, *and tomorrow is just a sick leave.*

24

Dushyant Roy

It was late and Dushyant hadn't gone to sleep. For the last two hours, he had been waiting for Pihu to come back from her *magical* date. It had been long, so it was going well, he guessed. He would have no one else to blame but himself if anything went wrong. After all, the stethoscope, the doctor's coat, the case files of interesting patients—it was all his idea for a perfect date for Pihu. Earlier that day, when Arman was doing a routine check-up, he had seemed to be a little tense. Dushyant wouldn't have talked, but he asked what was bothering him. Arman had asked him to fuck off and be busy killing himself, but Dushyant had insisted. Long story short, Dushyant had *suggested* what the perfect date for Pihu should have.

Earlier that night, when he saw Arman execute the date just like he had suggested, he smiled and prayed for her. On second thoughts, he knew a touch of flowers and candles wouldn't have been that bad either. It was two in the night when he saw Arman walk in, carrying her in his arms. *How heavy must she be?* As soon as Arman left, he wanted to go over and talk to Pihu. He also had to apologize and he had not got the time

203

to do so till then. But better sense prevailed and he thought he would let her soak in the moment.

As he lay down his head on the pillow, he wondered how different his life would have been had he respected the one girl to whom he meant the world. Unable to curb the urge, he took out his cell phone and called the number he should have called long back. The phone rang.

'Hi, Kajal. Dushyant,' he said and waited. It had been long since he heard her voice and he wondered if the raw, sugary sweetness of her voice was still there.

'Umm . . . Hi. How are you?' she responded. *Still so sweet!*

'I am good. The medicines seem to be working for now,' he lied. 'How are you?'

He wanted to ask her why she had come to the hospital but didn't know how to approach the topic.

'I am good, too. I came to the hospital that day,' she said. *Phew!* 'You were sleeping, so I ended up talking to your room-mate. Pihu.'

'Yes, she told me. I wish I could have seen you,' he replied. He wondered if it showed his vulnerability, but he was allowed to be so. He was dying, after all.

'I wish so too,' she said.

'Can you come over?'

'Now? Are you sure?'

'Can you?'

There was silence on the other side. An unending, torturous time between when he finished and she responded. He didn't know why he had asked her to come over. Was it because he had just seen Pihu come back smiling from a date? Did he want the same? As he weighed the possibilities of his womanlike proposition, Kajal said she would be there in a bit. He did a happy little dance in his head. For the first time since he had come to the hospital, he got up from his bed, dragged himself to the washroom and looked at himself in the mirror. *I hate myself.* He hadn't shaved in days, but that wasn't the only problem. Over the last month, he had lost a lot of weight and he no longer looked the guy whose bench press had touched 190 pounds in his bodybuilding prime. He even tried flexing his biceps in the mirror but a skinny arm stared back at him. No more of that protein-supplement-pumped, steroid-injected-in-the-bum bloated hands that would scream out of his XL-sized yet tight T-shirts. He shaved. Washed his face. Twice. Still looked as bad as he did before. Exasperated, he even washed his face with Pihu's strawberry-flavoured facewash, which left his skin surprisingly fresh.

He walked back to his bed and started to count time backwards. It hadn't been long when the door was knocked upon and Kajal walked in. In a blue tank top, slightly torn jeans and chappals, she didn't look like an engineering student at all. And then it struck him; Kajal may no longer be an engineering student after a few days. Although rich, she had never seemed like the type who would quit engineering midway because life was too short to do uninteresting shit and go dancing to London to do a course which had no academic value. And of course, to have sexual intercourse with white men with different accents. But then again, Pihu had added that Kajal's decision had something to do with her break-up with Varun. *That bastard!*

Dushyant's hatred for Varun was multilayered and very complex. The most obvious reason was Varun sleeping with his girlfriend. But then again, it wasn't the only reason. Varun was rich and accomplished beyond any girl's criterion. He came from a family of millionaires, but he had added a few millions of his own, too, into the bulging accounts of his father's clandestine bank accounts in countless European countries.

He hated almost everything about him. The cars. The places he went to. The first-class flights he took. The opulent flat he never lived in. The slicked hair. The perfect tone of talking. The first time he met him—and that's when Dushyant and Kajal were dating—he had decided not to like the guy and the feeling of revulsion had only grown with time.

'You look amazing,' he said as Kajal sat down by his side.

'You don't look too bad either. A little thinner, but I never liked your muscles anyway,' she chuckled. Dushyant saw her eyes rove over all the drips and needles that plunged deep into him and kept him alive.

'You loved them! You couldn't keep your hands off them!' he poked.

'Naah. That was just because you worked so hard and I didn't want to disappoint you.'

That was correct. She had never disappointed him. *I am an asshole.*

'Are you feeling any better?' she asked.

'A little. Though there is a shooting pain every time the effect of the painkillers wears off. My liver and kidneys are shot. They have put me on the transplant list, just in case,' he said. He conveniently missed out the fact that he might not make it to the next month.

'Transplant list?' The shock on Kajal's face was off-putting. He regretted saying it. He was no stranger to saying things he shouldn't.

'Oh . . . there is just a one-in-a-million chance of that happening. Nothing is happening to me,' he lied. Even though Arman's words rang clearly in his head. *We will get you on the transplant list, but I don't know if it will be any good. The list moves slowly and your record of abuse will not go down well with the people who decide. I think you should tell your parents. Maybe there is a match there.*

'Your room-mate thinks you're dying, too,' she said, her voice cracking.

'Are you crazy?' He put his hand across to comfort her. 'She is just a wannabe medical student. And moreover, she is the one who's dying, so quite obviously, she is slowly losing her mind.' He laughed. The room reeked of death and disappointment but there was still laughter in their hearts. She laughed.

'I heard you're going to London? Why is that?' he asked.

'Just like that.'

'Are you sure it's got nothing to do with Varun . . . or me?' he pried.

'Why would it be like that? Both of you are assholes. You cared too much, he doesn't care at all. I have always been wrong with my choices in men. Remember Charanpreet? That sardar guy who told me in first year that he would wait for me till the end of eternity? The guy with the big black SUV?'

'Yeah, the guy we beat up,' Dushyant said with pride.

'Yes, the same guy. But he was alone and you were with ten other guys.'

'I had to get extra help! He was big, wasn't he?' he defended himself. It was odd how the mention of other guys still made him squirm. Just imagining Kajal with someone else was distressing. During the period of time that they were together, Dushyant routinely found himself in drunken brawls and fist fights with guys who made passes at her. Sometimes, they blew up to the magnitude of fifty-people-a-side showdowns. His side usually won. He could get beat up and he could smash heads in.

'Yes, he was big. Maybe I should have gone to him. You know—he's still waiting? I still get flowers and chocolates at my doorstep every birthday and Valentine's Day. That's cute, isn't it?'

'Frankly, that's creepy and a waste of money!' he mocked.

They laughed again. In an instant, they were back to the times they had spent together, holding hands in the empty corridors of the department of mechanical engineering or the third floor of the library. Soon, they started gossiping and reminiscing about all the times they had spent together. A couple of hours had passed when Dushyant felt the pain shooting up from his stomach again. He grumbled and growled inside but didn't let it show on his face again. But just as the pain crept up, he thought he should call for assistance. The last thing he wanted was to bleed in his bed in front of Kajal and freak her out.

'I think I need help,' he snarled. 'The pain . . .'

'Oh, I will just call someone!' She panicked and rushed out.

Dushyant clutched his stomach as his insides burnt up; he heard choked sounds from the other side of the curtain. He pulled himself away from the bed and pulled the curtain away even as his body seemed to slowly disintegrate. On the bed, he saw Pihu wildly flapping her hands around, her eyes rolled over and her body furiously shaking. Before he could pull himself to her bed, she had stopped. Still. He cried out loud as he saw her stop moving. He shouted and shook her, but she didn't respond. Panicking, he slapped her a few times but her face just flopped from one side to the other. He screamed for help. With the last bit of strength left in him, he climbed over her bed, put both his hands to her chest and started to push it down. It was something he had seen on television many times before. He bent over her and breathed into her open mouth and again pounded her chest. The pain in his body rose. The legs. The stomach. The chest. He was falling. His eyes closed as his body slumped and fell from the bed on the cold, hard ground. Darkness.

25

Zarah Mirza

It was a gloomy morning, like many before. Muted light from the tinted windows of her bedroom made patterns on the mosaic floor. Her parents were back again and finally, she had figured out the reason behind the uncalled-for surprise drop-ins. Last night, her mother had dropped in five names, all doctors, who were really fond of the picture they had been sent. It was a picture of her from a wedding she had been dragged to by her mom. She was in a red embellished saree and carried a Chanel handbag—a gift from her mother—which her mom had bought for herself during her trip to Europe the year before. The photo had all three of them, but it had been cropped.

The recent visits had been bothersome. Her dad had tried to initiate conversation with her every time they were alone and she would feel queasy and nauseated.

Groggily, she stepped out of her room and called out to her mom. She was nowhere to be seen. After checking the kitchen, the balcony and the washrooms, she finally asked her dad.

'Where is Mom?' she asked.

'She has gone to the nearby masjid to pray for you. I think she will be back in half an hour,' he said and put the newspaper by his side.

'Okay,' she acknowledged and turned on her heel.

'Zarah?' her dad called out.

'Yes?'

'Can we talk? Will you sit with me for a while?' he asked. Zarah looked at him with revulsion. Every inch of her body wanted to run away from the man who wouldn't believe his daughter, but his questioning gaze kept her from going.

'Fine,' she said and plonked down on the sofa. 'But it better not be about the guys whom you have chosen for me. I am too busy to get married right now,' she declared.

'I am not talking about that,' he said. 'I want to talk about *us*.'

This can't be happening. Zarah felt someone had pulled the rug from beneath her feet. All of a sudden, she started to feel light-headed. She wanted to run from him. *Why? Why does he want to talk about us?*

'Why do you want to talk?' she asked.

'There are some things that I know that you think I don't. And things that you don't know.'

Oh no. This was only getting only worse. She wished he would stop and not go any further. It had taken her years to put what had happened that night behind her, and him digging out the past would only mean it was real. She looked at him with rapt attention and saw his eyes glaze over.

'I have been a coward.'

Yes, you have.

He continued, 'I know what happened that night. I have wanted to talk to you about this for very long, but I have never found the words. I tried to get close and make you understand how wrong I had been, but it never helped. I understand your hatred for me. I understand that it's hard for you to sit in the same room as me. I know I have failed as a father.'

'Can I go?' she asked. Her eyes had started to well up and she didn't want to cry in her front of her father. Despite all the years she had spent hating her father, she also had the lovely memories of her childhood when her dad doted on her and loved her like a little newborn baby. She didn't want to be reminded of all that.

'Yes, you can. I understand why. I know I should have believed you, but I didn't. Years later, I came to know what happened from the daughter of my senior and about what he had done to you . . . She told me that you had gone to the hospital when her dad was in a coma and told her that her father was a monster, a disgrace, a paedophile, a depraved pervert . . .' His voice trailed off. 'I was consumed by guilt. I was no less a monster than that man. I didn't know how to come to you and apologize. I didn't know what I could have done to make it better . . . I needed to die.'

'I need to go,' she said as a lone tear trickled down her cheek. She got up and turned her back on him.

'I tried to kill myself,' he mumbled.

She turned to look him in the eye, still fuming but a mush of emotions inside. Almost instinctively, her searching gaze caught his hands—both wrists had huge scars running through and through. Someone must have found him quickly after he did that because the wounds appeared deep enough to prove fatal within fifteen minutes. They were determined cuts that ran deep, not superficial grazes that suicidal teenagers have.

'Did you cut . . . ?' Her voice trailed off.

'Nothing worked. I drove our car off a flyover. I ate a bottle of sleeping pills . . . I lived. I lived to face you,' he whimpered like a little girl.

'When was that?' she asked with a trace of emotion in her voice. 'Wait? Was it when you and Mom . . . ?'

'We never went to Europe. I was in a hospital for a month,' he clarified.

'And Mom? You never thought about her? Does she know? Had you died, what would she have done? She has a daughter who doesn't talk to her and a husband who constantly tries to kill himself? WHAT THE FUCK WERE YOU THINKING? And just because you tried to kill yourself doesn't mean I will forgive you. How can I forgive all those years you were right in front of me and I couldn't tell you anything. HOW DO YOU THINK I FELT when you were going to parties with the SAME MEN WHO RAPED ME! How can I forget all that? JUST BECAUSE YOU TRIED TO KILL YOURSELF? You know what? I wish you had died! *You deserve to!*' she bellowed and melted into a big pool of tears.

She slumped on the couch, scrunched herself into a little ball and hoped she would disappear. She wept and she could hear her father sob like a little child. She was angry, distraught and vulnerable. Slowly, a montage of pictures with her father and her started to float in front of her eyes, interspersed with images of her dad lying on the bathroom floor in a pool of blood, lying with broken bones in a hospital bed, frothing at the mouth because of an overdose of sleeping pills. Slowly, she felt the anger melt away. She couldn't help but think about what it would be like not to have her dad around. It was a sinking feeling.

She didn't know how it happened, but she found herself in her dad's arms and both of them wept profusely. Every passing second made the presence of her father near her easier to bear. With every tear that she shed, she could feel the animosity melt away. The flood of tears slowly reduced to a trickle. Zarah didn't know what to say, all she knew was that after years of bitterness and hostility, this tiny moment of love made her feel alive again. Just then, the door bell rang.

Zarah stood up straight. Both of them wiped their tears away and she felt her lips curve into a little smile. Next, she smoothened out her clothes and walked to the door. She opened the door and hugged her mother. 'Good morning,' she whispered. Her mother looked at her, shocked.

'I got aloo-puri for breakfast,' her mother said and held out the polythene in her hands.

'I will just take a bath and come back,' Zarah said and smiled. As she walked to her room, her eyes met her father's and they smiled. She blushed. In more ways than one, it was one. The shower went on for a little longer than she had intended. For the longest time, she stood there and thought about how life would have been different had her father come out earlier and apologized. She realized her anger was aimed at her father keeping mum about the whole matter.

She came to the living room after she dried herself and dressed. Her parents were already waiting on the table for her. The salty, yummy aroma of the aloo-puri overwhelmed her senses. She sat down and started to eat, her mother slightly perturbed by the glances and small talk between Zarah and her father.

'When do you have to go to the hospital today?' her mom asked.

'Late night,' she said and reminded her mother of her weekly day off.

'You're staying at home today?' she asked.

'No, I am going out with friends for a movie. The new *Avengers* movie is out. People are saying it's hilarious. So, I might go catch that. Plus, Robert Downey, Jr is really nice looking,' she said. Her mother was still perplexed at her daughter's sudden chatty mood.

'And what about the guys we have chosen for you? Beta, you're anyway too busy on the days that you're working. At least meet them? There is this really nice guy—'

'Oh, c'mon! She is still young. Let her live her life for now. She can get married later!' her dad interrupted.

'See? At least someone has the sense!' she said and laughed with her dad. Her mother's face contorted in utter bewilderment.

'And who knows, maybe she has already found someone she wants to be with? Zarah, is there somebody in your life that you really like?'

'As a matter of fact, I do,' she said with an evil smirk. 'Though I am not really sure about it.'

It looked as if her mom was struck by lightning. She froze like a mother from an '80s shoddy Hindi movie who had just learnt that her daughter had been impregnated by her college sweetheart.

'What?'

'I am just kidding, Maa. There is just this very cute patient in my ward.'

'So, you like someone who is not well? Whoever he is, he is sick. How can you like him? I hope he is not a Christian or a Hindu. Oh, God. Why didn't you tell me that before?' she asked frantically. 'You knew about this?' She looked at her husband, who shook his head vehemently.

'Maa. Calm down. It's nothing but a crush,' she clarified.

'God knows what I have done to deserve this,' she grumbled. For the rest of the meal, she found some or the other reason to curse her life, which Zarah found adorable. After a while, both she and her dad ignored her and talked about other aspects. Since her mom was never interested in her work—in fact, she never wanted her daughter to be a doctor and be around diseases—it was a relief for her to actually discuss her work with someone from her family.

After dilly-dallying for a bit, because she didn't want to leave the family she had regained after so many years, she left the house. She met her school friends after a really long time and they were surprised to see Zarah in an ecstatic mood. After making them cancel the plan to watch the movie, she dragged them from one shop to another to get her father a gift. Careful consideration and rebukes from her friends, who progressively got more impatient, made her decide on a beautiful Tag Heuer watch that she had seen Shahrukh Khan wear in an advertisement.

It was a day of colossal shocks for her mother as she saw her daughter give her father a gift far more expensive than anything he had ever owned. Had she been carrying a tray of teacups, she would have promptly dropped it like the quintessential soap-opera mom.

On the watch, there was an inscription which said, '*We still have time.*'

~

Later that night, her father offered to drive her to the hospital but she refused. She got into her car and left, and her parents waved her goodbye from the balcony like they used to in her schooldays. As her car lazily zipped through the traffic, she wondered about all the times she had cursed her father for her wretched life. Everything that didn't go according to her plans was attributed to a failed father. But that day, she was amazed at how easily she had forgotten everything and had gone running into his arms. She argued that it had been too long and her father had suffered enough. Probably even more than she had. As penance, he had tried to kill himself thrice and none of them were half-hearted attempts. *The guilt must have driven him to madness*, she thought.

On certain levels, she even felt guilty about it. Maybe things would have returned to normal a lot earlier had she mustered up the courage to pick up that topic again. All said and done, there was a sinking feeling in her stomach that all the years of hatred and loathing would never come back. She parked the car and as she entered the hospital building, a winning smile found its way to her face. She wanted to shift in with her parents. It was a crazy thought and it would in no certain way be pleasurable, but there was nothing to lose.

The spring in her step and the glow on her face, even when it was one in the night, were apparent. She put a new pot of coffee in the machine and waited for it to brew. Her body sprawled across the couch, she was thinking about a vacation they could go on. Maybe, this time for real . . . Europe. Just as she closed her eyes and imagined her family on a gondola ride in Venice, she heard a commotion in the corridor and saw a doctor and a few nurses run past her office. Instinct told her they were running towards the all-familiar room no. 509. She jumped up and ran in their direction.

She was there fifteen seconds after the nurses and saw the door ajar. Pihu was coughing violently on the bed while Dushyant lay on the floor, his hand twisted in a strange angle, motionless. On the door, she saw Kajal with her hands covering her mouth as the nurses and the doctor made a mad scramble for the two patients. Zarah froze, her legs numb, unable to move or think.

Dushyant was put on a stretcher and rushed out of the room towards the Intensive Care Unit; he had suffered a major bleed again. From the little experience that she had, she knew Dushyant's liver had given up. The alternatives started to crop up in her head. *Transplant? Living donors? Dead donors? No insurance? Maybe his parents?* She just sat there on Dushyant's bed, petrified, as the doctor got Pihu to breathe normally again. She called Arman to let him know about his patient.

Kajal was still standing in the corner, watching in horror as the scene unfolded.

Finally, she stepped towards Zarah and asked, 'Will he be okay?'

'His liver just gave up. He needs a transplant,' she said mindlessly. 'But . . .'

'But what? Are you looking for a donor? Can I donate? If that's okay? I mean I am healthy and we even share the same blood group! What else do you need to match?' Kajal panicked.

A fear-stricken Zarah looked at her in shock. Her feelings towards Dushyant, which she thought were genuine, were dwarfed in front of Kajal's proposition.

'I need to talk to my seniors,' she said and got up.

'Can I come?' she asked impatiently.

'No, I think you should be with Dushyant right now,' she said and told her where they had taken him.

'I don't think I can watch him like this,' she cried out and crumpled into a heap near the bedpost. Zarah, on noticing there was someone who was much more disturbed than she was, finally jolted herself back to her senses. She helped Kajal sit on the bed and reassured her that she would do anything and everything to get him a donor. Kajal, still weeping, whispered that she would be ready to donate if the need arose. Zarah knew finding a donor was tough, given the red tape, shortage of dead people with usable livers and the rising number of old alcoholics with plenty of money to spare. Transplanting livers from living patients was monstrously expensive and she wondered if Dushyant alone could afford it. It was a long, complicated surgery and usually cost more than 15 lakh rupees. As she sat there patting and consoling

Kajal, Pihu's parents came rushing in, crying. They sat beside their daughter and kept asking her what had happened. Pihu had no answers for them—she just stared at them with a blank expression on her face.

'You just stay here; I will be back in a bit and update you on how he is doing,' she said and got up to leave the room and talk to Arman about it.

Just then, a voice called out her name: 'Zarah?'

Zarah looked back to see Pihu call out her name. 'Yes?'

'What happened?' Pihu asked. 'And . . . And . . . I can't move my hands.'

'You were about to choke to death. I think your heart stopped too. The nurse just told me that Dushyant resuscitated you. He saved you,' she said and left the room, as four pairs of stunned eyes followed her.

26

Arman Kashyap

Arman paced about in his room, angry, frustrated and really scared. He waited for Zarah to come back to his office and tell him exactly what had happened. For the first time in many years, he felt like he would pass out from anxiety. It was his third cigarette and he was far from being calm. If the surgery failed, he would have to schedule another one and quick. Reversing the process was improbable and even more dangerous than just going ahead with the treatment and finishing it.

At a distance, he saw Zarah walk towards his office with slow, unsure steps. He held the door open for her and as soon as she got in, he said, 'What happened?' His hands were crossed firmly in front of his chest, bracing for impact.

'Dushyant needs a liver transplant. He might not see another day. Pihu is dying. She can't feel her hands any more and she nearly choked to death,' she said and took a seat. 'She needs to be put on constant breathing support if we don't want it to happen again.'

Silence gripped the room as both the doctors faced the reality that stared them right in the face. Arman's head was

219

a mashed pulp of angst and failure. Sitting on his seat with Pihu's reports in front of him, his demeanour transformed from a headstrong, unemotional doctor's to that of a parent who is about to lose his or her kid. As tears threatened to peek out from his eyes, he made a few calls for some tests to be run on Pihu. Next, he called his college buddy–surgeon to let him know that he would need his help again. As he looked around helplessly, often running his hands over his head, he noticed Zarah sobbing softly with her head buried in her palms.

'I will see what has to be done. You should talk to his parents. They can be possible donors,' he said, trying to regain some grip on the situation. His words had no effect on Zarah whose stifled sobs only got louder. 'I will pay if money is a problem,' he added as another assurance. But deep down, he knew all this wouldn't matter. A liver transplant would make him live for another few days, maybe a month, but his kidneys were still shutting down. The survival chances of someone with donor kidneys and liver were slim, and that is *if* the patient got the organs in the first place.

'I think I should talk to his parents,' she said and left the room.

It was time for Arman to accept the truth, too. He had most likely failed. She might or might not survive the next surgery. From the cabinet he hardly ever opened, he took out a bottle of Scotch and poured himself a drink. The tan-coloured liquid slipped down his throat smoothly, burning it a little, soothing it a little. He picked up the phone and asked for Pihu's parents to be sent to his office. As he waited for her parents, he downed two more drinks. The pain, the agony was still there. He saw the parents walking to his door, her father stoic, her mother hysterical.

'What happened to her?' her dad asked, his forehead riddled with criss-crossed lines.

'I am afraid our treatment didn't work,' he said, trying to be as doctor-like and straight-faced as possible.

'What do you mean?' her mom said, looking at him with the veins in her eyes popping out.

'We have to do another surgery and see if we can make her live a little longer,' he said. 'There are chances . . . but they are minimal. She might not have more than a few days.'

'YOU KILLED HER!' her mom shouted all of sudden and lunged at Arman, her hands flailing wildly at him as she tried to grab him. Her father tried his best to stop her. Arman just sat there waiting to get hit, thinking it was just. He felt responsible, and if in any way he could assuage the pain of her mother, he was up for it. Her mother kept shouting and repeating that her daughter would have been much better without him, even though her father knew she wouldn't have. For five minutes, she kept trying to swing at Arman. She threw an odd stapler and the punching machine at him, both of which hit his head as Arman sat there unflinchingly. Finally, tired and wanting to spend time with her daughter, she left the room on the insistence of the father.

'I am sorry,' Arman said, shaking his head.

'You did all you could do,' the father responded. 'Had it not been for you, we wouldn't have seen her walk again. We would have lost her a long time ago. It's all thanks to you. I am sorry for my wife. She knows it, too, but you know how it is. She is . . .' His voice trailed away as he looked everywhere but at him. If he had worked hard at anything in his life, Arman knew it had been easier than not breaking down in front of Pihu's dad. Gathering himself together, he patted the shoulder of the father whose eyes, too, had glazed over. And then Arman watched as Pihu's father couldn't keep the barrage of tears from streaming down his face. He had spent a year controlling himself, trying to be strong as people around him showered them with sympathy, ignoring the crushing pain inside his chest as he saw his daughter become progressively sicker. Arman looked at him and his own pain seemed like a needle prick. *The loss of an only child is the worst pain any one can endure. After all, what do our parents live for? With the best years of their youth gone by, they don't have any yearnings for comfort or money or fame; all they want is to see us grow up as happy, healthy human beings with all the luxuries that they couldn't afford. To see years of love, care and upbringing reduce to dust, burnt and buried, takes away everything from a parent.* Slowly, the sobs became softer, the shoulder shrugs became more periodic and her father wiped his face with his handkerchief a few times before he thanked Arman.

'Can you tell her? I think she is happy when she is around you,' he requested, turned and left the room to join his wife.

The stress ball in Arman's hand was crushed to the maximum. Darkness enveloped him as he tried to imagine what it would be like to tell her that she might not have long to live. He had practised the speech many times in his head before and it never became easier. He thought he would wait for the test results to come through. Maybe, he had just panicked. It was just one seizure, one blockage, after all. For the next hour, he paced restlessly around the room. After the first few calls, the test lab assistants asked him to wait in the stern voice usually reserved for junior doctors. Finally, the results arrived. He mailed them to his doctor friend immediately. The results were unambiguous and clear. She was dying, and she was dying fast. The next surgery had to be performed as quickly as possible. He braced himself and left for room no. 509.

He entered the room and found the bed next to Pihu empty. He remembered Zarah's words: *he needs a transplant.* Almost to distract himself, he tried to think about how at least Dushyant could be saved. A few more steps and he looked straight at Pihu. She met his eyes and smiled. He knew that she knew, so he decided he wouldn't beat around the bush. It was as difficult for him as it was for her, he thought.

'Your test results are back,' he said, his face glum and devoid of happiness. 'We have to schedule you in for another surgery.'

'I know. What are my chances?' she said in a very throaty voice. It wasn't easy for her to talk any more. Her breathing was laboured and she looked drained and tired.

'I don't know, I can't say. Your immune system is a little weak for the procedure, but there is no way out,' he clarified.

Her eyes glazed over as she looked at the ceiling. 'I will die,' she whispered and tears flowed. Arman felt like cutting out his heart and giving it to the little girl whose spirit to live was undefeatable. There she was, confined to the bed, most of her limbs useless, and she still wanted to live.

'Don't say that,' he said and put his hand on her cheek.

'I am not afraid of dying,' she said. 'I have seen that happening to me before. I am ready for that. I am afraid of being forgotten. I am scared of where I will go after this is over. I am afraid of what will happen to my parents. All these months, I have stayed up nights, crying, thinking of how my dad will react when I am gone. I know he doesn't show much, but I know, inside, he is a broken man. My mother, who brought me up, whose only dream was to see me as a beautiful bride with many kids, what will happen to her? All they lived for was me. This isn't how it's supposed to be, is it? Why do *they* have to suffer? Haven't *I* suffered enough? What had I done wrong? I had always been a good girl. Why me? Why my family? Why should I die? Why can't I get married? Spend another night with you? I . . . am just going to die? Not be here any more?'

And then, she broke down into sobs; her tears rolled down and wet her pillow. Arman bent over and kissed her forehead.

'Everything will be okay,' he said, knowing that his promise was empty. He choked on his words.

'It will not be,' she said from behind the stifled sobs.

'I have something for you,' he said and reached into his pocket.

For a moment, Pihu stopped crying and looked straight at him. Had she been able to get up and hug him, she would have. She would have hugged her mom, her dad. She was leaving them behind and going to a world unknown. And though she didn't know what would happen to her after the last shred of breath would leave her, wherever she would go, she would miss them.

Arman took out what he had been carrying with him for weeks now. He dangled it in front of her. It was a gold chain. The yellowness of the gold had somewhat waned away, and hanging beneath it was a small diamond of 3 carats, and it was beyond beautiful.

'This is for you,' he said and gingerly took Pihu's hand into his and wrapped it thrice around her limp, senseless wrist. Pihu's eyes sparkled as she gazed at her newly acquired possession.

'That is beautiful.'

'It pales in comparison to you. You're the most beautiful thing I have ever considered my own. Before you came along, I was a loner, someone who didn't care about anything but himself, his work, his obsession. But one fine day, you walked into my life, with the help of crutches, no less, and turned it upside down. For the first time, I loved someone more than I have loved myself,' he said.

'You make even dying beautiful,' she purred. Her eyes roved around the room and she saw her parents walk inside. Arman noticed their presence, too, and it was his cue to leave.

'I will see you in a bit,' he said and turned.

'Arman?' she called out. 'To whom did this belong?' She pointed to the chain and the pendant.

'It was my great-grandmother's. She wanted my beautiful wife to have it,' he said and left the room with tears in his eyes. Pihu looked at her wrist and the words rung in her head, *a beautiful wife*. Her life had suddenly changed into an old, predictable movie from the '90s.

27

Kajal Khurana

Kajal sat in the passenger seat, rubbing her hands together, disappointed. It turned out her blood group wasn't the same as Dushyant's. Zarah had reasoned that guys in love often lie about having the same blood groups to make it sound like they are meant to be. Zarah drove on, without saying much. Kajal could sense that she was disturbed.

'Have you ever talked to his parents, Zarah?' Kajal said trying to break the uneasy silence, though even she was nervous. If Dushyant was ever intimidated by someone, it was his parents, and everyone knew Dushyant wasn't an easy person to intimidate.

'No, I haven't. He doesn't like them. I figured it would be better not to talk to them. I wouldn't have if we had found a match amongst ourselves,' Zarah said, her eyes still stuck firmly on the road.

'*Ourselves?*' Kajal looked at her in shock. Zarah was caught off guard for a minute—her left hand fumbled with the gear and her eyes roved around nervously.

'I thought I would help out,' she finally said.

Kajal didn't say anything. Slumped back into her car

seat, Kajal looked at Zarah's face. It was apparent that she was no longer just Dushyant's doctor, she was much more. That night, when Pihu had narrated every detail of every day since Dushyant was first admitted, Kajal had conveniently ignored the parts where she had described a nameless, faceless doctor who never left Dushyant's bedside. As she saw Zarah's contorted face, the protruding vein on her forehead, the tense hand that clutched the steering wheel tightly, she knew the faceless doctor was her. And she knew Zarah was not next to Dushyant because her responsibilities as a doctor demanded her to be.

'After the transplant . . . do you think he will live?' Kajal asked Zarah, who was lost in her own train of thought.

After a long pause, Zarah said, 'Only a slight chance.'

'You didn't test your compatibility as a donor because you wanted to help out . . . It was much more, wasn't it?' she asked.

'I don't want to talk about it. Anyway, the two of you seem to be happy around each other. I have seen the look on his face when he talks about you. So this conversation means nothing,' Zarah said.

'We have a history. I was his only friend,' she responded.

'Good for you,' Zarah snapped.

Kajal was taken aback at Zarah's curt, almost rude, reply. At a sudden loss for words, she looked away from her and outside the window. It went without saying that in the two years that had passed by, Kajal had missed Dushyant. Even when in Varun's arms, she used to close her eyes and think about Dushyant and how he was doing. Occasionally, she would get snippets of the fights Dushyant used to get into, the drunken brawls, the skirmishes with hostel guards and the like. Incidents like these had been on the rise after their break-up. Kajal could think of just two reasons for it. Either Dushyant was destroying himself or he was trying to catch her attention, after she had snapped all ties with him. Or both. After a while, he'd stopped. The breaking of college furniture and water coolers, the burning of staff offices, all of this stopped. Or so she thought.

The gossip died. The bad-boy legend of the college retreated to his room to die a quiet death. There were younger, meaner students baring their teeth in college. Dushyant was no longer trying to catch her attention; he had just spiralled down deeper into his addictions. Alcohol, weed, marijuana, ice, heroin . . . master of all drugs, jack of none.

Sometimes, they did cross paths on the streets of the college—Dushyant, often with a cigarette in his hands, Kajal with her eyes dug into her toes. They never talked, avoiding each other in the hallways and the corridors and the labs, if and when there was any crossing of paths. For all she knew, the break-up was a lot harder on Dushyant than it was on her. After all, months after, she was dating Varun with all her heart. Dushyant was the one who moped, cried, drank, destroyed himself further after the break-up, not her.

The car reached the address. They were modest apartments where people live on for generations, adding a room or two against the government regulations. Zarah double-checked the gate number before she rang the bell. The Diwali lights from last October still hung on the door. There was no conversation between Zarah and Kajal.

A middle-aged woman opened the gate and asked who they were.

'I am Dr Zarah Mirza, GKL Hospital.'

'What do you want?' the woman asked.

'We have been treating your son, Dushyant Roy, for the last few weeks. I am afraid his chances are slim and he needs a liver transplant. If things get worse, he might need a kidney transplant too,' Zarah laid out the facts threadbare, her tone stern. No false assurances.

The mother looked at her in disbelief and then the truth sank and her knees buckled and her eyes rolled up and she fainted. Both of them reached out to her and prevented her from falling head first on to the concrete floor. They carried her to the sofa inside the house, which was even more modest (or poor looking) than the apartment buildings from outside. A ragged sofa, an old box-type television, a chunky desktop on a table, a rusty single-door fridge and a landline on the small side table. The rest of the evening was easier. Dushyant's dad appeared, duly shocked to see two girls and his half-conscious wife. Zarah explained the same to him and his eyes had more annoyance and fury than sympathy. He asked for more details and as Zarah told them, the mother kept tugging at the father's sleeve to take her to the hospital.

Fifteen minutes later, the parents were following the red Santro to the hospital. The mother had packed lunch for her son who was far from consciousness. During the whole ordeal, Kajal had stood there motionless and not a word had escaped her mouth. Zarah, on the other hand, had been brave and stoic and had managed the father's anger and the mother's impatience. Kajal felt insignificant. Guilty. A liability.

As they reached the hospital, Zarah asked them to wait in Arman's office and told Kajal to find her own way around. Still taken aback with how Zarah was behaving with her, she felt lost. Or perhaps she had always been lost . . . ever since that day when she had decided she wouldn't be with him any more.

Maybe it was for the best.

28

Pihu Malhotra

Time had stopped for Pihu. Contrasting emotions flooded her head as she went through the motions of the day. Her surgery—the second one—was scheduled for the next day and her fear clawed at her. As long as Arman was with her, she felt calm, but now, alone in the hospital room, she was petrified. Later she would be wheeled into a hospital room and she wouldn't come out. The thought terrified her. How would her parents react? She started to see herself as a corpse lying on a surgical table with surgeons around her, shaking their heads in disappointment. She was dead. What if she wasn't? What if she was still trapped inside the dead body, shrieking and trying to catch the attention of the doctors who would just leave the room? Trapped inside her body, what would she do? Beads of sweat trickled down her forehead. She wished her parents were around. Her mother had told her that she would be back. They had some paperwork to take care of. She was sure there would be plenty.

As she lay there, moving her head restlessly from side to side, three ward boys and a doctor wheeled in a stretcher. Dushyant was back, worse than ever. Just gaining consciousness, his head bobbed from side to side as he groaned in obvious pain. His pain only made it worse for her. Big, round tears peeked out from her eyes. She tried to move her hand to wipe her tears, but she knew that she couldn't. The doctors left him on the bed and hooked him on to the monitors. They checked for his stats and nodded their heads before leaving the hospital ward. She kept looking at him, wondering if he would ever look her way. And he did.

'How are you?' he groaned.

She smiled. 'I am good. Or well—as good as I can be.'

'Are you scared?' he asked.

'Are you?'

Dushyant nodded. She nodded in return.

'What are the doctors saying?' she asked.

'I need a transplant. Liver, for sure. Kidneys, too. And still . . . Anyway, what's with you?' he asked.

'Thank you for saving me. I almost died.'

'It was nothing,' he said.

'You saved my life. It means a lot. But that also proves one thing. Although I am sure you would beg to differ,' she said with a grin.

'What is that?'

'We are room-mates, and we will always have each other's backs. We are 2-1 now. You're a better room-mate than I am!'

'Oh, c'mon. My favours were small.' Dushyant blushed. 'But fine, if you say I'm leading by 2-1, how can I disagree?'

Dushyant looked at her and smiled and then they both laughed. They laughed till their stomachs hurt. Days or even hours before their probable last breaths, they shared their first moment of camaraderie.

'What does Arman say?' Dushyant asked. 'Are you getting any better?'

'Worse,' she said and told Dushyant about the surgery and

about the possible outcomes. Pihu hadn't really expected any reaction from Dushyant and was positively surprised when his face turned pale and it looked like he had seen a ghost. He was agitated even behind the pain, his fists were clenched and his face was a tense tangle of muscles and veins. It was only after Pihu repeatedly assured him that she would be okay that he relaxed a bit.

'But at least I am not dying unloved,' she said and added, 'No offence.' With her eyes she pointed to the gold chain and the pendant on her wrist. 'Arman gave it to me. It was meant for his wife.' Her face was a million shades of scarlet. 'And should I add, he used the word *beautiful*.'

'He didn't have any choice! Who else would marry him?' he mocked.

'That's mean!'

'I am just kidding. And it's beautiful. I am happy for you. On the other hand, who wouldn't marry you!'

'Aw. That's sweet now.' She blushed.

'Where are your parents?' he asked. And just as he did, they heard footsteps approach the door of the hospital room.

'They are here—' she said and stopped as she looked at two unfamiliar faces staring all around the room, their eyes wide open and their mouth agape.

'Ishhhhh!' the woman shrieked and immediately rushed to Dushyant's bedside while the man stood at a distance with one hand on his chest and the other on his face in disappointment.

Pihu couldn't make out what the woman was saying behind the wailing and the sobbing. She kept caressing and kissing Dushyant's face and hair furiously. Pihu didn't get a single word she was saying in her weepy Bengali accent. For the next half hour, the high-pitched crying continued. Sometimes, the woman looked at her husband and said something to him in angry sobs. She couldn't get the words, it was in Bengali after all, but she could tell that Dushyant's father was being blamed for everything.

Meanwhile, Dushyant, who was at first unmoved, even irritated, had started crying and had taken his mother in his arms. His father still stood there motionless, watching the whole saga unfold. *What a jerk!* thought Pihu. It was only after his mom scolded the man that he came near the bed and sat on it. The revulsion and disgust found its way back to Dushyant's face and he couldn't meet his father's eyes. While his mom cried, he just looked away from his father. Seeing his son's antipathy, the father excused himself while the woman still had her face buried in her crying son's chest.

Pihu's parents walked in too, after a little while, and sat beside her. All three of them were looking at the woman who was sobbing feverishly on the adjacent hospital bed. Pihu filled them in on who she was and told them a little about how Dushyant and his father didn't see eye to eye. Her mother nodded disapprovingly as if to say, *'Who would want such a son?'* Pihu promptly reminded her of how it was Dushyant who had saved her life even as he was about to die himself. Her mother muttered something about the unlucky room number and her eyes glazed over.

For a change, her father, too, sat on the other side and held her other hand. Almost instantly, he discovered the gold chain with the little diamond and looked at her with questioning eyes. She blushed stupidly and it became apparent where it came from. Her father grinned approvingly. If only she had more time to go on unnoticed dates and night-outs without her father knowing and to stash Valentine's Day cards in the corners of her wardrobe, to save money to buy her boyfriend expensive gifts and to have her heart broken and lose her love to someone else and get married. If only . . .

Her father's grip tightened on her hand and though she couldn't feel it, she could sense it . . . the anguish, the irreparable loss, the defeat. Both sets of parents sat near their kids. Often her eyes would meet Dushyant's and they would both smile. A little later, Zarah walked into the room and asked Dushyant's parents to follow a ward boy for the blood and tissue tests. They wanted to check for possible donors. Zarah's face screamed anxiety and she never looked straight at Dushyant.

Pihu's parents, too, excused themselves for lunch after she forced them to. She was sure they hadn't eaten anything substantial in days. Her mom had been beautiful in her college days; now she looked dead and lifeless.

Zarah was checking Dushyant's charts when Pihu finally greeted her: 'Hi!'

'Hi, Pihu. How are you doing?' Zarah answered with a forced smile.

'You tell me? You're the doctor,' she chuckled.

'She is doing great. Ask me,' Dushyant butted in and Pihu gave him a reprimanding look. 'Oh, wait, you don't know, do you?'

'What do I not know?' a confused Zarah queried.

'Pihu almost got married,' Dushyant smirked. Pihu blushed. *'WHAT?'* Zarah exclaimed.

'I mean not *really* married. But look at her wrist. That's Arman's great-grandmother's pendant meant for Arman's wife. Now, if that doesn't sound straight out of a clichéd Hindi movie, I don't know what does. So symbolically, they are married. Who cares about the paperwork and all that shit! Right, Pihu?'

Zarah bent over to see the chain and the piece of sparkling rock dangling from it and broke into a big smile . . . which slowly turned into a big grin and she hugged the life out of poor Pihu. Obviously, she couldn't feel the hug, but she could feel the love.

'Yes, Dushyant is right. You're married now,' she quipped. 'So congratulations!'

'Oh, shut up,' Pihu snarled and blushed at the same time.

'But this is so sweet, Pihu,' Zarah said and sat by her side. Pihu's joy knew no bounds. It's a very girly thing to do . . . to blush and feel ecstatic when your girlfriends approve of the guy you have chosen. Zarah wasn't *really* her girlfriend but who cared? It was her moment. For a few seconds, she closed her eyes and imagined herself crying as she walked into a car adorned with flowers and with a number plate that said *Just Married, Rx*.

'I am glad I came here,' Pihu said, her mood wistful and her eyes distant.

'That's the first time I've heard someone be thankful to be in a hospital,' Dushyant quipped and they all laughed.

'I wish he was here,' Pihu said.

'Aw. He would have been, but he is preparing for the surgery. I have never seen him so tense before. I hope it goes well,' Zarah said, as the tension in her eyebrows returned. 'There is still hope, Pihu.'

'Fingers crossed!' Pihu said with false happiness. 'All I want to know are the chances of my coming out of that operation room alive.'

Zarah didn't say anything. After a long pause, she said, 'My guess is . . . one hundred per cent!'

She forgave Zarah for lying. She knew she might not ever open her eyes again after the anaesthesiologist pricked her with his injection filled with stuff that was supposed to put her under one more time. The feeling passed. It had come way too many times to mean anything now. She had told people she loved that she loved them . . . many, many times. Her goodbye to her parents had lasted over a year. Over the past year, she had been waiting for her death. As she lay her head back on the pillow, she smiled. Her wait had been long and weary and she decided she didn't want her last few hours to go by in dread.

'I will just be back, then,' Zarah said and hugged her.

'Be back soon. They will take me away in a few hours and Dushyant will be all lonely then. He really needs you.' Pihu winked.

Contrary to what she had thought, she didn't spot a smile on Zarah's face. If anything, it drooped a little.

'He has people to take care of him. I don't think he needs me any more than as a doctor,' Zarah said. Dushyant and Pihu looked at each other, shocked, not knowing what to make of it.

'Obviously, he needs you. Haven't you noticed the way he looks at you?' Pihu said excitedly even as Dushyant's face flushed with obvious anger and embarrassment.

'I am sure there are other people who would respond to his looks and overtures in a manner better than mine,' she said, irritably.

Dushyant was still confused and fidgeted with the tubes around him. Pihu, on the other hand, grasped immediately what Zarah meant and stayed shut. Before the light of realization dawned on Dushyant's face, Zarah had left.

'You know what she was talking about, right?' Pihu asked.

'I have a faint idea,' he said. 'Kajal.'

'Who do you like more?' Pihu asked.

'Does it matter? I might not make it tomorrow, or the day after, or the month after that.'

'It matters to them. Don't you think it matters to Zarah what you think about her? After you go, if you go, do you think it will be easy for her to grieve for you and yet not know what you thought about her?'

'I have no idea. It's a really hard question. I mean, Kajal and I have a history together. We have seen things, been through shit, but Zarah and I have seen worse. With Zarah, I don't think I have given her a single reason to smile or feel good about *us*.'

'Trust me, you have.'

'You think so?'

'She stands at the door for hours, watching you sleep.'

'You're kidding me!' he exclaimed.

'I am not. You mumble her name in your sleep too,' she said. 'I DO *NOT*!'

'Okay, yes, the last one was a lie, but she really likes you.'

'And Kajal?' he asked, confused.

'She loves you, too.'

'And I?'

'With that, I can't help,' she said and shrugged.

'Why? I am an asshole. Why would they even like me? It's horrible. Why can't they go out there and find someone who is cute and lovable and adorable and not dying like me?'

'For them, you must be cute and lovable and adorable and . . . you are not dying,' she said.

Dushyant broke down in tears like a little girl. He cupped his face, his lips looked like an inverted kayak, and his eyes were little puddles of tears.

'What happened?'

'I . . . am . . . so sorry I was rude to you,' he said and collected himself and wiped the tears off. 'I wish we could have talked before.'

'It's fine. Though a word of advice—don't cry. Like, *ever*. You're *the* bad boy. Movies get made on you, Dushyant. You can't afford to be a sissy.'

'What sissy? Roger Federer cries and he is pretty kickass,' he defended himself.

'Is Roger Federer more dateable and irresistible . . . or say Mick Jagger?'

'Whatever.'

'Don't whatever me,' she said angrily.

'Whatever.'

They both laughed. They lay there, talking about anything that wouldn't remind them of what was going to happen to them. The clock touched five. There was a shuffle of feet near the door. With Pihu's parents, the ward boys and Arman walked inside. Seeing her mother in tears, her tears came back, too. Only momentarily. They pulled the curtain between Dushyant and her and she could see Dushyant's horror-struck face hidden behind the curtain.

'Do we really have to do it now? You said seven, not five,' her father begged.

Arman's head hung low. He said in a soft yet assertive voice, 'I know, Uncle, but the surgery room will be inspected later, early tomorrow morning. We have to schedule the surgery right now or we won't be able to. Please try to understand.'

'But . . . but . . .' Her mother wailed and threw herself at Pihu, who felt helpless and a little scared. 'Don't take her, she is fine!' she shrieked.

'I will be okay,' Pihu whispered, with tears in her eyes.

Her father, too, joined Pihu in her bed and both of them hugged her. There was no stopping the tears now. Arman cowered in a corner and he looked scared, too. She waited for Arman to look at her and when he did, she smiled meekly at him as if to say, *I am ready*.

The ward boys shifted her to the stretcher and slowly started to roll her away, her parents still clutching both of her hands and walking beside her. She took a deep breath and braced herself for what was going to follow. She had led a good life. She had no regrets. As she passed Dushyant, she noticed the shock on his face, too. She smiled at him and moved her lips to say, 'I will be back. Don't worry.'

Dushyant smiled at her and the stretcher was out of the room. Her parents said a million things to her about how much they loved her. She closed her eyes and thought how superfluous and unnecessary those words were. *She knew.* If she died, their loss would be far greater than hers. She knew they knew she loved them.

As Arman bent over, pretending to help the ward boys roll the stretcher into the lift, he whispered in her ears, *'I love you, my beautiful wife.'*

29

Dushyant Roy

Time had slowed down. It had been four hours now. Dushyant had spent a major chunk of his time in the hospital not talking to the girl on the other bed, but he felt lonely without her on the bed beside him. He missed her cherubic, irritating presence. The empty bed and the perfectly ironed bedsheet, which had been changed since she last slept on it, scared him.

His mother had dozed off on the bed after some high-intensity sobbing and his father had been looking at Dushyant as if to ask if he was forgiven—or if he had driven Dushyant to the condition he was in right now. Or so Dushyant thought.

Constantly, his eyes went to the bed alongside his and he could still see all the books scattered around, the crutches Pihu had used when he first saw her, the wrapping paper of the gifts her friends got her. There was a crushing sensation in his heart like he had lost something important. No matter how hard he tried to shake off thoughts of Pihu's pulse dropping to zero, her lifeline flattening out and she breathing her last on the surgery table, he wasn't able to do so. His own heartbeat slowed down every time he thought of her not being there.

Zarah walked in a little later with an envelope in her hand. Dushyant didn't think anything of it before she handed it over to him.

'How's she?' Dushyant asked as Zarah started to walk away.

'It's still going on. I am too scared to go in and disturb them,' Zarah said.

'And what is this?' he asked pointing to the envelope in his hand.

'I have no idea,' she replied curtly. Her mood since the morning hadn't changed. It seemed as if she was still hurting from what had happened earlier that day. Dushyant would have stopped her from leaving the room but he wasn't sure himself about what he wanted.

Nervously, he tore off the top of the envelope. There was a slightly crumpled piece of paper inside with something written in a familiar handwriting. He read:

Hey Dushyant,

I hope you are doing well. I have always hoped.

I am leaving. I would have stayed, but I can't. It's my time to go. For the second time and this time it's because of me. You deserve better. I shouldn't have come back, but then I couldn't help it. As I leave, I want to let you know that every moment I had spent with you made me a better person, a better lover, a better daughter and a better sister. I know the world warned me against the obsessive, paranoid, angry guy that you no doubt are, but you're a lot more than that and they will never know it. I experienced it and I know that any girl who gets to walk into the sunset with you will be the luckiest girl there has ever been.

I lost you the day I left you. I don't want to go back in time and brood over what happened between us. But what happened is something that I will take to my grave, smiling. It's time for you to move on, find a new life, find someone who will accept you the way you are, love you for the person you are. And as I see it, that person is around you. You just need to acknowledge it.

I hope you have a good life. I will be thinking of you. I always have. No matter whom I was with.

Love,
Kajal

P.S. I am not disappearing from your life; I don't think I can do that any more. I am going to London. Call me if you need me. I will always be there. Stop drinking.

~

As Dushyant finished reading the letter for the second time, he realized two things: though Kajal meant a lot to him and always would, he had paid his dues, and that he had suffered a lot to love her again as insanely as he used to. The sleepless nights he had spent wondering if he still meant anything to her had extracted every bit from him. Loving her was tiring and he didn't know if he had the strength to go through that again. Even so, the last line brought a smile to his face. She would still be around, be a part of his life, be there when he threw the big parties, and be with him in his heartbreak if he had any. That in itself meant a lot to him.

Maybe he needed someone damaged, like Zarah, and not someone with the perfect life like Kajal. For one thing, he was sure he wasn't in love with Zarah yet. But it was an infatuation, and it was growing. She was with him in the worst of times and she had helped him keep his shit together. Who knows where it might lead him? He closed his eyes and fantasized about him asking Zarah out on a date. And he thought about how Pihu was doing in the surgery room. Quite a few hours had passed and, ideally, it should have been ended by now.

He closed his eyes and the monitor showed a flat line.

~

There were shouts across the corridor.

'CRASH CART!' Zarah shouted and two ward boys came rolling in with one. Dushyant's heart was a flat line, his body had had a violent seizure seconds ago and had now gone limp. His parents were shrieking, wailing, shouting at the top of their lungs, 'HOW COULD HE . . . !', their faces pale and hands flailing wildly.

Zarah rubbed the paddles together, ripped his robe apart and sent an electric shock flying into his heart. Nothing happened. She tried it again. Nothing. And again. Finally, the heart picked up and Dushyant started breathing again in short coughs. All his stats were still low and dipping. Zarah asked the ward boys to shift him to the Intensive Care Unit and rushed out, ignoring the pleas and the shouts of his parents.

'He needs surgery. NOW!' Zarah shouted to someone on the phone. Zarah face drooped. There was nothing she could do. There were no matching donors.

30

Fifteen Days Later

We all have our places in this world. I do, too. I, Dushyant, am the rotten apple of the basket. I stay in the basket too long, I tend to ruin everything. That's my place in the world. That was supposed to be my identity till my last breath. Like the identity of Zarah is to unscrew herself, for Arman it is to do what no one else would, for Kajal it is to try to find what her heart really wants, for Pihu it was to smile and make the world a better place. It's what defines us.

But that day when I had decided to do three extra shots of vodka and five extra drags and three extra snorts of cocaine and then passed out after a seizure, I didn't know I would wake up to a new morning and to a new identity. I was in pain, in considerable pain, and there was just one person who still smiled at the rotten assemblage of human tissues that I had become. That person was Pihu. A little girl with the brightest of smiles and the biggest of hearts who didn't think anyone was bad inside. And for someone like me, who has ten thousand layers of bad before the slightest of good, it meant a lot. What would have happened had I decided to do that one month later? Who knows? I would have died, that's for sure. But I would have died a bitter, angry guy.

Am I happy now? Will I be happy five years from now? I don't know. Do I thank her for saving me? Yes. Do I feel good about being saved? Again, I am not sure. Why should I be happy just because I have a few years more to live, why should I be happy just because I have more time with my parents? Why should I be happy because my folks won't grieve? For Pihu, these questions were the answers. Then why didn't she get those last few breaths? The extra few years?

As I look at the empty bed next to me and the missing books and the absence of her chirping laughter, I feel the world has permanently become a little darker, a little sadder. All I remember of her are her last words to me, 'I will be back. It will be okay.'

Well, she lied. I don't think I am forgiving her for that. Not now, not ever.

She left us behind to miss her, to yearn for her, to find things to distract ourselves from missing her. She is not there. She is not around us. I will never see that smile. She will not be on the next bed trying to irritate the hell out of me. She will not talk till my head bursts into little splinters and then irritate me some more. I have not met Arman, but over the last few days I have heard stories. He told Zarah that he was sure she smiled at him long after her heart rate dropped and the lifeline drew a flat line on the monitor and the doctors failed to revive her. Zarah tells me that Arman had spent the night at the morgue standing outside her frozen casket because Pihu was afraid of the dark. She tells me he had to be forced out before he caught pneumonia or something worse. She tells me how every night Arman comes to both the room and the terrace where they had gone on their first date. She tells me how her mother had fainted when she had come back to the unlucky room no. 509 and how she had to be pulled from Pihu's bed by her father. She tells me her father looked like a walking corpse when he heard the news. She tells me how both sets of parents had cried arm in arm. She tells me how her father comforted my crying father (crying!) when I was battling for my life while their daughter was dead. Zarah tells me that her father has not said a word since the day Pihu passed away on the operating table, lying on her side with her back cut open and a smile pasted on her face. It was painless, Zarah tells me.

Does knowing that it was painless make me feel any better? It doesn't. She was no stranger to pain. She was strong and she would have picked pain and life any day over comfort and death. People like her aren't meant to die. They never die because people don't forget them. Did she give us enough moments together? She would never have been able to even if she had died a hundred years later. People like her just don't live enough. No matter how long, how fulfilling their lives, how painless their deaths are, people miss them. Like I miss her, and I hardly knew her. We weren't even friends; we were room-mates.

She dies. I live. I cry. Where is the sense in that? I didn't even want to live. I thought the procedures, the medicines, the doctors and the drips were nonsense. All I wanted was to get injected with a few extra CCs of morphine in my drip and I would pass on to the next world, painlessly. I didn't want this. I hated pain. I have done everything to run away from it. I used to numb it by injecting and snorting everything I could find. I hated pain and I hated life. I get nothing, she gets everything. Nobody wanted this. How do you think I will feel when I look at her parents, childless, grieving at their loss? How do you think I will feel when Arman crosses my path? We were in the same room. Same room! How difficult was it to have our fates switched? How wrong can God get, if there is one? We were right there. How could he not see?

Did I find a donor? Yes, I did. It was her. *The perfect match. We were room-mates.*

But that's not the only thing she gave me. Fifteen days after my surgery when I was shifted back to my room, the bed next to me was empty but for a little note on top of it. I opened the note and it said:

'You were the best room-mate ever. Now, we're 2-2. Don't waste it.'

I cry.

If It's Not Forever
It's Not Love

Durjoy Datta • Nikita Singh

To the everlasting power of love . . .

When Deb, an author and publisher, survives the bomb
blasts at Chandni Chowk, he knows his life is nothing short
of a miracle. And though he escapes with minor injuries, he
is haunted by the images and voices that he heard on that
unfortunate day.

Even as he recovers, his feet take him to where the blasts
took place. From the burnt remains he discovers a diary. It
seems to belong to a dead man who was deeply in love with
a girl. As he reads the heartbreaking narrative, he knows that
this story must never be left incomplete. Thus begins Deb's
journey with his girlfriend, Avantika, and his best friend, Shrey,
to hand over the diary to the man's beloved.

Deeply engrossing and powerfully told, *If It's Not Forever . . .*
tells an unforgettable tale of love and life.

You Were My Crush
Till You Said You Love Me!

Durjoy Datta • Orvana Ghai

Would you change yourself for the love of your life?

Benoy zips around in a Bentley, lives alone in a palatial house and is every girl's dream. To everyone in college he is a stud and a heartbreaker. But is he, really? What no one sees is his struggle to come to terms with his mother's untimely death and his very strained relationship with his father.

Then once again his world turns upside down when he sees the gorgeous Shaina. He instantly falls in love but she keeps pushing him away. What is stopping them from having their fairy-tale romance? What is Shaina hiding?

It's time Benoy learned his lesson about love and relationships . . .